Monroe

Stina Rubio

[Type text]

Printed in the United States of America

Monroe

To Mom

Ordination

Hi, my name is Josephine, but everyone calls me Monroe. In this business, it is better to keep things classified. I'm used to not sharing anything about myself. I have no family—so I have no ties. In my business, no family means no problems, no family means no one to hold you back. No family means no one to embarrass you when things go south. What am I you ask? I'm your daydream wrapped in your worst nightmare. However, I am more helpful than not. I have a 98.9 % completion rate, not trying to sound cocky, I'm just an extremely confident woman, and I have to be to get the job done.

What I do is not what you think it is. I do not have sex with these clients or the men they want info on. What I actually do is quite mastermind like. I seduce the men into trusting me. I take what I have learned and relay it to my, let's call her Jane Doe. They pay me when they get what they are looking for and I am off to another client. Why you ask? They want to know if this new man they are dating is going to cheat on them or fuck them over. They pay me to find out if they are the Prince Charming they portray themselves to be. Most aren't, but some of them are honest. Either way, I am paid.

Easy right?

No, wrong. It takes skill and patience, and a whole lot of being felt up. Let me take you back to my first job and see if you get the picture of why I got into this game in the first place. Life back then was something I, to this day wouldn't wish on my worst enemy. It was the life of a rat.

Let me explain.

Tuscon, Arizona was the hottest fucking hellhole I have ever been in. It made me want to peel my skin off to cool down. I wanted to submerge myself in a bucket of ice and live there until winter. But I learned early on dreams were something meant for gutters and not heads. I was riding shotgun in this shitty F-150 listening to this asshole drum his fingers on the steering wheel. Contemplating pushing him out and watching as he rolled on the road, but I couldn't. I promised my friend, slash roommate I would get the info on him. See, she didn't want to get involved with another prick that was just going to fuck her over and break her heart again. So I volunteered to scope him out for her and come back with the all the dirty details she wanted.

It was proving to be the worst thing I have done in my entire life, and I have been dragged through shit and back, but that's another story altogether and I don't feel like getting into it just yet.

"So, where did you wanna go baby?" he asked me as he leaned over and rubbed on one of my tits. I didn't know why men thought this was going to turn us on. First: I didn't know this asshole from dick. Second: you have to do a lot more than just a nipple rub to get my engine running.

But I responded the way he expected me to. "Wherever you want to go, big boy. I just want to get my hands on you." I said in a sugar coated mousy voice, which made me sick to my fucking stomach. I put my hand over his and rubbed harder. The friction caused my bud to harden.

"Just the words I was waiting for! You don't know what you're in for baby. I'm going to make you cum so hard you'll be seeing stars." Great, I was going to be so dry if we did fuck that my vagina was going to rip.

"Um-hum, you know how to get me wet, sexy. I bet you'll have me squirting in a hot minute." Lies, all lies. If he could read my mind, I would be lying face down in a ditch somewhere, which meant I was going to have to go through with this or come up with an excuse. I told her I wasn't going to sleep with him, but I couldn't think of any way to get out of this. My mind was still in the ditch where I pictured my body. I have always been good at getting out of sticky situations. In my lifestyle, you had to be quick on your feet. It was either that or you would die. The world was cold blooded and it swallowed up the weak for breakfast.

"Shoot, faster than that when I get my hands on you girl. You're going to start screaming for me to stop it's going to be so good." He was overly confident. This wasn't going to be good. I've been around men like him. Men who thought they were entitle to more than they had. It never ended well in these situations.

"I bet baby, I'm going to ride your dick like a stallion." Again, why like this shit, 'Ride your dick like a stallion'? It made me question the sanity of some men. A horse had a huge wang and I'm sure no woman in her right mind would get on it. But he seemed to eat this crap up.

Monroe

He pulled onto a dirt road, surrounding us in thick green trees. I kept my face calm and my smile wide and open. We drove for another five minutes before he pulled onto the side of the road and got out. He walked over to my side and opened the door, pulling me into his arms. I wasn't a small girl, I was a good five-ten and in heels, I was six foot. But I fit into him like I was a little girl. 'Get it together!' I reprimanded myself. This was nothing but a job to me. I needed to start bringing something to protect myself. I told myself I was never going to have sex with anyone ever again. He ruined it for me. There was no feeling in it, there was no love.

Whatever-his-name-was, bent down and kissed me on my lips leaving a trail of saliva in his wake. It made a slimy line down my face like a snail. I focused on the flowers in the clearing up ahead, appreciating the way they moved it the light breeze. I was admiring the colors that the sun amplified. Trying to concentrate on anything but him. "Did you hear me love?" Had he spoken to me?

"Did you ask me something? I was lost in the moment." I didn't lie. I was lost in the moment of my absolute hatred and repulsion.

"I asked how you want it, on the car, in the grass? I could pick you up and screw you just like that." He winked at me as if it was a great accomplishment. I threw up in my mouth at the thought.

Miraculously something popped into my head, a way out. "Oh my gosh, I think I might have started my period." It was lame, but it was the only idea I could think of, and in my experience there were many men who didn't care if you were on your rag or not.

"It's okay, baby. I got a condom, don't worry there won't be no mess." Spoken like a true sleaze. I was thinking quick on my feet. There had to be a way to get out of this.

My father's voice vibrated in my head. "Stay still, you fucking slut!"

"I don't like to fuck when I'm on my period, you understand, right baby?" I haven't prayed this hard since that night. Please, just hear me Lord. I will be better, I'll stop what I've been doing. Which wasn't much. When I met with a client, I broke it down for them. I told them what my job, and what it was not.

He looked at me for a while before he smiled, "Okay. No problem. Let me help you. You can at least let me see that sweet pussy." Shit!

"You don't really want to see that, do you? " My mouth fell open at him for even suggesting it.

"I want to at least see what I am going to be getting the next time I see you." He started to back me into the corner. I was trying to gauge his facial expression. Did he know I was lying? Why did I take this on as my first job? I knew Jimmy was an abusive asshole when I met him. I told Mackenzie he was a douche when I moved in and he was lying on our couch eating all our damn food. I wasn't nice to him at all, and I bet Mack he would go for me if I flirted with him. She told me no, that her Jimmy loved her and only her. I knew what men saw when they looked at me. I was beautiful and they wanted me. My mother would beat me because I looked like my father, and she was jealous that her old-man wanted some of me and took it. When she found him on top of me in my room, she blamed me. Told me my long blonde hair and emerald green eyes were the work of the devil. That no one should be this pretty. That any man would have done the same. I ran away three years later when I was fourteen. Let's just say I have trust issues that will never go away.

He pulled me to him and started to unbutton my pants. I did the first thing I thought of. I punched him in his nose.

"You fucking bitch! I am going to kill you!" he dashed for me grabbing me around my waist and banging me into the cold asphalt. Trying to slow the concrete as it approached, I heard a crack from my wrist. I tried to break my fall, but ended up breaking my wrist instead. My life was a hallmark card of natural disasters.

"I said no, you son of a bitch! Leave me alone!" As I hopped up and ran for the opposite side of the truck, he followed me. Yanking my head back and thrusting me head first into the side of the truck. To say I saw stars would have been an understatement, I saw the whole damn sky. It took a moment for my vision to come back. He was going to have me whether I wanted it or not. Once again, I hit the asphalt with a sickening crunch.

I'll save you all the gory details. In the end, she didn't leave him. She told me I was a bitch and asked for it. Thank God I asked her for half of my payment beforehand. Yes, it started as a bet but I wasn't stupid. I knew how she was going to see things. From there on, I only took on women who made money. I sought them out in bars. I would get them drunk and they would spill their guts on the men in their lives. After the water works calmed down, I would proposition them. Tell them about the services I offered. I was raised in a life were hustling was the only means of income. My brother made sure I had a quick mouthpiece.

The next few years consisted of me helping old rich women. Getting information on men they were interested in. These women had money. It was more about loyalty and faithfulness, companionship and love. They want things that people told them they couldn't have because they would be used. And in all honesty it's true. They were women who made a name for themselves and men think they are vulnerable just because they have a vagina and not a dick. I got it, and I wanted to help them. I wanted them to have happiness, but more importantly I want to get the assholes out there that were fucking over these women and talking advantage of them. Men who rape women, hit them and do whatever they want.

I have been in their shoes and it wasn't a good feeling being a bug they thought they could step on or control like a pet. I didn't like to relive what had happened to me in my past, but there wasn't any way to escape it.I was sitting here waiting for my next client to arrive. It's dangerous when I have too much time on my hands and I start thinking. The server put my tea down and walked away. I took a sip as my eyes roamed over the crowd of people. The scraping sound of a chair being pulled out in front of me snapped me out of my daze.

"Monroe?" A beautiful red headed woman asked. She was young, nothing like any of the other women I work with. Her hair was long and straight, freckles sprinkled lightly on her straight pert nose. She made me do a double take as I glanced over her freshly pressed clothes. What intrigued me were her black eyes. I could describe them as an abyss. Everything that went in never came out.

"Yes, that's me." I was used to working with older men too, the ones who could barely keep their dicks hard.

"Hi, my name is Vera. We talked on the phone last week." She extended her hand to me and beamed. Most women who came to me were looking for a lifeline someone to pull them out when they were sinking. Desperation brought them to me. A shitload of money kept me here.

"Hi, nice to meet you Vera. I am Monroe, as you know. So how can I help you?" It was a standard question I asked when I met with someone. This part was more of an interview. It was my chance to rate what I was dealing with and what kind of person she was. I could tell by the way she shook my hand she was lacking confidence. I have no idea why because she was gorgeous. More than likely, it was a man telling her she wasn't good enough or there was something wrong with her. They do that to keep you where they want you. It's like a predator adapting to a change in climate. It's adapt or die.

"Well, as you must know, I have been talking to this man my father thought would be good for me. At first, I didn't want anything to do with him, but the more we met, the more I started to like him. He isn't like other men in my father's company. He's young, handsome, and funny. Goodness is he funny! I want nothing more than to be with him, but there is something about him. I feel I fell too fast and he isn't on the same page as me, if that makes any sense." A man with his own money and daughter of the company's owner? Smells like a business transaction to me. Her father was going to sell her off the highest bidder. Or in this case, the person her father knew would take his company places when he wouldn't be able to.

"Right. Are you sure you like him because you do, or because your father does? I don't want to come off as arrogant, but it seems like your father just wants him for himself. How many times have you met him, or went out?"

"I have been seeing him for the last couple months. All together I have to say we have been on four dates." She smiled as if it explained everything. Like it told me he really wanted her and there wasn't anything going on.

"Where did he take you?" This was the million-dollar question. It would let me know if he liked her or her father's money.

"Twice to my place and twice to his." She explained.

"Have you guys slept together?" He was trying to hide her. If he liked her, he wouldn't care who saw them as a couple. He would be shouting it to the world. He would tell everyone that she was his girl. Therefore, the sex question would let me know if he was a jackass. Most men wouldn't care if they loved her or not. She was hot and they would fuck her senseless, with or without daddy's money.

"No, he told me he didn't want to take things too fast. He wanted to wait until the time was right. He wanted it to be perfect for me. Isn't that so sweet?" she beamed.

18

Monroe

"No, it isn't fucking sweet." I said deadpanned. "Will
you listen to yourself? Who the fuck in their right mind
wouldn't want to bang you? I am straight and it's hard
for me to think of anything else. Him keeping you behind
closed doors is another dead giveaway. He doesn't want
anyone to see you guys together. Use your head woman,
think first, and act last. You can't be that naïve, can you?
Your father needs someone to run his business. I'm going
to take a shot in the dark and say you are an only child,
not because your parents didn't try. Mommy went barren
and couldn't conceive after you. Daddy doesn't trust his
princess to run his big old business. So, your asshole of a
father is trying to pawn you off to the highest bidder, and
in this case it's…?"

"His name is Roman." she confided.

"Ah, even a douche bag name. Well, Roman will do anything for daddy. Including marrying you. How old is he?" I asked as all the pieces fall together.

"He's twenty-five" she said in a whisper. This was the hard part where I had to tell them the truth and shatter all their dreams.

"Roman is too young to think of love or having a family. Fresh out of college, he is thinking of one thing: his career. And how to get himself where your father sits as CEO ." This was where they either ran or were all in. There wasn't a half way mark. This was the point of no return. You were all in or you wasted my time. I took the time to examine my shirt, letting her process everything I said.

"You don't even know him." She spouted in contempt.

"Neither do you, doll. Four dates isn't a partnership. Hell, it isn't even a friendship yet. If you can tell me his favorite color, I will admit I'm wrong. And I will tell you there is hope for you and douche-bag."

The smile fell from her face, "I don't know." She gritted.

"I know this is hard and I know you like this guy, and I'm here to help, really, I am. But, I will never lie to you. I have been doing this for years and most men are the same. They think with their cocks and nothing else . I'm sure he would have really liked you if he were a bit older and he had climbed the company ladder . But right now all he is thinking about is pleasing your father. If you

21

don't want me to do this, if you will walk out of here and tell him you will never see him again I won't charge you a dime. But if we go through with this, it will be ten thousand dollars down and another ten when I am done, regardless of what I find out." I waited tapping my fingers on the table.

"What? It isn't that easy. I can't just tell him no!" outrage covered her beautiful face.

"Vera you're very beautiful. Your someone is out there looking for you as we speak. Roman isn't that someone. If he were, he would be head over heels for you."

"But how do I know that? I don't.So I still want you to do it. I have the money, don't worry." She took out a very plump envelope.

"Wait, I need you to look this over and sign it before you give me that," I pointed to the envelope. "There is also a questionnaire in there. Just simple things like: where can I find him, where he likes to go on his time off, or things he likes to do. And Vera, if this doesn't work, no matter how unhappy you are with the results. I do not exist. I'm a ghost. Got it?" She nodded her head yes and took the packet. I put money on the table and left. When and if she were ready, she would call. For now, I would wait. My number one rule is to not become attached or involved with clients or suspects. I wasn't lying when I told her I was a ghost. It's the way it had to be. If people knew who I was it would be easier for my past to find me. I even legally changed my name. My real name was too innocent, nothing like me. Nothing like the person I was and who I became. It was a way to keep all the pain and hurt locked away. It would drive me crazy if

I was still the sick, stupid girl. No. I was more than that now, and I wasn't going to be her ever again. If I was meant to never have anyone in my life, so be it.

I walked into the hotel I was staying at and smiled at the man behind the desk. I didn't have permanent housing. I took cases and clients all over the place, so it was just easier to stay mobile. I knew the client was going to call within twenty-four hours or I wasn't getting the job. It would suck because I used jobs to pass time. When I got into the room, I went through the routine of getting settled in for the night. I placed all my things neatly on the table next to the door. In a row from biggest to smallest, depending on what the items were. I placed my shoes side by side under the table and my jacket on the hook. Order was a necessity in my life. It was the only thing that was consistent. I walked into the bathroom and started taking my clothes off, every item I folded and place on the counter in an arrangement.

I took baths in scalding hot water. To some this was weird, to me it was my life. I wanted to scrub off all the feelings, emotions, and dirt of the day. When I met with clientele, it was like the stink of their souls stuck to the fabric of my clothing. My mother used to tell me I felt what others were feeling. As I got older, I realized how true her words were. I didn't like it. I didn't want to feel what these women were feeling. So, I adapted a poker face. A lot of people call it the resting bitch face. If they knew how I was feeling they would think I was weak, and I was anything but.

I sat in the hot water letting it soak in and wash away the stress of the day, feeling relaxed and somewhat myself after. It was a ritual. When I met with them, I wasn't me. They weren't paying for me the sad girl from Alabama, they wanted Monroe. The woman all men dreamed of. Monroe the fearless, who could get any man wrapped around her finger. I wasn't the latter, but they needed to believe I was. They needed to feel like they could trust me. They needed to know I wasn't a woman with problems and I could get the job done. I was a pro at keeping everything to myself. Emotions, feeling, humanity, whatever it was.

In the distance, I could hear the phone. It was a soft melody, it had no lyrics. Just a sweet song. It was her, Vera. This was a test of her confidence. This was her taking back her life. Feeling as she never accomplished or followed through with most decisions she has made. Money was one of the reasons. What did you give a woman who had everything she wanted? She was brought up with a silver spoon shoved in her mouth. I know what I could give her that no one else could. Him.

"Hello?" I said into the end of the phone.

"Monroe, this is Vera. I want to employ you. I filled out the paperwork you gave me and there are a few things I would like to discuss. One is that there wasn't anything in here stating if you were going to sleep with him or not. I would prefer that you didn't. I am unclear on to how this all works, but I would like you to just flirt—if that is possible." I didn't put that in the paperwork because they should know this is my job and like any other professional, they should know I wouldn't take part in such scandalous affairs.

"No, I do not sleep with client's prospects. I didn't put it in there Ms. Calvin, because I would hope it didn't need explaining. This is a business, not a brothel, and I understand if this isn't what you were looking for, but this is all I have to offer." It seemed like I was waiting for a response most of the time. Either she was stuck on stupid, or she loved dramatic pauses.

"No. I was just wondering about it and all."

"No, I do not, nor have I ever slept with a client's interest, but that doesn't mean it was for a lack of them trying. No, that would be too easy or hard whatever way you look at it. They try. I play shy and tell them no. Does that answer your questions?"

"Yes. It's just that… I think I'm …"

"You think you're in love with him. I've heard it all. Remember, I have been doing this for a while now. The one thing I want out of this more than anything is for you to be happy, whatever that means." I was pretty cut and dry when it came to explaining what I did and what my services were.

"When is the next time we can meet up and discuss this?" she asked.

"I would like to get started as soon as possible. Can you meet tonight?" If I was lucky, I would get the info in a day. If not ,the worst would be a week.

"Tonight? I'm at my fathers for a dinner and Roman is here" she explained like this was supposed to mean something to me. Roman was there! Oh no, call the police! Something about men who labeled themselves as high end got to me. They thought they were better than the rest of us, and it was the other way around. Nothing in life would let me give in to these men.

29

"Tonight. Yes. There is a lot to do and the sooner I get it the sooner I can start interacting with the subject." I picked at my nails, still waiting impatiently for her to make up her mind. My foot started tapping and it reminded me of my mother.

"Jo! Get your ass in here! You know he doesn't like it when you're dirty!" My mother whispered aggressively as she pulled me through the door by my arm.

Every now and again little things sparked my memory, bringing me back to my life from before.

"You talk of him like he is nothing more than paperwork to you!" anger coated her words.

"Vera, at this point he is paperwork to me, and when I am finished I will file him as such. I do not know this man and everything that is going to happen between him

30

and I is going to be such. I don't want to be his friend and I am not here to be yours. Though this sounds rude and I don't like coming off that way, I will not lie to you. This is a business deal and he is my subject, my goal, or my mission. I get what I need out of him, whether it is what you want to hear or not. Do we have an understanding?" When I first started out, I would have never talked to a client like this. I would have stayed on my toes and bowed down to them. After all, they were the ones who paid my bills. Now I had a choice in who I worked with. I could be meticulous if I felt like it.

"Yes." A simple response, but it was what I was looking for.

"Now that that is settled, I will meet you at the hotel on First and Bradshaw. Do not come late and make sure you knock once." I liked order and control. If I can get women who pay me, to listen and follow orders quickly, than the men should be a piece of cake. I hung up without another word. She could find me. It wasn't that difficult and my name was now legally Monroe. Plus she didn't seem that stupid, but I could be wrong.

Ten minutes later, there was a quick knock on the door. I walked over and looked out the peep hole. Even though I knew who was there, I still had the feeling of unease. Yet, there was Vera on the other side of the door, looking back and forth down the hall with the envelope in her hand. I pulled the door open and motioned for her to come in. She strolled in and looked around. She would be disappointed because there was nothing in the room that told my story, and there never would be. It was the bed and my clothes that was it.

I pushed my hand out, and she looked at it as if I had lost my mind. "The envelope please." She handed it to me and began ambling around the room. Normal people would go to the only chair there was and sit in it. Not Vera. She sat on my bed. Where I slept.

"That's it?" Vera questioned.

"That's it. What else can I do for you Ms. Calvin? I know you said there were things you wanted to discuss, or was the sex thing all?"

She slightly tilted her head and eyed me, "No one is that cold hearted." It shocked me, but I kept my face neutral.

"I have no idea what you mean. I have told you this is business. You don't go to your gynecologist and try making friends with her, right? After all, she has seen

33

your pussy and it would be completely inappropriate." I placed the papers on the desk and looked to her expectantly.

"No, but normal people are not as rude as you, Monroe. You come off as cold and callous." She stood up quickly.

"I come off this way because in the end they all hate me. No matter what happens, these women blame me for what's going on in their relationships. They don't have the balls to leave, so it's easier to blame me. You will be no different, because the man that holds your heart is an asshole who doesn't give a shit about your pretty ass! I can tell you what he does care about though. Your daddy's money." I don't know why I told her any of this, but it came out like a tidal wave and it smacked her.

Astonishment crept into her beautiful features, consuming them.

"I'm sorry… I just assumed…" What pissed me off more than someone judging me was someone who pitied me.

"Don't fucking look at me like that! I don't need your fucking pity! I am who I am. I am here because I want to be. Having friends only causes problems. This is my life and you know nothing about me!"

"I apologize. I understand if you don't want to work with me. Of course this is a business arrangement. I should have been more professional with you." She stumbled on her way to the door because she couldn't get out fast enough.

When I was alone, I marched over to the paperwork and took it out. Regarding the details of Mr. Roman's life there were tons. You knew a lot about someone you loved, and from what I read, Vera had it bad for the douche. He was a consultant at Calvin industries. What he consulted beat the fuck out of me. He was born in New York to John and Sarah Pierce. He was their only child. He went to Duke and was on the football team. He was quoted as saying, 'Football was fun, but it wasn't what he wanted to do in his life.' What struck me as odd was that earlier she didn't even know his favorite color, but she knew everything else it seemed. It was my first red flag. Why was she lying?

I placed the papers back into the envelope and got into the left side of the bed. I fanned my hair out on the pillow and got snug into the sheets. Thinking about the picture that was included, I could tell why she was going for him, he had a good job and he was drop dead gorgeous. He looked like a Ken doll walking around in a suit. He had black hair, but what was most peculiar was the color of his eyes. One was green and the other brown. He was blessed with a strong muscular jaw and a small dimple in the middle of his chin. In the photo, he was smiling and the happiness on his face was blinding. The picture spoke volumes about him. He was happy. He loved life. So why was he agreeing to marry Vera? I was rarely ever wrong when it came to reading someone, but looking in his eyes I prayed I was wrong. He had kind eyes and an inviting mouth. I wanted to tuck his hair back behind his ear and run my fingers down his jaw.

It wasn't only his looks that baffled me. Vera and him would make a lovely couple, and together they would have money and power. Not to mention their snot nosed kids would have the world readily available to them. I imagined them holding hands as their kids ran in front of them, playing tag. Roman pushing a stroller, where their new edition sat staring into the unknown. I played with the idea of me having that one day, but it evaporated like a promised rain into nothing.

Monroe

According to her paperwork, she said he had lunch at the same café every day. Now all I had to do was get a seat where he would be able to see me. It was a crowded place. I didn't like the feeling of being surrounded by people, and I dressed to attract attention. I wanted him to notice me. I hope I would be so irresistible in my black mini dress that he wouldn't be able to take his eyes off me. I ordered a large coffee, and I brought my laptop to act as if I were working on something. Why anyone would work in this outfit was beyond me, but they did. I was minding my own business when some random dude came and sat at my table. I was just getting cozy, and he had to go and ruin it.

"Can I help you?" I asked as sweetly as I could, because at this moment all I wanted to do was kick his chair from underneath him. He irritated my soul.

"I was just wondering why such a beautiful woman was sitting all alone," he leered.

"Believe me, it's by choice. I have a lot of homework to do." I forced a smile, nodded my head and returned my eyes to my computer.

"You don't have to act like you don't want it baby," with that, he ran his hand over my bare leg. At first, I was too shocked to reply. I just stared at him like I was lost. The nerve some people had.

A hand appeared on the douches shoulder. "I think the lady would appreciate you leaving her alone and taking your hand off her leg." He grinned at the jerk with no humor.

"What? Are you fucking her?" Dick-face asked.

"No I'm not, and if I were that would be none of your fucking business. It would be between her and me, I don't think your mother taught you manners. Should I take you outside and show you what my father taught me? When it comes to a lady, you must have respect. Or you make the rest of us look like shit." I was shocked when I looked up into the strangers eyes. My eyes briefly met his eyes for a minute, as he returned his gaze back to the dude and removed him from the shop. It was him. Roman. Not the ideal way to meet him, but I will take what I could get.

When he came back inside, I thanked him for what he'd done.

"It was nothing, if I could save a beautiful woman every day I would." He wasn't trying to impress me with his admission. He was being genuine, something you didn't find a lot of these day. He was my savior. I had to admit I was wrong from my first impression of him. Most of the men who were my targets were womanizing assholes. This could just be a trick, but my gut feeling was usually right.

"Thank you, regardless. Please allow me to buy you a coffee." I insisted. Even if he was heroic, it didn't stop me from doing my job. He was the mission and I would conquer him.

"I couldn't let you do that." He shook his head and chuckled softly.

"You're right. You can't let me do anything. I offered," I am not a woman who can be forced to do anything." I got up and walked with him to the counter as he placed his order. I took my wallet out and paid for his coffee.

"Thanks for the coffee." He raised it into the air and bobbed once again, before he proceeded to walk away.

"Hey, if you really want to thank me you can sit with me and protect me from all these other hooligans." I flirted playfully and went back to my seat sure he was going to follow me. They all did. However, when I looked back at him he was still standing by the counter looking at me like he was at war with himself.

"I don't think it would be a good idea. I'm seeing someone and I don't want anyone to get the wrong idea." His words put me into a stupor. I wasn't used to men telling me no. Usually they would look at me and see ass and tits. It was ok with me. I didn't mind, whatever it took to get the job done, right?

"Okay, no problem. I guess I'll see you around, hero." I picked up my coffee and strode to the door. I must be off my game if I couldn't pull him in. It was weird, but I never back down from a challenge. I would get him no matter how hard to get he made himself out to be.

I made it back to my hotel just before sunset. I like to document what went on with every meeting so I can tell the client everything in detail. I don't know if I was being a bitch. The facts I tell them will hurt, and I didn't blink an eye as the women sat in front of me crying like they lost their minds. Expressing emotions to a person you hardly knew eluded me. Not even people I knew would see me cry. Trusting no one was complicated at times, never knowing who was out to get me. I guess I just wasn't a people person.

Target: Roman Pierce

Occupation: Marketing executive. (Under the thumb of dear old daddy Calvin.) But he doesn't come off as a person who can be told what to do from first observation.

Description: He is taller than I assumed from his pictures. Though it was an error in judgment. From how Vera looks (which is small) I thought he would be less than six foot. I need to know measurement just in case something goes wrong and I have to defend myself. It has happened before and I will not relive it. He has one blue eye and one brown. His hair is black. It looks like a night without stars. In all honesty, he and Vera make a cute couple. The red with black hair had always been a combination favorite of mine. He also has a genuine smile. Not sure if this was trick or he was honest. Either way I will find out.

Objective: Finding out if the motives of Sir Roman are one hundred percent authentic or if the company and the CEO position is all that is on his mind.

Plan: At this point, my looks alone aren't going to show me the results I am looking for, so I am going to have to dig deeper. This one poses a challenge that I will gladly meet head on. (He had no idea who I was).

After I write something about my target, I like to evaluate the client and guess if she is going to lose her shit if all this starts heading south, but at this moment I kept thinking about when the mission went wrong and I ended up with four cracked ribs and a missing tooth. It was a client in the Alabama area. I didn't want to take it, but the money that was being offered to me, I couldn't turn it down. Going home was one of the toughest things I have ever done. It was a couple cities over from where I was raised. When I met the client, my instinct was telling me to turn it down, and I had. But she kept telling me she would pay more. With that much money, I wouldn't have to take another case all year if I didn't want to. I know it's sad to say that I had grown accustomed to a certain life style. Missing out on the money would have been a hard blow. I've taken cases that left a sour feeling in my gut before, but this was different. Everything in me was saying to high tail and run as fast as my legs would carry me, or more accurately get in my Porsche and get to another state by nightfall. I chucked it up to being in my home state and nothing was going to hurt me. After all, doing this for a while left me feeling as if I could take on the world.

This was a case where they both had money and they had been married for fifteen years. She wanted me to find out if he were offered a chance, he would cheat. I told her before that this wasn't a good idea, and if he was given an opportunity with a pretty young woman he was going to take it. Men thought with their willies most times. It might be sexist of me to think of it like that, but I have had enough experience with the opposite sex to know what I was talking about. Even the ones you thought were faithful, if they were in a position with a girl naked throwing herself at them, in the end she won.

I took it after she offered me half a million dollars. It would have been stupid not to. In the end, he was a cheating asshole, and you could add woman beater to the list. He almost killed me when he found out I was there to investigate him. His wife is the one who told him. I mentioned I was close to cracking him and that night he was going to give in. She ran to him, told him everything, and begged him not to fall under the power of my witchcraft. I went in there blind and once I walked in, he hit me in the side with a baseball bat. I went down instantly. I took self-defense after it was all said and done. To this day, I meet with my trainer at least twice a week, and with all the money I'm forking out, he meets me where ever I am. I know how to defend myself and expect the worse. Too many times I've ended up under a boot, or behind a balled fist.

I needed to write my findings about Vera, but the day wore me out and I needed to get something to eat. The thought of eating room service again was not appealing. Some fresh air and people watching is just what the doctor ordered. Tomorrow was a new day. I would start over with Roman then.

———————————————————

Going to a restaurant alone was most women's worst nightmare. Me? I took it as an opportunity to get new clientele. A place like this was littered with money. It was by reservation only, but I knew the chef so I got in whenever I was in town.

"Monroe," he kissed both my cheeks. "So nice to see you again, love. I haven't seen you in over a year" he said in his thick French accent. Ever since I met him, he would hint to me that he had a crush on me. He was nice, but nice wasn't going to turn me on.

"I know and I have missed you too, Jean, really. It has been a very long year." I smiled and rubbed his arm.

"Yeah, well, you are here now, and at such an exquisite time. There is a whole new menu and so much I want you to try, belle."
"It sounds lovely, and I will have whatever you recommend, old friend," he took my hand and lead me to

my seat. I always sat at the same one. It had a view of the town outside and it was in the middle of the restaurant so I could people watch well.

He placed a basket of bread on the table that they baked with freshly picked almonds and a divine butter and sugar dip. There were other things in it but he refused to confide in me. It was heavenly and it was one of my only comfort foods. He was one of the only people I connected with and it was only about food. Something we both held close to our heart.

"Josephine, didn't I tell you none of that food was for you? Your daddy is going to be so mad if he gets home and you touched it. Do you want to make him mad child? Now, get your scrawny behind away from that table!"

"Yes, Momma."

My brother spoke up. *"If we can't eat that, what are we going to eat tonight momma? You only cook for daddy while we eat bread split between me and Jo."* My brother Ira was one to stir up things. He was a troublemaker, but I loved him with everything I was. My big brother who protected me, and took the beatings that were directed at me. There wasn't anything he couldn't do, he was my own personal superman.

"Boy, if you don't stop talking to me like that I'm going to blister your ass! Now both of you get out of my kitchen!" My brother did know when to take a hint and leave. He grabbed my hand and we ran down to the quarry right when my daddy pulled up in his truck. Ira would catch fish sometimes and we would eat it by the fire. He would tell me ghost stories as we watched the sky

53

turn from blue to pink. When the stars appeared, we heard our daddy call us.

That night he leaned over and told me, "One day Jo, we are going to get out of this place. We're going to get far away from them and we won't ever beg for food again. I swear I will put the prettiest shoes I can find on your feet. We will. Just watch." I believed every word that came out of his mouth because I knew he would save me. My brother was the only thing I had, and I will forever blame myself for what happened to him.

A plate was placed in front of me and I snapped out of my daze. At times, I feel like that life was a different one altogether. A life I didn't want to remember, but knew I lived so long ago.

"The first course we have for you Madame," he presented the food to me. "Is a sweet and sour spring salad topped with a poached egg. Enjoy." If only Ira could see me now, he would see I was doing everything I could to make him proud. The salad was great like everything Jean made. I was in heaven from the first bite. I finished the first plate just in time for the second course.

"The next course Madame, is veal chops with wilted lettuce and oysters smothered in a garlic-parmesan sauce. Enjoy." He came back and filled my cup with a rare red wine, and every course after was delivered the same way. I was the chef's number one guest and he was treating me like a queen.

I excused myself to the ladies' room, asking the waiter to hold the next course. He informed me he would be happy to comply. I nodded my thanks and went about my way. The red wine was catching up to me. I never drank because it altered my judgment. I needed to be able to think quickly on my toes, and I knew better because I was on a job, but the need to feel something was overwhelming. Not what I wanted to feel, but it was something.

Stalking leisurely back to my table, I took in all the couples cooing over one another. The sight drew my eyebrows together. I wondered what love felt like. When I was younger, the lack of affection caused me to look at the world inversely from others. When people would show each other emotions that I had no understanding of, I would study them, trying to pick apart every look and touch. It was one of the main reasons I got my Master's Degree in social sciences.

Where my empty table was supposed to be, a man sat. His dark raven hair slicked stylishly back. His body was perpendicular and at attention. It confused me to why someone would be sitting at my table.

"Excuse me sir, I think you are in my seat." I said with authority. Making sure he knew I wasn't playing around, and just because I was a woman, alone didn't mean he was going to steal my table.

"I am well aware whose seat I am sitting in, Madame." He kept his back to me as he spoke. Curiosity got the best of me and I walked to the other side of the table to get a good look at the man who had a hearing problem.

It was him. Roman, and he had the biggest smile pasted on his face. "And what pray tell is so funny?"

"You, Madame." he said mockingly. "Yesterday, I get the pleasure of meeting you at a regular coffee shop, and now I run into you at an extremely high end restaurant run by Jean Luke himself. And you seem to be one friendly terms with the culinary god no less." He got up and offered me my seat. I took it graciously and waited as he pushed me in.

"I don't see why that is so weird, sir. Now days coffee is a major necessity, and if you weren't aware, I feel bad for you. As for Jean, he is a dear old friend. I see him every time I am here." I smiled up at him.

"Friend huh, or more?"

"I don't recall that being any of your business, Roman! It was made clear to me you were taken. Which it's a shame, but she is one lucky lady," Flirting was one of many tools I had in my arsenal. They were suckers for a pretty smile and cleavage.

"That I am," he said with a frown.

"You don't look so pleased to admit such things." I placed my hand on the table and looked at him through my thick lashes.

"It's complicated, but nothing I can't handle." He smiled. "Enjoy the rest of your meal." I thought he was going to walk away from me, but he did the damnedest thing I have seen. He took my hand, bent, and laid a kiss on my knuckles. I was used to men making all kinds of advances at me, but this was polite. He kept his lips on my hand a little longer than necessary.

Bingo. Got him.

"You don't have to leave. Friends can eat and make conversation. No need to run off just yet. I can tell Jean to make another plate, of course, on me, for your chivalry." I was grinning so big it was starting to hurt my face. I can't remember the last time that I smiled so much. I was losing my mind.

"I don't…" he was going to say.

"Then stop thinking and act. We aren't going to leave here together, and nothing is going to happen. If I wanted you, you wouldn't be able to say no. I am simply asking you to a meal, as a friend. Are you going to turn down a lady in need of companionship?" If he were loyal, he would have said no either way. A man with no intention of cheating wouldn't have thought twice. It was my open window, and I was going to take it like a twenty dollar bill someone dropped on the street corner.

"Just sit, and don't think about it." I raised my hand and told the waiter I was going to need another plate and a glass of wine. He looked over at Roman and lifted his chin a bit. They weren't used to me bringing someone in. It was as if I was getting dinner and a show tonight.

"He didn't seem so happy about me sitting here," Roman said as he took a seat on the other side of the table.

"They aren't used to me having someone here. I wouldn't be surprised if Jean comes out to see who you are, and he isn't going to be nice about it." I laughed. Sure enough, there he was trotting over to us.

"I was told you were going to have a guest this evening, Monroe." Jean stood by my chair and placed his hand on it protectively.

61

"Yes, if that's not a problem, Jean. This man saved me from the hand of a frisky young man today. I don't know what I would have done if he didn't show up." I placed a hand over my heart, dramatically bobbing my head. Jean's attitude evaporated.

"Of course there isn't a problem. I wanted to come out and introduce myself personally. Any friend of Monroe is a friend of mine." He smiled and walked over and clapped Roman on the back, leaning down and saying something I couldn't make out.

"Enjoy," he said and he was off.

"What did he say to you?" I knew Jean wished to be more than a friend to me, but he never acted on it. I was curious to know what treat he instated on Roman.

"He told me he would gut me if I hurt you, and that no one would know because he cuts all his meat himself." His eyes were as big as saucers. "He was kidding right?"

I just nodded as my shoulders shook in a silent laugh. I couldn't help it. I knew how Jean felt and he knew it was never going to happen. I wasn't the relationship type. I was a lone wolf.

"He was kidding, don't take it seriously. He has a thing for me and I told him I don't do relationships." I didn't mean to tell him that. It just slipped out. I never told anyone the truth about myself.

"I sense a story, care to share?" It wasn't going to happen.

"No." I simply said.

"So cryptic. And Monroe, huh? What a beautiful name." It was. That's why I picked it. I wanted people to associate my name with the sex icon. It's like marketing in a business. You name your company something that is going to grab the customer's attention.

"Thank you. It's a family name." I lied.

"Tell me something about yourself, Monroe." He probed. When someone started asking questions, it never stopped with one. They would keep asking and invading. It made me uncomfortable. When I was around Roman, I lost sight of the mission. I didn't want to lie to him. I was starting to behave normally, showing him bits and pieces of myself.

"Okay, I like expensive wine. I am an erotic writer and I love coming to places like this alone so I can watch the people." Another bit of truth. I was breaking every fucking rule I had. For who? This guy? Who was he to me? The answer: No one. He was going to be some other woman's husband soon, and for a company no less. He was the guy I told myself to stay away from. I didn't need this in my life. It was complicated enough. It would only cause pain and anger once he figured out he couldn't fix me. The truth of it was, I was broken beyond repair and I deserved to be like this. I didn't deserve anyone in my life, I was worthless and unlovable.

"I like to watch people too. I like to make up conversations when they talk. You know, kind of like lip-syncing their life story. It can be fun, want to try?" Was he serious? By the look on his face, he was. This was a game, something to keep you entertained when waiting for food.

"What the hell, it's something I haven't done before, let's give it a go."

"I'll start." He said as he searched around. "Them, there!" he pointed to a couple sitting in a booth right in front of us.

"You are so delicious, I can't wait to get you home and devour you," he said in a fake Russian accent.

It was my turn and the girl was obviously swooning over whatever he said. I chose to play along. "Oh honey, you can have me any way you would like," I mimicked in my real southern accent. I didn't use it much because people assumed you weren't as smart as them.

"Good," he said looking at me. "If you aren't careful, I am going to take you on this table, right here in front of everyone."

"I dare you to, sweetheart." What's funny is, the woman didn't look southern at all. She had long black hair and olive skin. If I had to take a guess at her nationality, I would say she was Hispanic. She was stunning.

"If you think I won't, you are sadly mistaken, love. I will do more to you in five minutes than anyone has done to you in a lifetime." He was no longer looking at the couple. He was looking at me. He swallowed loudly. The awkwardness saved when our lovely waiter placed our plates on the table.

I cleared my throat. "I hope you like it. He always serves me what he creates. He is a genius and I don't question him." I chuckled and busied myself with my silverware, not wanting to look at him because this all just became real. Normal to me was a man trying to get into my pants. This was anything but ordinary. He was trying to get into something else.

"I think this meal will be one of the best I have ever had." he boasted, sticking a piece of meat into his mouth, with a newfound elation.

"I doubt it, you're here after all. That means you have been here before." I probed.

"Nope, I was here checking it out. I was going to take…" he stopped.

"Your girlfriend here? Will this be your first big date? A man only takes a girl here when they are getting serious." I lifted my eyebrow in question.

"Yes, there is that. This was nice, but I must be going." He stood abruptly, knocking a cup over in his haste. Why would be going? It was just getting interesting.

"Why? You haven't even finished. Sit. Talk. There is nothing going on, don't get nervous. I know about her and it's fine. I've told you I don't do relationships. So don't worry about me, because if I did want you, you wouldn't be telling me no." I admitted. Roman had a way of bringing out the honest woman in me. When I was with him, he made me want to be truthful.

"You don't do relationships? You sound like a man, and the reason I should be going is because you intrigue me. I want to know about you, everything really. You see, when I saw you in the coffee shop I knew you could handle yourself. I stepped in more for the boy's benefit. Your eyes had death in them and you looked like you were going to kill him. I couldn't leave without saying something to you. There was no guarantee I would ever see you again. My life is a bag of shit right now, and to be honest, there is nothing I could offer you, and a girl like you deserves the world." He looked me in the eyes, like he was looking for something. It felt like he was digging around in me. I did the only thing I could do. I laughed.

"You're absurd. You can't possibly know my life from just two meetings." However, he could, because I do. I can tell someone's personality from the emotions they put out. I now knew why Vera was falling for him. He was acting like such a gentleman. Me on the other hand, I was well versed in the acts of men. Just because he knew how to work a woman, just as much as I knew how to work a man, didn't mean I was stupid.

"You don't think so? I can tell you are trying to hide something. I can tell you don't let anyone in from the way you carry yourself. I can tell you don't let anyone close enough to touch you, because when I kissed your hand earlier you were trying to pull away. I have no idea how Jean got into you, but I sure as hell would like to know." All of these things were true. It didn't take a private eye to see I was withdrawn when it came to people. I should wear a warning sign that said stay the fuck away.

"Okay, let's say you're right, and I'm not saying you are. Just hypothetically. Anyone could tell these things. I have Obsessive Compulsive Disorder, so I need to be in control. It must show." Fuck me, with my fucking big mouth.

"People might believe that, but me, not so much. I can see through the poker face you wear so well, and all it does is make me want to peel it back and chip it away. That in itself is a dangerous thing."

"Then why stay? Why are you here if I'm so dangerous? If you were as loyal as you come off, you would have walked out the first time you said you were going to." The attitude was a coping mechanism. It came out when I felt attacked. I was calm most of the time, people never got under my skin.

"If you remember correctly, I was going to, but you asked me to stay, and what would I be if I left a beautiful woman to dine alone? When I look at you, all I see is the things you are trying to hide. When I look at you, I see someone I could see myself with." Abort! This was a trick! No man in his right mind thought about being with a woman forever so soon.

"I think it would be best if you left. I have told you I don't do this, no exceptions." I pointed from him to me, and looked at him with a stern face. The crazy bitch is coming out to play and she doesn't let hostages go. It was all of nothing with her. This was who Monroe was. This is who I am. "You can't know that from seeing someone twice and meeting them in one day. This is the reason I stay the fuck away from men! All you guys want is ass, and you don't give a fuck who you hurt in the process. Well, guess what? I am not her! She is the poor sap you claim to be dating. Poor thing, someone needs to break it to her." What the fuck was I doing? He was my goal, and here I was pushing him away. This was the first time I lost my cool with a client. I have always remained impartial to them. I keep telling myself the same thing over and over again, "I have done this so many times, I know men like the back of my hand, I let no one in." It wasn't for them, it was for me. I was trying to make myself believe it. I told them I wanted nothing, but truthfully, I didn't deserve anything. Loving me would be their death. I was like a siren luring sailors in and drowning them. Sure, I was nice to look at, but my inside was dark and evil.

Monroe

My alarm went off at its normal time, five a.m. I was up getting ready and studying my subject. Roman was something else altogether. He wasn't wrong in what he had said about me. He was actually on point. No one had been able to do that in a long time. I was very hard to read because I showed no emotion. Over the years, I had perfected it. My brother Ira used to tell me I was an empath and if there was someone in some kind of mood around me, I was going to feel it too. I told him to shut his dirty mouth and leave me alone.

"Come on Jo, I didn't mean it in a bad way. Don't be mad at me." I was sitting on the curb in front of the ice cream shop. My head was resting in my hands and I was

still crying over what I had seen in there. I was used to not getting things I wanted but if we were lucky, the owner would give us something the customers didn't like. So, my brother and me would go there to see if he would have anything to give us. It was something we would look forward to. Mr. Molt did his best to stand by us. Everyone in the town knew what our home life was like, and he wasn't any different. The Alabama sun was beating down on my neck, as sweat pooled on the curve of my throat.

"I know I can't help the way I feel, Ira. That doesn't mean you gotta be so mean to me." I stuck my tongue out at him.

"I'm not mean Jo, and you know that. I've been taking care of you since you was knee high to a grasshopper. You just gotta learn how to hide it, or

people are going to take advantage of you when you get older. I'm only trying to look out for you." That was the day I realized how much my brother held on his shoulders. For someone his age, he was mature and he didn't lie. Ever since my mother had me, he took care of me. He was always taking the punishment when daddy would come home drunk and momma wouldn't do anything to stop him. He was one of the best people I knew.

"Ira, you want to go swimming? We still got some time before the sun goes down." I smiled at my brother brightly, and his head popped up.

"Sure, let's go. I'll race ya!" he was off like a rabbit in heat.

"That's no fair Ira! You got longer legs than me, and this time I want to win!" I whined and my brother slowed and kept pace with me.

"I was gonna let you win, cry baby! You just didn't give me the chance. I was gonna make it look like you really won and I wasn't letting you, but now you blew it."

Ira was the last person I allowed myself to love, I wouldn't even get a dog. Getting someone else involved in my drama was a no-no. I was going to make Ira proud if it killed me. He taught me so much in life, and this is what I could do to repay him. I dreamt of him every night. Of the last time I saw him. It's burned into my brain for eternity.

It was time to write the report on my and Roman's meeting last night and the report about Vera. I was meeting her today to go over what my evaluation of the situation was. I need something to present.

Client: Vera Calvin.

Occupation: Fuck if I know. (Probably lives with her parents.)

Description: Red hair, blue eyes, naïve, and a fucking brat. Using her parents' money to control people. I don't fucking know what it is about her, but there's something wrong. I don't mean to be catty, but God! She looks like a fucking model, so why doesn't Roman like her? Beats me, I have no clue. This case is going downhill fast. Maybe after today, I will have something more to add.

Objective: The objective is to acquire Roman for her. (Fucking Bitch!!!)

Plan: At this moment, I am clueless, I hope today is more progressive, but my hopes are low.

What I wrote was completely ridiculous. What was wrong with me? I think I should just drop this case and move on. I wasn't tight for money yet. There was no reason why I was putting myself through it. He was getting under my skin only because I was letting him. Now what I was going to tell the little brat, and why was I calling her that? Why was I judging her when I hardly knew her? I had to get my mind straight. I had a couple hours before I had to meet her. I needed to do something that was going to relax me.

Monroe

A swim sounded wonderful right now, the cool water running over my warm body. It was just what I needed. A couple of laps in the pool. As I walked into the shallow end, it reminded me of the time Ira insisted I learn to swim. *There weren't any adults around where we went, and he wanted to make sure I knew how so I wouldn't drown.*

"First, you start off in the shallow parts to make sure you have something to fall back on if you can't tread the water." He told me to float on the water. He held me at my waist as I floated. "Now kick your feet, as fast as you can. Good, now move them out like a frog when he swims. Okay, good, now you got to do the same with your arms." To me, he was everything, my protector, my provider, and my teacher all in one.

We didn't leave the pond till I was good and wrinkled, but I left with more pride than ever because I knew how to swim. Ira will always be my hero, for the rest of my life. I will always try to make him proud. I vowed, as I watched my brother shake out his shoes and slip them on his wrinkled feet.

It was one of the best moments in my life. I would give anything to relive it just once. I missed the soft curl on the back of Ira's neck when his hair got wet. I miss the way he would let me win all the races. Hell, I even missed when he would win some. Life without him was hard, I counted the days till I returned home and returned to him.

I waited on Vera in a donut shop of all places. I ordered coffees for her and me. The paper work I had on Roman was tucked under my arm, ready for her when she got here. There shouldn't have been anything sexy about what I was doing or the way I looked, but some men didn't read the signs.

"Hey honey, you looking for a good time?" I held in a gag. He must have me confused with someone who gave a fuck. Why did this have to happen all the time? Couldn't they just leave me alone? I was sitting here minding my own business, and here they go, thinking I needed saving or something worse… their dick.

"You sure you sat down at the right table?" I said as I looked over the brim of my glasses.

"I did if you want to get out of here." He winked. This is why I had little faith in the male species.

"There is no chance of that happening. I suggest you take your lame ass pickup lines and shove them up your ass, were they will never see the light of day. Let's be honest, they were shit to begin with." I averted my eyes back to the papers in front of me.

"What a bitch!" He got up and pointed a finger at my face. "You're one of those bitches who thinks she's better than everyone else, huh?"

"I won't even dignify that with an answer, because you are one of those assholes that thinks every woman should just fall over him." I peeked up at him just in time to see his face turn ripe as a cherry.

He kicked the chair as he stormed off. It was like watching a toddler have a temper tantrum. Someone should have put him in his place eons ago. Fucking prick! I didn't think I was better than anyone. Matter of fact, I thought I didn't deserve most things normal people had. The chair scraped as it moved out across from me. I thought it was the idiot coming back to get another piece of my mind. I peered at the person who was now in the chair. It was Vera.

"Just in time," I told her.

"What was all that about?" she pointed to the guy who was still glaring at me in the corner.

"Nothing I couldn't handle, don't worry." I placed a paper on the table and slid it to her. "These are the notes I have taken on Roman from the two encounters I've had with him." She picked it up and squinted as she read.

"There isn't anything of significance in here." She looked at me over her paper.

"I have only been on this case for a day, and getting to him when he's involved is more trying than I originally thought. Roman has some... unique characteristics. He is not blinded by my first advances. He seems like he is more than interested in you, and it might come out positive in the end." I nodded to her. It was total bullshit and I had to stop my stomach from turning. I was still getting the feeling of betrayal from her.

"So you're telling me Roman might not be a cheating bastard?" she looked shocked. I was expecting happiness, joy, something other than what I was getting. Another flag was raised. It looked like she was disappointed.

"Yes. That is exactly what I'm saying. I can't be sure until I spend more time with him, but his motives in being with you might be as he tells you. After all, you are quite nice to look at." I told her this to see if she would let her guard down. If Roman was interested in her, it was purely for money. A faithful man wouldn't tell me he saw himself with me.

"I'm paying you a shit load of money for you to tell me I overreacted?" She placed her paper down and leaned back in the chair she was sitting in.

"What you are paying me for, Vera, is to gather information for you, whatever it may be. You pay me for the job. I can't determine what the end results are. We still have time and I might get something more substantial. I told you when we started, either way I get paid. This is what you hired me for, if I didn't know any better I would say you were disappointed in him not cheating." I stopped just to see what my words were doing to her. They slipped slightly, before she molded it back into an indifferent expression.

"Let us hope." And with that, she took the paper and left. The first time I met Vera she came off as young and naïve. This time it seemed like she was playing a game, and I was the main player. I didn't know what her motives were yet, but I was going to find out. The fact that I didn't trust anyone helped me weed out the people who were trying to screw me over. My brother Ira always told me, 'If you wanted to trust someone, trust yourself. Your instinct will never lead you astray.' He was right. I followed the feeling in my gut, and it saved me from death. It lead me to college where I got a degree in in social science and human behavior, and I busted my ass waitressing in a little crap in the wall diner. I paid all my loans off and graduated with honors.

"When you get older, Jo I want you to go to college and make something of yourself. I want you to show our parents that we are more than what they told us we could be. I swear it on my life Jo, you will go no matter what it costs me."

"What about you Ira? Don't you want to go and make something of yourself?" I said between licks of my ice cream. Mr. Molt gave us chocolate today it was my favorite. I always got to eat some of Ira's too, he would talk my ear off as the ice cream melted down his arm.

"My goal in life is to make sure nothing happens to you, Jo. I'm your big brother and seeing you happy will be enough for me."

"Ira, you always get so sappy," I laughed.

"Promise me Jo, promise me right now!" I have never seen my brother with so much determination on his face. I stopped licking my ice cream and wiped my face.

"I promise," I looked at him in the eyes and stuck out my hand for him to shake. He took my little hand in his and squeezed.

I meant to keep my promise, because the promises I made with Ira were the only thing that kept me going when I was hiding at night in trashcans or abandoned buildings. It was always somewhere new, I didn't want anyone to find me, and they were looking. That night when he told me to run, I ran and never looked back. I love you Ira.

I had to get back to the hotel room, I promised Jean I would accompany him to a gala of some sort tonight. He was catering a company's annual party, and he wanted to show up with the most beautiful woman he knew on his arm. Since I wasn't doing anything tonight, I thought what the hell. I had a sexy black strapless dress I had been dying to wear. I bought it months ago and never wore it because there was never an occasion that called for its extravagance.

I was ready at ten minutes till eight. When someone knocked on the door, I strode over to it and pulled it open. Jean Luke was there in a three piece, all black suit looking dapper.

"I didn't know the cook could wear such beautiful attire when he was catering the event." I smirked and leaned against the door.

"That's what sous chefs are for, love. All my creations and ideas, I'm just not me cooking them." He offered me his arm and I took it graciously.

"What if they mess up and ruin your good name?" I touched his shoulder lightly. If I was ordinary, I could see myself with Jean. He was handsome and was as sweet as a peach. I didn't deserve someone like him. I would weigh him down with all my fucked up-ness. It was like a disease and it caught fast.

"No chance in that happening. If it did, I would have their heads. They know. There is no need for me to tell them." He placed his hand on my arm where it rested in his.

"Fabulous, so I get you all to myself tonight. I haven't spent time with someone I liked in a long time." It was going to be a refreshing evening, and difficult all in one.

"Dressed like that Monroe, you could have me for life if you wanted." I just laughed because we had this talk before. No matter how much I wanted average, I wasn't. I couldn't allow someone to love me and be dragged down. I wouldn't survive this time.

"Tonight I am all yours Jean, but for life, that isn't in my cards." We got to the car and he opened the door for me.

"Ah, the nomad life. I understand, but it doesn't mean I have to like it." He smiled as he closed the door and walked to the other side to join me in the car. "I will take tonight, if it's the only thing I can get."

"Why wish for tomorrow when we have tonight," I smirked placing my hand on his leg and flexed. I was giving him false hope, and I didn't mean to, it was just who I was.

"Tonight it is," he looked out the window.

We pulled up to an old magnificent building. The architecture was stunning and it left me in awe. The building was enormous and stone. It had stone columns topped with frowning beasts. Put there to scare the life from you, no doubt. I marveled at its size alone. I had to crane my neck back to see where it ended.

"If you think this is nice, wait till we get inside." He took my arm once more and led me up the stairs. The wind blew at my neck and a chill ran down my back. I felt as if someone was staring at me as walked up the stone steps. I looked around and found nothing out of character. It must be the dress. It wore me, a black strapless dress with a lace flower print that was sheer on the lining of my body with random silver sequins. You could see my tan skin down the side, and it was scandalized because I wore nothing under it. My hair was in a fashionable messy braid bun pinned at the nap of my neck. I felt like I looked. In the dress, I could take on the world.

Jean was right. When we got inside, it was nothing like I had imagined. Everything was modern and in steel. It was as if tastes had clashed when it came to designing this marvel. He introduced me to the important people who were there, and when we came up to a red headed older gentleman he said, "Monroe, this is Fredrick Calvin. Mr. Calvin this is my lovely date, Monroe Wilkes." He took my hand and kissed me gently on my knuckles.

"It's a pleasure to meet you, Monroe. And may I say, you look lovely tonight. You outshine every woman here. Well, except my wife." He beamed down at her. And she was beautiful. She looked lovely in a light pink chiffon ball gown that was one shouldered, and pleated out at the waist.

"She is stunning," I said and introduced myself to Mrs. Calvin.

"It is always nice to meet friends of Jean," she replied and looked at him sarcastically. If I didn't know any better, I would say there was history between the two.

"Yes, Jean Luke and I go way back. I have been coming to his restaurant for years now." I smirked back.

"I would marry her if she would just say yes," he looked at me adoringly as he spoke.

"Ah back to this. If I ever change my mind about commitment you will be the first to know." I joked playfully, but if he waited, he would be waiting for ages.

"What an outlandish idea!" Mrs. Calvin claimed. "What woman wouldn't go for a catch like Jean Luke?"

"I am afraid, madam, that I am a very peculiar woman. Though I love Jean Luke dearly, I do not see the need for such frivolousness. It is, after all the twenty-first century and women have been doing things on their own for a while now. I am sure a woman of your stature can relate. Though it isn't right for me, I do not take judgment on those who choose love for their lives. I think love is beautiful and is to be celebrated. I just wasn't lucky enough to find it yet." I was selling this crap. I didn't believe that at all, but I didn't want them to look too closely into what I was.

"A shame that is too," Mr. Calvin chimed in. "Enjoy the party, Monroe. It was nice to meet you." He departed with his wife by his side. She gave one more glance over her shoulder. She seemed vaguely familiar. I felt like I had met her before. Maybe it was from another case.

"She seemed to know you," I pointed at Jean's chest.

"It was all history, water under the bridge. There is no one in this room that has my attention, but you." It was a nice notion, but I didn't need to get into any catty exchanges with any other woman when I wasn't in it for the long run.

"Will you excuse me? I need the powder room." I took my leave and found the bathroom that was bigger than my hotel room. It had a woman in there ready to help you or spritz up with perfume. I told her no thank you and washed my hands, taking a moment to collect myself. I just met my client's parents, I was getting too close to this case and my gut was telling me to back out now. It wasn't just telling me, it was screaming it, get the fuck out.

I walked down a hallway that lead to the main hall. Right when I stepped out of the corridor, an arm snaked around my midsection, pulling me behind a pillar and pinning me against it.

"What the fu…" I started.

"Now that's not proper language for a lady, and if you're not quiet everyone is going to hear us." Roman said.

"Why are you touching me?" I asked though I really wanted him to stay against me. He had one leg pressed between mine. Any passerby would assume we were lovers.

"I didn't think I was going to get a chance to talk to you and I wanted to tell you…" I stopped him.

"You wanted to tell me how lovely I look. I know I've been told all night."

"No, I was going to tell you that I have had a fucking boner since I laid eyes on you. I know you don't respond well with niceties. So, I thought I would try my hand at vulgarity." He ran his middle finger down my chin as he bore into my eyes.

"I don't respond well to anything you are giving. If I remember, you are here with your girlfriend. You better hurry up and get back before her daddy gives the CEO position to someone who is willing to pay attention to his little petunia!" I pushed him off me and attempted to dust off the feel of his touch.

"You might not respond to me, but your body likes what it sees." He pushed my back into the pillar.

"You went from saving me from assholes like this to being the asshole I need saving from. This world is going to hell! I have zero faith in humanity." I sighed.

"I couldn't take it anymore, I feel something when I'm around you, and no, I wasn't going to say love. I was going to say you made my dick stand and it won't listen to me anymore. Did you want to kill me with that dress?" Tilting his head to the side, he devoured my skin that was under the see through fabric. "Nothing on under there is there?"

"Is that any of your concern Roman? Go back to Vera." He looked confused for a moment.

"I don't think I mentioned her name before."

"You must have or how else would I know it?" I pushed back once again. This time he took the hint and stayed away.

"Save a dance for me, Monroe, I will look for you later." I was left there, breathing heavily and wondering how the fuck I got myself into this. He was my mark, my target. I didn't catch feelings for anyone, but yet it seemed like he was cracking my inner bitch.

When I got myself under control, I moved from behind the pillar and looked for Jean. He was talking to a group of women who were pawing at him. I had to admit he was a catch. I understood why they would want him, he was everything you looked for in a man. Caring, warm hearted, easy on the eyes, and he was stable.

He looked up and saw me walking to him, and immediately moved in my direction. "There you are," he smiled and placed an arm around my shoulders. It was to show the women that he was there with someone. It was a polite way of telling them to back off.

"Sorry, I almost got lost. It was a palace in there." I smiled at the women as I spoke.

"I told you it was truly amazing in here." The music began to play and everyone seemed to just couple up for the dance. It was weird. It felt like they were drones. Jean placed his hand on my waist and guided me to the dance floor. "Care to dance?"

"I would love to." I gently place my hand on his arm. Enjoying the small things in life like dancing was something I dreamt of but couldn't quite touch. I was so busy with work, and I had to remember when I was on a job. Moreover, no matter how much I liked Jean, I was going to be leaving soon and I didn't know when I was going to be back, if I ever did return.

He guided me across the room, and it felt like we were gliding. He was a good dancer and the authority that he possessed showed in the way he held me. I looked up into his eyes and he pulled me closer. Resting his hands right above my ass, he rubbed his hands softly over the thin fabric on my skin.

"You know, I wasn't lying when I told you I would marry you if you would have me," his head bent down slightly.

"Not this again, I've told you. I am not the marrying type. I am poison and I will kill you right along with me." After that, he didn't say anything to me and we danced two more songs. The third song started and we were still mingled together, until someone came up and tapped Jean on the shoulder.

"Can I have the next dance with your lovely date?" Roman said with a cocky smile. I was going to object, but then thought twice. Jean had death in his eyes. He remembered Roman from last night. I pleaded silently with him not to say anything. He nodded and walked to the sidelines.

Dancing with Roman was completely different from dancing with Jean Luke. Roman didn't seem to care if anyone thought something. He placed his hands on me possessively, almost like he owned me. "Why are you doing this, Roman? I'm here with someone else, and you want to make a fool of me."

"I am doing this because you are here with someone you don't want to be here with. I was simply saving you, like the first time we met. You told me earlier that I went from being a gentleman to being an asshole. I was just showing you I can play both roles."

"I don't need both roles. I need you to leave me alone. Like I told Jean, I am not the commitment type."

"So, I was right. He wants more than just to be your friend. I was wondering why he keeps giving me dirty looks." Jean Luke must have seen Roman before I did. He didn't like him so it made sense that he was giving Roman bad looks. It would explain why he was more hands on than usual. It was men trying to mark their territory.

"It would explain why the men are acting barbaric tonight. I thought someone slipped something in the punch." Having his arms around me was different, but in a good way. With Jean's, I felt like I was with a dear friend, there was no chemistry at all. With Roman, I could stay like this all night and never realize the time.

"If you didn't want anyone acting like a fool, you shouldn't have worn that dress. You are like a present every man in this room wants to open. Somewhat of a surprise, yet it has my stomach in a knot."

"Flattery gets you nowhere, and I can tell you now, the woman you are looking for isn't here right now. She is where?" Get in the game, Jo. My brother's voice echoed and it didn't matter if I was here at this party or somewhere Roman and I were alone. I was paid to do a job so I needed to get my head out of my ass.

"You sure?" I was positive it wasn't my heart he was tugging at, but muscles lower.

"You know what, fuck it!" I said and placed my hand on his ass and squeezed. "Might as well do what I want since you aren't going to leave me alone. I have been dying to get my hands on that ass all night!" It was firm in my hands as I imagined, but to my surprise, it was thicker. Now it left me wondering if the front was just as thick. If only.

He was shocked and I took pleasure in his discomfort. "What are you doing?" he whispered. "Everyone is watching."

"You want to play with me? I am going to have fun destroying you. Don't act like this isn't what you wanted. I was just making your dreams come true. Let's play. I'm game. Buckle up baby, this is going to get crazy." When it came to pleasure, I was all in, and if it was a battle he wanted, I would win.

"Wait, I thought we would take it slow and get to know each other," he shrugged and moved back from me a bit.

"Is that what you had in mind when you pinned me to the column earlier? Let me tell you something, I don't give a fuck who sees, when I want something, nothing is going to stop me." I ran my hand up his back and asked. "Are you ready, do you want to start this with me, because there is no backing out." I was bluffing and nothing was going to happen. I wanted to see his squirm. I wanted to watch as everyone in the whole building looked down at Roman for what he was doing.

"I... all I wanted was for you to think about it. You wouldn't even look at me if I was the person in the café." He looked at me grudgingly.

It took me aback for just a second. I knew this was a game he was playing, but for what? Why were he and Vera plotting against me?

"I don't get to know anyone. Did you think I was just going to fuck you and what…? What was the end game? You have me completely confused." He was smirking now and I wanted to slap him. The music stopped and I moved from him and found Jean, I needed to get out after I just grabbed him like that and I was here with one of the important people here tonight.

"Jean I am so sorry, but I must be going." I gathered my dress into my arms hastily making my way to the front door. Usually I was reserved and I didn't get physical with any man in public. I did the only thing I told myself I would never do—I had embarrassed myself. He didn't say anything to me as I left, and I was almost positive he wasn't going to talk to me anymore. It was a friendship I was going to miss. Even though I told him there was nothing between us, it didn't excuse my behavior.

I flagged down a cab and went to my hotel. Thinking needed to be on my list of top priorities. I was getting to close to the subject. Yes, that was my goal, but I faked it all. This was not fake. I wanted him, and I was going to give in. I hadn't been with a man in a long time, and my hormones were going crazy. My body felt like it needed him, and I wasn't going to deny myself for much longer. The best way to avoid breaking my rules was to get out of this town and far away from Roman. Getting into my hotel room, I pulled the pins from my hair and placed them in a row on the dresser. Scrutinizing over them being perfectly aligned.

The urgency to write Vera a letter was strong. Getting these feelings out was going to be the death of me. I couldn't believe I was letting such a little thing ruin my life, a man at that. Was it worth everything I built, everything I have poured my blood and sweet into for years?

Dear Ms. Calvin,

I regret to inform you that I will not be able to work on your case anymore, for there have been things that I just can't work around. I would like to say that being professional, that I could handle any situation that presented itself to me, but I just cannot. It has nothing to do with you, but Roman. I feel he is deeply in love with you and do not want to force myself on him. I wish you and Roman the best of luck with everything in life.

Monroe

Yours truly,

Monroe

I gritted my teeth as I wrote the last words, thinking to myself how I felt anything but happy for them. I wanted nothing more but for them to break up. He was never going to be mine, and I just met him. In my line of work there was no happily ever after. There was only heartache and pain. A knock on the door snapped me out of my angry thinking. No one knew I stayed here except Jean, and him coming here would be insane.

Right?

I opened the door to find Roman. I stopped myself from being pleased. It was getting more dangerous as time went on. He didn't get the concept of leave me the fuck alone.

"Aren't you going to invite me in?" he asked and started forward as if I had already extended the invitation. I didn't ask him how he knew where I stayed. It was obvious he followed me.

"No, I am not. You shouldn't be here, you should go." I pushed him back and started to close the door.

"Why are you acting like that? At the party you couldn't seem to keep your hands off me, now you act like you don't want anything to do with me." He pushed past and sat on my bed. What the hell was up with people? Did they not believe in personal space?

"That was all an act. I wanted to teach you a lesson. You wanted me, and you wanted your fine fair-haired woman too. I don't like sharing. If I ever wanted to be with a man, he would be mine. All of him." I went and sat in the chair and watched him. He crossed him legs and gazed at me thoughtfully.

"You weren't playing, and what if I told you, you could have me? What then? Would you still be running right now?" he said knowingly. He asked questions that examined my personality.

"It wouldn't make a difference. I was leaving town already. I thought I would just get some extra time packing. I have an early flight and need to be ready tonight." I never said making excuses was beneath me, I just preferred to tell the truth. Lies came out of my mouth and tasted nasty. The bitter taste would linger there and make me wonder why I told them in the first place.

"You think you can lie to me? Like I don't see it written all over your face. I'm not stupid, and I'm not telling you I want to marry you. All I'm saying is try at least." He looked hopeful like most men in his position. Thinking if they sold themselves well enough, all women would have a difficult time saying no. He didn't know me as well as he thought.

"There is no try in my vocabulary. I haven't thought about being with someone in an extremely long time. Why would I do it now? A pretty face and sugar sweet words? You might as well marry Vera. She is the one who will give you 2.5 kids and a white picket dream." It was intense between us. The words coming from my mouth were different from the language my body was speaking. I was shaking from the sexual tension. The need to have his hands on me again, to feel the first excitement when he pushed himself into me.

He got up from the bed and started stalking toward me, never breaking eye contact as he walked. It was the most penetrating staring game ever. When he reached me, he stood there looking down at me, trying to intimidate me. I wouldn't break for my asshole father, so no man would have an effect on me.

"I think you are trying to talk yourself out it. I think you want it so bad, it's scaring you. Funny thing is, I didn't think anything could scare you. Your eyes say you are fearless, but your emotions read something completely different." He ran a hand over my loose wavy hair.

"Please stop." I swallowed and closed my eyes, willing him to disappear, because if this was going where I thought it was, I wasn't going to have the strength to say no any longer.

"Tell me truthfully, do you want me? If you can make me believe you then I'll leave. I will never bother you again, I'll never talk to you. I won't even look at you if I see you again. All you have to do it make me believe." He let his arm fall back to his side and waited for me to answer. My eyes were still sealed shut. I was trying to gain my composure, looking at him would make me lose all my senses.

"I don't want you here," I said through a tight mouth. It made my words sound muffled and crazed.

"I don't believe you," he said as he took my hands and pulled me to my feet, pressing my body to his.

"I need you to leave, get out!" I shouted. My chest vibrated as I breathed heavy.

"Just because you yell, doesn't mean it's going to make me believe you." This time he took my arms and raised them above my head. As he brought his hand down, he caressed the side of my breast. I moaned unexpectedly. "Make me believe you, Monroe" he breathed as he kissed the side of my neck.

I gave up screaming. He wasn't hearing me even with my words loud. "Please leave me alone," my voice shaken and my body trembling.

He didn't tell me he didn't believe me. The silence was overwhelming so I opened my eyes and looked at him. It was a mistake, his eyes bore into mine. Desire was laced in his stare.

I was in trouble.

He turned me around so that my back was to his chest. I started to put my arms down, "Don't." he said simply. "I want you, Monroe and I know you want me. I'm just done fighting it. I will make you believe it with my hands," he said and started to unzip my dress. "I will have you believing it as my lips trail your body." He kissed down my skin as the zipper revealed it. As the dress fell to the floor, he kneeled with it. "I will possess your body and make you mine. When I finally get inside of you, my mission is to have you so far in ecstasy that you can barely breath, and Monroe I will have it before you leave." I wasn't used to men being so crude with me. Yes, catcalls and pick up lines were horrible and disrespectful at times. But what he was doing to me, it went against everything I learned from the world.

"I don't want to be yours! I don't want to be anyones." I said pathetically. There was nothing on under my dress, my skin rippled with goose flesh from the cool air coming in from the window. Roman was on his knees, his eyes locked on my ass. He ran his finger lightly up my bare leg.

"You will be, and I'll have you begging me to do more." He grabbed my thighs and pulled my ass to him, kissing each cheek then smacking it playfully. "Now tell me what you want me to do." The slight sting from his slap thrilled me.

What I wanted him to do was leave. I was still holding hope that he would get out so I wouldn't cave. He looked so fucking good down there staring up at me. I wanted to sit on his fucking face and smoother him. It had my pussy wet just thinking about it. He had the most remarkable eyes, one brown and one blue. I could imagine his eyes looking at me and he rolled his tongue over my clit. I licked my lips and moved from him. Turning, I sat in the chair.

I thought about calling someone to get his ass out of here, but my body refused to let me. I needed him to fuck the shit out of me and leave the next day. I spread my legs as I leaned back in the chair. His eyes went from desire to hunger, trained on my sweet spot. My stomach knotted as he crawled to me and placed his hand on my thighs and extended them further.

"Is this what you want me to do to you?" he asked and moved forward and inhaled my unique smell, further driving me crazy. I wanted to see my juices leaking down his chin. I wanted it to glisten on the tip of his nose.

"I want you to leave, but since you aren't going to. I might as well put you to good use. You are going to eat my pussy like you are starving." He must have liked what I said because he lowered his head and swiped his tongues over my slit. It was electrifying, causing my body to convulse slightly.

"Sounds like a plan." As he stated those last words, he began to devour me, consuming me whole. I must have blanked out for a while from all the pleasure building in me. I pushed him on to his back and straddled his face, looking into his eyes as his mouth found its way back to my pussy. It was the most intense moment my body had had in, well, forever. The orgasm squeezed at my stomach, demanding its release. I busted on his face, and he rewarded me with a wicked grin.

"I have no words to describe what just happened! Now it's my turn!" he declared as he hoisted me up and pinned me to the wall. He was so rough my head slammed against it.

Just how I liked it.

Men usually had no idea what to do with me in bed. They bore me. I required someone who challenged me and wasn't afraid to be rough. I jumped up and he caught me in his arms. He kissed me as if I were everything he ever wanted, and everything he ever needed. I tasted myself on his lips. Salty and sweet. He placed me on the bed and stood back admiring me.

"If you aren't the sexiest fucking thing on this planet!" He started to undo his tie. I was getting impatient looking at him, so I started rubbing my nub, watching him as he undressed.

"Stop that!" he scolded as he slapped my hand away. "I'm hard just watching you. I want to give you every orgasm you receive tonight." I moved side to side as he took his belt off. He stopped and watched my expression. He slapped his belt against my inner thigh and told me to be still.

He let his pants fall loosely to the floor, kicking them to the side. What I saw wasn't what I expected, but it was mouthwatering and I needed to get my mouth on it as soon as possible. I sat up and scooted to the edge of the bed, pulling him to me by the hips. His thickness was intimidating. The thought of it pushing into the back of my throat gagging me caused my pussy to weep.

Licking it would have been pointless. I dove right in, taking him all the way into my mouth. He hit the back of my throat and made me gag like I knew he would . Most women wouldn't like the choking. I loved it. It turned me on. My eyes watered and I looked up just in time to see Roman's eyes roll to the back of his head. I popped it out like a lollipop and licked the tip as his tangy pre-cum invaded my mouth.

He grabbed my hair and pulled my head away from his dick. I fought against the sting on my scalp. "Ahhh! If you keep that up, I am going to cum before I want to."

He fell to his knees once more, making him eye level with me, he took my nipples between his fingers and pinched them until pain shot through my body. I wiggled and a noise escaped my lips. I thought maybe he would apologize for being so rough with me, maybe he would think I couldn't handle it. Most men would ask because if it hurt. It gave them an ego boost. Not Roman. Whatever he was dishing out, he knew I wanted it. He knew I fucking reveled in the pain. My body needed it. Part of me felt alive when pain was inflicted on me.

"I am going to fuck you, Monroe. Do you want me to? Tell me how you want it." I wanted everything he wanted to give me, and I would take the beating with no complaint.

"I want you to do what you want to me. I don't care what it is. I just want to feel it." It was enough for him. He pulled me up and pushed me onto my stomach. He arranged my hands so they were wrapped around the metal headboard.

"Do you trust me?" he asked.

"No. I fucking don't." I retorted and smiled.

"Okay, I am going to ride you hard. So hard, in fact, it's going to make you want to cry. I know that pussy is tight and no one has been in it for some time. My cock is going to have you walking funny for weeks, and I don't want you to move your hands from that spot, do you understand?"

"What are you my fucking father?" he bent over my back and grabbed my face in his hands and squeezed.

"That mouth is going to get you in trouble. You are going to wish you never met me. I was nice before, but nice isn't what I like in bed." He shoved my face away.

"Are you going to keep talking, or are you going to fuck me? I can get some tea while we talk about your day." He slapped my ass hard. I felt it run up my back.

"Keep talking to me like that, and I will shove my dick in your mouth and keep it there till you can't breathe." He had no idea what his crude words were doing to me. I might be acting like a badass, but I couldn't wait to feel him push into me.

I didn't have to wait long as he pulled out a foil wrapper, ripped it open and rolled in onto himself. God, if he wasn't the finest thing I have ever laid eyes on. He noticed me gaping at him over my shoulder. I wasn't secretive about ogling him. He whacked his length on my ass and rubbed it in between my crack. "You like what you see?"

"It's fan-fucking-tastic." I said and reared back.

Without another word exchanged, he spread me wide and drove into me. He was right when he told me it was going to sting. I adjusted to him quick enough. Either way, he wasn't giving me more than a couple seconds.

"So fucking wet," he moaned and began pumping into me. It was rough and painful, and every fucking inch of him was exquisite. As his pace quickened, I found it difficult to keep my hands on the headboard. I was slipping off.

He stopped and looked at me. "I told you to keep your hands there." When he stalled ,it was more torture than what he was doing to me. I liked the pain, and he wasn't going to give it to me. The only way he knew how to tease me was not giving me what I wanted.

"I want to nut in your mouth and you are going to let me." I wasn't thrilled over swallowing bodily fluid.

"No thanks. You can keep it to yourself." I panicked.

He didn't say anything else as he continued his brutal attack on my pussy. He yanked my head back as he rode me like he promised, and all I could do was enjoy how he was making my body feel. I let out a scream as the orgasm took over my body. It was so intense it hurt as he continued to move in and out. It wasn't long before he came. It felt like a jolt surging through my entire being. I came undone once more. Just from the thought of making him cum.

I laid there for a while, relishing in the sweet bliss. When my head started clearing and my thoughts became coherent again. I remembered that I fucked up and I recalled someone coming to my house and helping me with my misguided decision.

"As much fun as that was, you need to leave." I said and grabbed my robe.

"What?" he asked, stunned. He was still lying there with the condom still wrapped around his dick.

"I didn't stutter, did I? I said you have to go! That was fun, but that was all it was. I told you, I don't do relationships. Please don't over think this, and don't make it something it isn't." I wrapped the stings of my robe around me tightly, feeling dirty and like I did something wrong. I needed to shower, and the sooner he

133

left the sooner I could get one. It was what I felt after I had sex. Like I was dirty and my skin needed to be scrubbed. It was my father's fault. The bastard took so much from me.

I gathered his things off the floor and tossed them to him.

"I don't even get to clean up?" he looked stunned as I picked his shoes up.

"No, you live somewhere I assume, so you can clean up there." I threw his shoes at him. I walked to the door and opened it looking at him expectantly.

"Wow, I guess you are heartless."

I laughed and placed my hand on my chest. "You didn't think it was going to mean something did you?

What was your plan? Fuck me good and expect me to fall into your arms and adore you forever." I cooed and puckered my lips. "You are so adorable. You think if you fucked a normal woman like that, that she would just let it happen. You would have killed that poor girl. I am what I have always claimed to be." I waved my arms as if I was showcasing a fucking prize on the price is right. I was offering him the door and that was all.

He shrugged into his pants ,creeping over to me with his slacks still open. He didn't bother to put on anything else. He smiled and moved into me, "If you think you're going to scare me away, you're going to have to try harder." I slammed the door as he went through.

I sat on the bed and thought about his words. What was I going to do? Thinking hard to myself, I laid back. Completely mortified at what I had done. A loud bang on

135

the door brought me out of my mind and I got up to answer it. I was still in my robe with nothing under it. I should feel inappropriate going to the door like this, but I had no fucks to give,

I opened the door expecting Roman to come back to try to sleep in my bed, but when I opened the door Jean was leaning against the frame looking disheveled and out of place. His bow tie was draped around his shoulders. His hair was mussed as if he were pulling at it.

"Jean, what are you doing here?"

"What do you think I am doing here?" He moved into the room, looking straight at the messed up bed. "Please tell me, why were you in such a rush? I noticed someone following you so I thought I would come and check on you, but it seems like I am not needed." He backed into me, making his way back to the door.

"Let me explain… Jean," I said as I placed my hand on his arm trying to calm him.

"You don't have to explain anything to me! You made it clear that you aren't looking for anything. But maybe I should have tried to fuck you. Maybe then you would have liked me more." He grabbed my arms and looked at me. The anger there was crippling. "Why, Monroe? I have loved you for so long. I wanted nothing more than to make you my wife. I would have taken care of you. You would have never have to work again. I could have saved you." I felt like shit when he first came into the room, but his last words sobered me up.

"I don't need anyone to save me. I am fine with everything I am. I will not be told I am anything less than great. My life is my business and I will do as I please. You are right about one thing, Jean. I did tell you I didn't want anything. I will never love you .You get that, right? You get I'm the heartless bitch that everyone says I am." I pulled away from him and he let go without a fight. His mouth was hanging open a bit, because I just ripped out his heart and served it to him on a silver platter.

"I guess I will be leaving," he said as he slumped to the door.

"I think that's best." I closed the door when he was gone. I slid to the floor and rested my head against the door. What the fuck just happened?

When the sun shined through my open blinds in my room, I got up. I had been awake for a while now, but I didn't want to move. Everything from last night kept repeating itself in my mind. My brother used to tell me not to be the girl everyone expected me to be. At the time, I didn't know what he was talking about, but now as a woman I understood.

Monroe

Don't be the woman men want, the fast loose type.
Don't be the woman other women will hate, the one who
is all flash and talk. I was being judged because I was
blonde and I was beautiful. Automatically, they thought I
was stupid, and I knew nothing.

*"Jo, you ready?" Ira asked. He had gotten us into the
public school, something my parents didn't think needed
to happen. No matter how much the school board
harassed them. They would say they were home
schooling us, when in reality daddy just didn't want to
lose slaves around the ranch.*

"Yes," I said.

*"Shhhhhhh... If they hear you, we're going to get it."
He wasn't lying. It was early. We had to get out of this
house before my momma woke up. If she found us, she*

would tell daddy, and he would beat us. Ira would get it worse, he was the oldest and he was condoning it.

"I am," I whispered and took my bag to the window and tossed it outside. I sat on the ledge and jumped off landing in a soft crouch. Ira followed me and we ran off. The sun wasn't up yet, but you could see the orange poking over the horizon. We were going to sleep for a while under the steps at the school and wait for it to start.

Little did I know, my brother let me sleep and stayed up to watch what was going on, to make sure I was safe. I missed him with every memory I had.

I couldn't stay in bed all day no matter how much I wanted to. I had to meet with Vera. I needed to get ready. I told her to meet me here in the lobby, there was no reason to be secretive anymore. I was leaving today, right after our meeting. I was on the first flight.

I chose something sweet and comfortable for our meeting. I was thinking comfort for the flight, but cute just in case I met a future client. I grabbed the letter off the table and my recent notes on Roman, though most of them were made up. She deserved to know something. She did make a deposit that was nonrefundable. I did consult her after all. I walked slowly, taking the stairs. I was going to be there too early, and I wanted to think out what I was going to say to her. After all, she was going to be pissed off. The first five flights were quiet. When I got to the sixth, I heard someone talking. I peeked over the banner slightly to catch a glimpse of who it was.

Roman was there with Vera, and at first I saw red. Thinking to myself he was with me a few hours ago, yet he is here in the staircase with her. I was silent so I could hear what they were saying.

"Look Roman, you need to get more on her. I told you to bring her down, not fucking fall in love with her. How does that happen anyways? You just met that bitch!" Vera was agitated and talking out of her ass. All my ideas of her being innocent went out the window as she went out. "What's your plan now?"

"I don't have one!"

"Well—fucking—done! You sleep with her and can't manage to actually bag her! That was supposed to be a deal breaker remember? 'What woman could say no to you?' Do you fucking remember that?"

"She isn't like normal women, Vera. She doesn't have the normal emotional problems women have." Damn right I didn't, I did have baggage that no one knew about and I was going to keep it that way.

"I have to go, I have to meet her in a couple minutes, and I have to collect my damn thoughts!" With that, Roman left the stairwell.

"Why the fuck can't I seem to take this bitch out?" She screamed and punched the wall, leaving a streak of red on the titles. She is a fucking unhinged bitch.

I snuck out of the sixth floor stairwell and went to the elevator. I was still going to meet with her. Feeling guilt and sadness over something I had done was something Josephine would do—and I wasn't her anymore. Vera's mother looked familiar to me the night I met her, and I kept telling myself there was something about Vera herself. There was always something off with her, as if her soul wasn't there. As if she let anger rule her mind. I could tell now, it was the connection I felt with her. I was missing my soul also.

Kindred spirits and what not.

I would play her game if she wanted me to, I would go in there like nothing happened. I was going to dig and get what I was looking for. My mission changed and I would not be leaving. It was all a set up, and they just made this the biggest game of my life. I walked into the lobby and scoped the place out. I was on high alert, and everything I took in was in focus with great detail.

No shocker, she was there before me looking devious as hell, like there was nothing in the world that could upset her day. If I hadn't seen her and the way she was acting, I would have thought everything was sunshine in her life. But I knew she was a snake, and she was here to try and destroy me. People who held grudges were deadly. She would do anything to take me out, and that included murder. I knew, because I felt the same way. She just didn't have it in her to do whatever it took to get her revenge. Too bad for her, I did.

"Vera, always lovely to see you." I blathered as I sauntered up. All I wanted to do was uncover why she was so angry.

"Monroe," she nodded curtly.

"So, straight to business then?" I placed the paper with my notes on the table. She snatched it up and looked it over.

"What do you mean your findings are inconclusive at this time?" she seethed.

"Is there something wrong with you today, Vera? You are looking under the weather." It was the nicest way you would say someone looked like shit.

"I am fine, and I really would like to know what "findings" refers to." She mumbled through clenched teeth. She placed the note down, looked at me, and smiled. Now that I knew what I knew, she wouldn't be able to trick me, and I would never believe she was innocent and caring. She was the fucking devil and she was out for blood.

"It's simple really. Roman is a man, he has been forward with me, but he hasn't touched me in a way deemed inappropriate. I don't know if he's interested or if he's just bored. Sometimes men get uninterested in who they are with. It's like you playing with the same toy for years and it loses its shine. They will be boys and look for something shiny and new. It isn't that he doesn't want the old toy, but when you get something new it is always more exciting." I crossed my legs and picked at an invisible fuzz ball on my pants. I was giving her time to digest my insult. I want to bask in her anger. I wanted to eat her up and spit her rotten ass out.

"So what? Is there any point to continue doing this? Are you telling me he's eventually going to lose interest in me?" I had to say, Vera was an exceptional actress. If I didn't know any better, I would say she was really in love with Roman. But Vera was taught that mixing business with pleasure wasn't how daddy ran things.

"I am saying that if you really want him, you're going to have to work your ass off to get him and keep him. You're going to have to do things you normally wouldn't like. You need to ask yourself, is he worth it? There is a

148

chance you'll put all the effort into it and still not get anything." I shrugged and got up. As far as I was concerned, this little powwow was over. I didn't like being around conniving women, or people in general.

"That's it? All I get for twenty racks is a half assed shrug and a maybe if you work for it?" I smiled at her and it seemed to piss her off even more.

"What else do you want me to do? I am like a private investigator. I get what you ask for, and I am telling you what I found out. He doesn't want to cheat on you. He doesn't want to marry you. He does however want his job. To me, it would be like taking candy from a baby. You're the daughter of his boss. I am sure you can think of something to get what you want."

"I want you to find out more. Can you just stay for another week? I want to be sure. I don't want to marry someone who doesn't want me." She was grasping for straws, and I loved it. I didn't plan on leaving. I was going to dig up everything I could on her, and I was going to make her pay for ever trying to fuck me over. As for Roman, I had something just as devilish planned. I was going to make her watch me fuck the love of her life, and I was going to take the only thing Roman loved more than himself. His job. My plan was to turn them against each other and watch from the sidelines as both of their lives fall apart.

"I will make you a deal Vera. I will stay—since you are so desperate…"

"I'm not…"

"Don't interrupt me, it isn't polite. I'm going to stay because you begged me." She gritted her teeth. I could feel the waves of rage rolling off her body. "But, I have one condition. I will not be meeting with you more than once a week and I will be taking my money in advance. I also want forty thousand now. Things seem to be getting sticky and I want to insure that I get all of it, just in case. No matter how this ends, I want you to know one thing." I waited to give it a dramatic pause.

"What?"

"I always get what I want, and no one will stop me. Bring my money here by tomorrow. If you don't, I am on the first flight out." I knew she would do it because she hated me so much. I could see her contemplating murder.

"Fine!" her fury was my joy. It was a sick, twisted game we were getting into and I was willing to dance for life. I had an idea of what I was going to do, and it wasn't going to leave any survivors.

When I got into my room, I sat on the bed and smiled to myself. Now to get ready and find Roman. I was going to make him fall so fucking hard. He was going to be left in a coma. I submitted last time, but this time I was going full on dominant. He wouldn't know what to do with himself.

Shopping was a must and it would clear my mind.

Let the games begin.

Staring at my reflection in the mirror brought on sad memories. When I was growing up, my mother would hit me in my face trying to make me ugly. My nose was broken so many times, it had a bump in the middle. I didn't mind it and I used to think it made me hideous. But looking at it now, it gave me character. The dress I chose to wear tonight was more revealing then even last nights. It was a cocktail dress. Snow white and it had a hole cut out in the middle of my abdomen. It showed off the curve of the bottom of my breast, and with no bra on, my nipples were standing at attention. The dress was so short it barely covered my ass. If I bent over in it, everyone would get a show of my nudeness. I didn't understand why the dress was long sleeved. To me, it showed too much skin to have a purpose.

I was aiming to kill, and I was going to make heads roll tonight. A little birdy had told me Roman was going to be at Haven, a club in Manhattan. My little birdy was never wrong, so I got dressed and made my way down to the lobby. Every man I walked by stopped and craned his neck in my direction. I smiled to myself, it was impossible not to. My long blonde hair was down to my waist in long, loose curls and thanks to my hair extensions, it was thick and full. My eyes were smoky, and my lips were a pale pink, creating an illusion that my lips were full and pouty.

The door attendant opened the door for me but not wide enough, I had to rub against him to make my way out. I teetered on my six inch Manolo Blahnik heels that were silver and black.

"I apologize, Miss—I didn't mean to do that." He was lying his ass off, but it was okay. Tonight, everything was going to be alright. I had a plan, and I was ready to put it into action.

"No need to apologize," I smiled and dropped a fifty into his hand as I walked out and waved down a cab. My right boob was close to popping out. If I wasn't careful, tonight would be all tits and no ass. Pun intended.

The cab pulled up to the club and the bouncer pulled open the door. He must have been expected something else, but when he saw me the grin that night, his face was radiant.

"Welcome to Haven, Beautiful. Let me know if there is anything I can help you with. I mean anything." He opened the rope for me without even looking at the guest list.

"Thank you, sexy," I ran my finger over the seam of his blazer, causing his pants to tent. Men were so fucking easy. I felt like I was dreaming as I walked in. There were strobe lights of different colors and a DJ in the corner playing some sweet hip-hop . The dance floor was live and the crowd was gyrating in a sexual fashion. I couldn't wait to get out there and move with them.

I decided on going to the bar to get something to drink first. Drinking wasn't my thing, but I wanted to have fun and let go. The plan I had mapped out before I got here should be put in a hall of fame for completely diabolical mastermind schemes. I drank whiskey straight, so when a Cosmo was placed in front of me, my eyebrow shot up in question.

"I didn't order this." I shouted to the bartender over the blaring music.

"No, but the man over there did." I looked to where he was pointing and saw an older gentleman making his way over to me. The look on his face was predatory and when he reached me it became perverted.

"I thought a pretty girl like you could use a tasty drink." When he said tasty, he dragged his s to make it sound like a snake. Tasssty. What it was was nasty.

I smiled at him and handed him the drink. "Sorry, my mother told me not to take drinks from strangers. I don't like fruity. You can give it to someone else." He looked at me as if I had lost my mind.

I moved away from the man with a small dick complex and aimed for the dance floor. Before I even got my feet on the floor, a hand grabbed my arm and stopped me. Thinking it was Roman, I smiled before I turned. It was Mr. Small dick.

"You are one rude bitch!" he shouted into my face. What was it with men and calling me rude? They didn't like that I was blunt and I stood up for myself.

"So I've been told. That doesn't change the fact that I don't want anything to do with you!" I yanked my arm but he had a good grip on it.

"Doesn't change the fact that I will fuck you if I want to! You look mighty fucking tasssty." Yuck.

"Get the fuck off me," I said lightly. "Or you are going to be tasssting your own damn balls for life!" I like to think I grew out of my fear of men. That I now thought of them as any other object I could own. It worked for a while, but I couldn't fool myself. When I was confronted in situations like this, it scared the shit out of me.

My daddy was telling his friends I was going to be a nice piece of ass when I got older. He didn't know how I got to be as pretty as I was. He said my momma wasn't a spring chicken anymore. Ira held his hand over my mouth trying to muffle my sound. Daddy told him not to go around me. He didn't want Ira to see what he started doing to me. He didn't know I told Ira everything, I trusted no one but Ira.

"I told Betty, she wasn't as tight as her sweet little daughter." He laughed. I cringed at his words. This was my father who was talking about me. He hadn't done anything to me but touch me. I knew it was wrong, but he told me if I moved or screamed he would kill Ira and give me to his friends.

159

I said nothing the whole time, not even when he told me to get up so he could remove my princess panties. Ira stole them for me, so I would have some when I went to school. I would never look at those princesses with the same innocent eyes. I was ashamed of what he was doing to me. It was my fault. If I stopped making him mad, he wouldn't be hurting me.

The whole time my father did this to me, I was emotionless. You would think a child of my age would cry, or beg him to stop. I did neither. He didn't deserve my tears. I already knew what life was like, partly because my parents were shit. What I went through then would only make me a stronger woman in the end.

Snapping back to reality, I pulled the man's hand back so fast I heard his fingers snap. Breaking the bones in his hand played like a symphony in my head. Thoughts of my father littered my brain, bring me back to my eight-year-old self. Wishing so badly that I could hurt my father, I wanted to kill that stupid son of a bitch. And I hoped to one day.

"What the hell!" The man screeched and I laughed. He got what was coming to him for being a sick pervert.

"I told you not to touch me, now you're going to be in a cast! It's going to be hard touching any other poor girl. You need a lesson in how to treat a lady!" I waved over the bouncer from earlier, and he came promptly.

"This asshole was just leaving." The security guard looked down at the pervert's hand and then to me again.

"Should I even ask?" The bouncer examined.

"You can have him tell you. I'm sure it will all be very entertaining and accurate." I maneuvered through the crowd. Roman was nowhere in sight. There was a balcony overlooking most of the club, it was the best place I could think of to see him. Maybe he would be in VIP. He did strike me as a pansy who would sit in VIP all night and didn't get up and dance. I needed a drink after what happened with the snake, so I got another shot from the bar and went off in search of this exclusive room.

The whiskey burned as it moved down my throat, a drip trailed over my chin and I wiped it away. The liquor was making my blood warm. I needed to slow down before I ended up shit faced. I stretched the fabric over my breasts and secured them into place. I went back to the bouncer and asked him if there was a VIP section and if so, where it was located. He told me everything he knew and gave me his number. I promised I would call him if he could get me into VIP.

He told me he probably couldn't, but he would try if I gave him a hug. I did and he grabbed my ass. I knew what he was going to do before he did it. I playfully slapped him on his shoulder, but I was really pissed off. I followed him to a door that lead to another part of the club. I had no idea this was even here. The door said it was for employees only, which usually was a broom closet.

"Damn! I didn't even know this was here! You guys are sneaky." I smiled and moved away from him before he tried to grab me again. "Thanks, and I promise to call." I waved and dropped the fucking number on the sticky floor and watched as people trampled over it. Fucking ingrate.

It was a different world behind the velvet ropes. I walked with confidence, like I belonged here, and I did. I spotted Roman in the corner with some other men wearing monkey suits. He looked like he was having an after work meeting. What a peculiar place to have it, since the lights were so dim it was hard to see my own hands that were right in front of me. He didn't notice me because he was deep in conversation with them. I decided to act like I hadn't seen him either. I took a seat at the bar and ordered another shot. The bartender brought my drink and waved my money off, telling me the man at the end of the bar had bought it for me. One of the best things about being a woman is the free drinks, and I don't feel like I set feminists back. They are going to buy them and try their hand at you either way, so why not?

I saluted the man with my drink and then drained it. The music in here was different then in the main room. It was more sexualized and slow. The atmosphere they were setting was not lost on me as I scanned the room. There were couples hooking up in all corners. My muscles tensed involuntarily, I was only human, and seeing the woman in red with long black hair riding her suitors dick as if she was on a bucking horse got to me, and I liked it.

Another drink was placed in front of me. I looked over at the end of the bar to thank my drink donator once again. He looked at me, raised his eyebrow, and looked at the couple I had been studying. Sex. It was normal. It was a basic instinct. It was something that connected us to our animalistic side. I might have issues with it, but I loved the way it made me feel. And this guy who was buying me drinks wouldn't be able to handle me. My problems in the bedroom ran deep. I would hurt him… and like it.

I licked the rim of my glass and tossed my head back. If I kept this up, he was going to come over here thinking he was going to get lucky. I loved flirting and this was what it was. The only man I had eyes for tonight was Roman. He was the only one I wanted to go home with. He was the only one I wanted to be riding. I returned my eyes to the woman in red and watched as she threw her head back in ecstasy. Her pleasure almost got me up out of my seat. I wanted to know what her eyes looked like as her face contorted in passion, I wanted to taste her moans as they escaped her lips.

I closed my legs tightly, not wanting anyone to know what I was thinking, or how I was feeling.

"You like what they're doing?" a whisper came from behind. I turned and stared into the eyes of the man at the end of the bar.

"Yes, I do." I admitted. I was so turned on at that moment, I couldn't hide it.

"Would you like me to make you scream like that?" I really didn't. But right now all I kept thinking about was Roman at the table adjacent to where I stood. He had finally noticed me, and he didn't look happy that another man was so close to me. He was getting up to come over when the man placed his hand on my thigh and started trailing it up my leg.

"No, I can handle it myself." I took my last shot and moved away from him. Fuck! I was vibrating with need. I strode to the dance floor right as one of my favorite songs started playing. It was dark, and so sexual that it made my condition worse. On the end of the dance floor Roman stood as I started to move my body. I kept my eyes trained on him, I knew he was hired to do this. He didn't really want me but I couldn't help the pressure flowing through me. I needed him.

He stood there watching me. He loosened his tie and wrapped it around his hand, balling it into a fist. He must have had enough, because he stalked over to me and grabbed my arm pulling me off the dance floor.

"What the fuck Monroe? Are you trying to get people killed?" he walked me to an empty corner and all I kept thinking about was the woman in red. I pushed him back onto the couch, and straddled him.

"I want you," I said and rubbed my hands over his cock. His pants were in the way but I could tell he was ready.

"Not here." He moved me to the side and got up. "I don't know what got into you or why you are here in that fucking rag, but you need to pull your shit together.! After I am done with my clients, I will come and find you." Everyone he was here with was staring at me. No one has ever blown me off. He made me feel like I wasn't good enough, as if he wanted nothing to do with me. The feeling was foreign to me. He could have it back.

"Don't bother!" I said, storming away.

He pulled me to him, pressing his chest into my back. "Do you know what I thought about doing when I saw him touching you, running his fucking hand up your leg? You have no clue what I felt. I shouldn't feel this way! You are fucking up everything I have worked for. You are making me question everything I have thought to be true. So please, get mad and walk away like I did something to you. I can't even fucking think straight with you around!" He pulled his hair and laughed dryly.

"Bye, Roman!" I called over my shoulder and walked away. Or more like wagged my ass at him. Getting out of the club was hard with all the dancers and people jumping all over the place. I was bumped into every few inches. I had sobered up from Roman's words. Again, he had left me feeling ashamed. Like I was a slut or a tramp selling herself.

Monroe

"Josephine, where are you girl?" My daddy called. I didn't want to go. He was going to touch me again. My mother would just sit there and watch it happen. "Josephine, girl if you don't come out, I got the boy here and I'm gonna slit his throat!" He tapped the tip of the knife on the metal gate of the front door.

"Jo, don't come! I'll be okay!" Ira screamed and my father bent his arm behind his back. I watch as the tears rolled down Ira's face. He was going to choke him to death. I couldn't take it anymore. I came out from the bushes where I had been watching.

"I'm here! Don't hurt Ira no more, please!" I begged and walked up the front steps.

He threw my brother down the stairs. It knocked him out. I cried silently and looked to my mother for help. All

171

she did was avert her eyes. She didn't shed one tear. She didn't give a fuck about what he was going to do to me. She didn't give a damn that he just threatened to kill her son. What kind of mother would do that to her child?

I got to my room and didn't feel like doing anything. The night was long and I felt like I needed to burn it out of my memory. Roman turning me down had hurt. It hurt more than I would admit aloud. I was usually able to keep the memories of my father at bay, but something about Roman has brought them out. My mind was unravelling and I didn't know how long I could hold on. Love was killing me. It was my curse.

Love. Roman. My father and Ira. My sweet Ira, who I missed more and more each day. Maybe it was time for me to give it all up and just be. I could take a vacation. Matter of fact, after I got out of here that was what I was going to do. I was going home to visit my brother. It had been years.

Someone was at my door, and I knew who it was before I opened it. I had taken off my dress and was only wearing my heels. I thought about putting something on, but I said fuck it. If it wasn't Roman, I would give someone a good show.

"Why the fuck are you opening the door like that?" it was him luckily, but he wasn't happy with what he was seeing. I thought I was going to have the opposite effect on him.

"Well, hello to you too! Why are you here Roman?"

"I told you I was going to come see you. Or were you too drunk to recall? If it wasn't me you were expecting, why the fuck would you open the door naked?" Why was he giving me this attitude?

"Why, so you could scold me? I can wear whatever I feel like and I can dance with anyone I want." I grabbed my robe and threw it on.

"Why put it on now? Why not just flaunt your body in front of everyone? You don't care. You might as well hand it out." He walked to the sink and washed his face.

"You might as well leave. You are projecting onto me, and I don't like it. You're acting like I'm your girl or something." I waved my hands wildly at him.

"Why do you act like that's a bad thing? Why couldn't you be my girlfriend or my lady or whatever you want to fucking call it."

174

"Because love isn't in my future. There is nothing for me down that road. I am worthless, don't you get it?" screaming wasn't going to help anyone but it felt good to finally let something out. I always have to keep my cool.

"You don't mean that. You can't be serious." He stalked the room as he watched me.

"But I am, I'm dead serious. There is so much you don't know, and you will never be able to wrap your head around it. Just leave, I am tired, and today just needs to end." I tried pushing him toward the door but he didn't budge.

"Stop. I'm not leaving. You annoyed the shit out of me today. You show up there in that dress and you expect me not to get mad. Please, don't tell me you weren't there for me. I know you were. I want to know how you figured out I was there?" he grabbed my arms and shoved me onto the bed.

I was supposed to be the dominant one. He wasn't supposed to be taking control. I was a fucking nut case. All these damn delusions and flashbacks were killing me. It was throwing me off my game.

Monroe

"You are the most confusing woman I know. What do you mean you're worthless? I have been trying to figure you out, but I keep running into dead ends." He was pacing the room.

I kept giving myself a pep talk. This was a job. This was the game to end all games. I was going to be out of here in a week, and I was going to be like, 'Roman who?' I just needed to get my mind right.

"Never mind what I said. I didn't mean it." I threw back.

"This is what the hell I'm talking about! You are one place and then another. Hot and cold, what am I to do? I have no clue how to approach you." He stopped in front of me and dropped to his knees, placing his head in my

177

lap. "Please, tell me what you want?" Either his feelings were real, or he was playing me. My past didn't let me trust anyone and it pushed everyone out.

"All I want you to do is fuck me and tell me what you want. I'm the one in control tonight." He looked at me with his beautiful eyes, one blue and one brown. They were like a clear river on a muddy shore.

"You can have me any way you want." he stood and consumed me with his hungry eyes. "What do you want me to do? I am all yours." Guilt swamped me, I peeked at the vent I had set the video camera in. Why feel bad? He would ruin me if I let him.

"Take your clothes off!" I commanded. He started rushing with his buttons fumbling over his own fingers. "Slowly." He is doing a job just like you, and he probably doesn't have real feelings for Vera, but Vera's feelings were very real. I was out for her fucking blood. If Roman got hurt in the crossfire, it would be a casualty I was willing to accept.

He was glorious in his nudity. Everything about him was hard and ready. My mouth went dry as he stood there at attention. "Play with yourself," I said.

"I would rather play with you." He smirked.

"Did I tell you to speak?" I shouted at him. His cockiness pissed me off. The feelings he was causing me pissed me off.

"No," he stood like a good little solider a smirk gracing his full mouth.

"Good, I didn't tell you anything. All I want right now is to look at you." I walked circles around him touching him, stroking him. All while his hand kept moving up and down his shaft. "That's right, keep stroking, and think of me when you are doing it. Imagine it's my tight pussy enveloped around your dick." He moaned. "I feel so fucking good? don't I baby?" I bit his arm.

"You feel fucking amazing!" he muttered. I dropped my bathrobe, and stood before him nude. He reached out and tried to pinch one of my nipples. I wanted him to do it more than anything, but I was making a point. He was going to beg me.

"No, you don't get to touch. Just look at what you could have been in tonight." I walked behind him and rubbed my tits on his back. "Tell me what it feels like. I want details. I want you to tell me how much you want me, and if I like the answer maybe I will give it to you."

"Monroe, you are a fucking tease and when I get my hands on you, you're going to regret what you're doing." His knees were bending and I nudged them back a little.

"I regret nothing and I can take anything you can give me. Stand straight, pump faster and Roman, you will not nut, you will not get pleasure from this." I laughed.

"I'm fine with that as long as I get you." His hand that was stroking his cock was moving rapidly and it made my cunt clinch.

"I'm not sure if that's going to happen. I haven't decided. After all, you didn't want me earlier." I pouted at him and twisted his nipples. It had to hurt, but all he

181

did was bare his teeth and rub his dick harder. He enjoyed it as much as I did, I would say he loved it.

"You are driving me crazy! I am going to cum," he whimpered.

"If you cum when I've told you not to, I will punish you." I watched as sweat collected on his forehead. He was trying so hard, and who was I kidding. He was going to get it. I needed him, I wasn't lying about that. I walked to the bed and sat down in front of him. At first I kept my legs closed as I watched him. I was entranced by him, I rubbed my legs together but the friction wasn't enough. I leaned back on my elbows and spread my legs slowly. I was going for seductive, and from the look on his face, it was working. I stuck two of my fingers into my mouth and sucked on them, my eyes never leaving his body.

I started slowly, rotating my hips as I circled my clit. "Ahhhhh… fuck!" my bud was swollen. I stuck both fingers into myself and rubbed my g-spot. I was still watching my blue and brown eyed monster. That was what he was to me. My monster. He made me feel so much in so little time.

"Can I please touch you?" he asked as if he was in pain.

"You can come closer because I want to touch you. Watching you is so beautiful. Everything on your body is perfect." He moved to me as I asked, keeping the pace of his shifting hand. His endurance was impressive. Who was I to deny him release? He wasn't going to get to bury himself in me, but I was going to give him my mouth. "Lay down Roman." He did as he was told.

"What are you going to do to me?" he wondered out loud.

"Don't concern yourself with my business." I stopped his hand and moved it. "No matter how good it feels, I don't want you to touch me. Just stay the way you are." I took him into my mouth and moaned. I could taste the saltiness of the pre-cum he used to slicken himself. I moved up and down, twisting and twirling my tongue over his head. He placed his hand on my head and pushed it up and down forcing himself in more than I could take. I gagged, causing my saliva to pool in my mouth. I loved the feeling of gliding up and down his shaft making him feel good. The sounds filtering out of his mouth were going to be the cause of my own release.

"Monroe," he moaned. I longed to hear him call my real name, but it would make me feel like I was ten and with my daddy. He used to call out my name as I gave him head in my room.

It was always late when daddy would come into my room. Ira was sleeping and he told me if I acted like I was sleeping, my daddy wouldn't bug me. He didn't know what he was talking about because daddy didn't care. He was going to take it no matter what.

"Jo, get on your knees, I know you ain't sleeping." If I didn't get up, he would pull me up by my hair. I did what I was told and dropped to my knees, watching as he unbuckled his belt and dropped his pants. The smell of his unwashed skin tickled my nose. Bile raced into my mouth and I swallowed it back down. "Don't look at me like that. I'm going to make you a woman. I am going to teach you things your momma don't even know how to do right." He was a disgusting excuse for a man, and at ten

Monroe

I knew this. I knew he was nothing, and one day I would be standing over his dead body. He would force my head down, and the sides of my mouth would bleed, but he wouldn't stop fucking my face. He would laugh and look at me and say. "It's ok Jo, that just gives it more lube." This sick twisted bastard was going to die.

I jumped off the bed and looked at Roman, breathing heavily. Roman had a way of making the memories resurface. I didn't want to remember the things that happened before. It made me lose my mind. As if I was living someone else's life. Like I wasn't even there.

"What the fuck was that Monroe?" Roman shrieked. He was holding on to the end of his shaft. When his hand moved from it there was a slash of crimson left on his hand.

"I… I'm so sorry, I don't know what came over me." I was breathing hard as my body trembled.

"It's fine—I think it's only a scrape. Come here," he called and I ambled over to him and gently kissed his cheek. "I really didn't mean to do that," I said softly. I was completely mortified. He was the reason these memories were coming up and if I wanted them to go away, I was going to have to stop seeing him.

One more week.

"Hey, it's okay, we can just… talk. That was more than an accident. We can talk about it if you want, or something else." I was too tired to be mean and I didn't have it in me right now. I wasn't going to tell him but he was right. There was something wrong with me.

"You're right. There was something else, but I don't think I can talk about it. I don't trust anyone. There is no way I could tell you something so personal about myself." I yawned.

"That's fine. Just let me comfort you. Is that okay?" Comfort me? The concept of emotions left me baffled. What he was asking me scared me. After what I just did, how could he be serious?

"Why would you want to comfort me? All I want from you, Roman is fucking. There is nothing more I need from you. Don't get the wrong idea."

"The only thing I get—is you! You think you can hide things so well. You think just because you walk around like you have no emotion that it really works?"

"You know nothing about me. All you see is a pretty face and a nice ass." The bathroom was calling my name. I wanted to hide in there and never come out.

"I know enough, and was still willing to look past it. I was willing to try to see everything you were trying to hide from everyone else. I thought, hey if she lets me in a little it would be a miracle. But no, you're too hard-headed and stubborn to let anyone care for you. Let me ask you something. When was the last time you actually acted like yourself? Not the person you think you turned into?"

Good question. I had no idea when the last time was. I couldn't even recall the last person I laughed with. I mean really, really laughed. People just assumed I was who they thought I was and I let them. It was easier than telling them who I really was. They didn't want some sob story about how my dad raped and molested me. People only wanted to hear the happy shit. The stories about babies and childhood memories that consisted of going to Disneyland or the time you and your mother baked cookies.

"This is who I am. This is what I became. Don't you get it yet? If I wanted to be saved, I would have asked a long time ago. I wouldn't have waited for you. I wouldn't have waited for anyone."

He remained silent as I ranted. He looked at me like I was wounded. Like I was a child he could scoop into his arms and care for.

"Will you ever let me in? Are you always going to be so cold and distant?" It was a simple enough question, but it was one I didn't have an answer for.

"I won't lie and tell you I haven't thought about letting you in, Roman but in the end, I won't be able to trust you." At this point, we were just standing in the middle of the room looking at each other, completely naked. It wasn't uncomfortable. There was no need to cover up. There was no need to rush to him and throw my arms around his neck. I didn't get butterflies in my stomach from looking at him. When I looked at him, my stomach pinched and my pussy got wet. He was the man I wanted to have buried deep in me every night, and that's as long term as I got.

"What are we going then?" he asked and slapped his hands against his leg.

"All we are is what we are doing now. It's simple. This is all I am offering you. I don't know if I'll be able to ever open up to anyone, but if this is what you want to keep doing, I am all for it." I shrugged.

"This is all, and what if feelings start getting involved? Are you just going to leave and not let me know?" he quizzed.

"Roman, after this week I am out of here anyway. I am on to the next person, the next city, and not knowing what it is thrills me. What I'm telling you is just that. Let's have this week. I will give you as much as possible, but no promises." Looking up at the vent, I remembered what was behind it. An uneasy feeling swam in my gut, but I had to follow through with my plan. He after all, was still listening to that bitch Vera. Thinking about it made my blood run cold and Monroe peeked through and showed her face. There was a devil on my left shoulder and an angel on the right one. They muttered evilly sweet things to me. The angel was no better than the devil. Both were debating their sides, but they both wanted the same thing. Roman. While my angel whispered tales of love and glory, my devil sang of passion and pain. They both had a point. Seeing Roman run through fire to please me, lit my insides up. Chills broke out on my skin. My mini devil was pleased with the thought. In the end, I knew what side would win. I was already lost.

"I'll take it, if that's all you are willing to give me. What the hell do I look like turning it down?" Roman accepted.

"You would look like a smart man. If I were you, I would walk away from me. I come off a little strong and most people don't want anything to do with me." I smiled.

"Now, are we done talking?" he asked. My eyes fell to his manhood. He was getting hard again just from listening to my laugh.

"I was waiting for you to get over yourself and realize what was waiting for you." He touched himself and lifted his eyebrow at me. The sideways smile always got to me. He was going to be my undoing.

"I see, and what makes you think it's what I want?" I bent down and squinted my eyes. It was a joke and he laughed and looked down at himself.

"Hey, that's not funny!" he covered himself like I had embarrassed him, but that would never happen. He was too full of himself.

" I'm trying to inspect the product, before you go telling me I want it and if it's not funny, why are you laughing?"

"Okay, I'll admit it is a little funny." He moved toward me and placed his arms around me. "It isn't small, and until you admit that, you won't be getting any of this." He made a show of his body. He was still smiling. It put me at ease to know he understood some of what I was going through.

"It isn't small. It is the biggest I've ever seen, happy?" I placed my hands on my hips and looked at him with a smile.

"When you stand like that, I don't see how I could be anything but happy." He smirked and pulled me back to him. "Did you notice, even when we weren't covered up, it didn't feel awkward?"

"I did," I backed him up until his knees hit the bed.

"Well, that is what normal feels like. Not the nudity alone, but the arguing while naked and coming to an agreement." He fell into a sitting position and I mounted his lap.

"It felt like something alright. I don't know if you can call it normal." His erection was stabbing me in my lower abdomen.

"Don't freak out when I tell you this, but I wanted you to know. I'm going to try my hardest to get behind the wall you have built." My face must have done something funny because he started talking fast and his words started coming out wrong.

"I mean…just… where were we?" The words finally made it out of his mouth and I licked his lips.

"Ah, just the words I craved to hear." He tasted magnificent.

He slipped me on to my back and gazed down at me. "You are stunning."

"So you've told me, let's get this show on the road." I sang.

He didn't reply to my sarcastic antics as he lowered himself onto me, rubbing my body softly as he went. There was nothing to take off this time. He licked circles around my navel as his untamed eyes drifted over my face. When he was done with one spot, he would blow on my skin. It created a hot and cold sensation that left me breathless.

197

He touched me like he was in tune with my body and its response. He knew where to touch and caress, like there was a button he only knew existed. I didn't have to tell him where to go and what to do. It was nice. He pulled my pebbled peak into his mouth and bit it lightly. This time felt different. It wasn't hard or rushed. It felt like he was making love to me. He had claimed me last time. This time he wanted to make a point. I arched as my nipple popped out of his mouth.

"I love how you respond to me." His eyes became dark with desire. He stuck one of his thick fingers into my mouth and told me to suck on it. I did as he asked. He pulled it away and trailed it over my body. Making his way down my stomach causing it to quiver and shake. When he reached his destination, he looked at me wickedly and circled my clit. The feeling building in my body was intense. I wanted to scream, I wanted to claw at his skin. All these feelings being born inside me left me confused. He was lovingly caressing and exploring my body. His fingers slipped into me, and the euphoria I felt was beyond words.

I heard rumors about love and pleasure being mixed. They said it was something you had to experience. It wasn't something that could be explained, but if they had to, it would be described as an out of body experience. It was as if you were feeling, hearing and tasting everything around you, but you and the person you were with became one and everything you felt, he felt. This is what was happening. I was feeling everything Roman felt, and it hurt. Or it was going to hurt. There were too many feelings behind this already. I was too selfish to walk away, and he was too blind to give a damn. We were at a stalemate, but I was going to take what he was giving me and love it.

The beginning of an orgasm was tugging at my stomach. If I could sprout wings, I would be flying from the intense feeling. I laughed when it spread throughout my body.

"What was that? Are you laughing at me?" He didn't know what he just did to me was something that most men couldn't accomplish. I was in complete bliss. The laugh was a good sign.

"No, no, nothing like that. Everything is fine," I laughed loudly.

He reached for his pants and began pulling them on. I was lost for words because I've never had to explain this to anyone. "I don't think this is funny Monroe. I was baring myself to you."

"It's isn't funny. You're right, I wasn't laughing at you. It's just something that happens when I cum sometimes. Now, why don't you come back and finish what you started?" I patted the bed beside me and laid back. I spread my legs so he could see what he did to me. I was soaked and determined to have him inside me. He wasn't leaving until he came too.

He didn't bother taking his pants off. He just unzipped them and pounced on me. "I guess it's just something I have to get used to. I've never had a woman laugh at me during sex." he kissed me gently and ran the back of his hand over my face. I closed my eyes and swallowed. I should leave. I shouldn't have even started this knowing where it was going to take me.

"I wasn't laughing at you," I pushed him off me and told him to lay back. I wanted to ride him and watch as he came undone. I wanted to watch as he lost control under me. "I want to watch you cum." I said and slid onto him. I wiggled to adjust myself. I almost came again from the pressure against my cervix. I placed my hands on his chest as I began to move up and down. Slowly at first, but as the raw passion took over, I rocked faster. I pinched my own nipple and licked my lips as Roman gripped my hips, and slammed into me.

"Cum for me baby," he said through clenched teeth. He was close. He was extremely close. I felt his shaft throb inside me, pushing me over the edge, claiming me completely. Roman followed soon after, calling out my name as he came inside me. It was the first time anyone had cum inside me.

I wanted to stay in our bubble and feel this way for a little longer. It would end soon enough, but I was going to hold onto it as long as it allowed me to.

"That was intense! You didn't laugh that time. I guess it isn't every time." he rubbed my back as I lay on his chest. He was still pulsing inside of me as his erection began to soften.

"No clue why." Sometimes it happened and sometimes it didn't.

"I should clean up, and you should too." He started to move from me, and when he pulled out, I felt lonely. I have worked years to hide who I was from everyone and in one night he came and destroyed everything I have worked so hard on. It put me in a rage. This isn't who I am. I was the bitch no one liked. I was the fucking cunt who would bury you.

Sliding into my nightshirt, I ambled over to the bathroom where Roman was washing up. "Time to leave," I said and placed my hands on the frame of the door. His back stiffened, but he continued to clean himself. I watched as his ass cheeks flexed as he moved and bent. He was beautiful and I would have liked him to stay. My pride was being a bitch, and him breaking through my wall wasn't going to fly with Monroe, but Josephine wished he was the exception. He wasn't because I knew what he wanted to do with me.

"Monroe, are we going to do this again? Stop pushing me away." He was in front of me faster than my eyes could adjust to what I was seeing. He had my arms in a tight grip, and he shook me lightly.

Monroe

"What are you doing Roman?" I looked into his eyes and saw crazy written all over them.

"I am trying to get through to you. What has happened to you in life that you can't let anyone in?" his grip on my arms didn't loosen. If anything, it got tighter.

"You can't get through to me. You can't save someone who doesn't want to be saved. I told you this once. Do I need to remind you what this is?" I was a cold hearted woman. When did I get to this point?

"I don't believe you, and you are screaming it even if you don't know. I can hear you, and I am not going anywhere. I won't hurt you, Monroe. I think I'm…" I stopped him with my hand.

"Don't say what I think you're going to say. There is no way you can feel like that." I covered my ears and looked out the window.

He moved my hand and looked me in my eyes, making sure I saw he was serious. "How are you going to tell me what I feel? You can tell yourself you feel nothing. You can keep telling yourself these bullshit lies, but I can feel what I want to feel. I'm going to get through to you no matter what you tell me. I'm not going anywhere anytime soon." he strolled over to the bed and got into it naked. "You can either get in with me, or you can sleep in the chair. Either way, I am sleeping here tonight in this room with you." he looked at the side of the bed I never slept on and turned and covered himself.

I sat in the chair and watched the lump in my bed. "Monroe, I can feel you staring holes in my back. You can join me if you'd like to. You don't have to sit over there in the cold."

"I don't want or need you in my bed Roman! Vera is going to be missing you. I think it's best if you get going." Every time I talked about Vera, it pissed him off.

"Stop talking about Vera! I I don't live with her, and I am not tied to her."

"Yet, you mean. What game are you getting at? We both know what this is about Roman. You aren't going to leave Vera. Or should I say, you aren't going to leave Calvin & Co." It was blow I wasn't going to come back from easily. It was meant to hurt him, insinuating he was just in it for the money.

"I don't give a fuck about that job Monroe! I was looking for a way out a long time ago. There is nothing I need there, including Vera. She has it in her mind that I'm going to marry her, but I can't stand her spoiled ass. She gets everything she wants, and if not she's going to leave destruction in her wake." He didn't raise his voice. His tone didn't imply he was angry, he said it lazily, stating facts.

"I don't believe anything that comes out of your mouth. I was clear when this started what it was. I don't know how you fell in love from that point to now, and I don't see how it's my problem." He had to go. I could feel his nut starting to drip out of me. If I didn't get to the bathroom soon, it would be all over the place. I turned to go when an arm snaked around my waist.

"You want me just as bad." he whispered against my neck. "I can feel it." He took my hands and placed them on the door. "I am going to have you begging me when I'm done with you."

"Didn't you tell me that when we first fucked? It isn't going to change the outcome." I pushed back at him, causing his cock to push into my asshole. It sent chills up my spine.

"You can act all you want Monroe, but I am going to claim you in the end. You will be mine." He was such a confident bastard.

He kicked my legs further apart, so I arched back into him. He lifted my shirt up further to expose my entire backside. He slapped me on each cheek then rubbed it after. "The only way I can get through to you is to fuck you. Do you want that?" I thought about the come that was still inside of me, and it excited me to know it was going to slicken his dick as he pushed into me.

"Yes, please," I moaned out as he pushed into my entrance.

"Are you going to let me cum in your mouth baby? I want to release and you suck me dry."

"Yes, anything you want." I was lost in the motion he was creating. I surrendered to the motion, I let it claim me, as the devil in me leered, making promised of eternal damnation. He stopped and my body kept its movement. I bucked back but he stilled me. "Tell. Me. How. You. Feel." With every word, he slammed into me. Bringing me close to the brink but pulling me back as he stalled.

"I feel like I'm going to cum, so shut the fuck up!" I screamed into the door.

"I won't let you until you tell me how you feel." he pulled my head back by my hair and licked the length of my neck, kissing his way down my back. "Tell me how you feel, damn it!" He thrust into me, causing my knees to buckle. If it wasn't for him, I would have fallen, but he held me there as he continued his attack on my pussy.

"What does it matter Roman? It's not like it's going to go anywhere even if I tell you!" I shrieked.

"It matters to me. I need to know that what I'm feeling isn't just my imagination." he paused again and I cried out in frustration. "Tell me, please."

I shouldn't have looked back at him. I shouldn't have looked into those eyes. It was my undoing. "Yes, I feel it." I whispered. At first, I didn't think he heard me, but when he grabbed my neck and turned my face to kiss him, I knew he did. He didn't break the kiss when he started pushing into me. He stroked my g-spot and it left me in tears. The pleasure was so unbearable I thought I was going to bust open.

"Cum!" he commanded.

"I don't want to!" I shouted back.

"You are going to cum right now!" I tried to hold it in. I was trying to be defiant and hold on to some part of who I was. In the end, he won and I squirted all over his shaft.

He pulled out of me and told me to get on my knees. I did what I was told, opening my mouth to receive him. Every time he entered my mouth, it took some adjustment. The taste of his cum and mine mixed caused the heat to build in my sex. He grabbed my head and pushed inside my mouth, hitting the back of my throat making my gag reflex react. I pulled away from his grip, spitting the extra saliva on his head and rubbed over it.

"You like that?" I asked, looking up at him from my squatting position.

"You like this?" he asked and looked at me tenderly. "I love it. Now, open your pretty mouth." I smiled and listened as he forced his dick as far back as it could go. I lost it. I was so turned on by this man. I came watching him fuck my face. My juices were flowing down my leg. I moaned around his manhood and he stilled as he shot his load into the back of my throat. I swallowed all of his salty fluids and beamed at him.

"You taste so good," I licked my lips and stood.

"Now, was that so hard?" he asked.

"It was harder than you will ever know," I told him and walked into the bathroom. I left the door open just in case he wanted to come in and wash up too.

"You can hide from everyone else Monroe, but you will never be able to hide from me." he kissed my back before he turned on the shower. "You want to get in with me?" A shower sounded great after a long night like this.

Monroe

I went to sleep last night with Roman at my side. This morning, I wasn't shocked to see that his sleeping figure was gone. Even if he told me he didn't care for Vera, there was still a job to do. He was still going to have to go through with his job if he wanted to be paid. It left me wondering what he was going to do afterward? Would he try to love me after he pulled the rug from under my feet?

Though I didn't want to do anything to hurt him, I felt it was necessary to teach them a lesson. It would be harder than that to get to me, and I wasn't going to go down without a fight. The more I think about Roman almost telling me he loves me, the more it starts feeling like a ploy trying to make me love him, and then acting like Vera is the only one for him. Vera was going to get hers. I recorded everything last night and I was going to hack into the company's electronics and put the video up for everyone to see. Of course, I was going to block out my face, but Vera would know it was me, and that's all that mattered in the end. The thought of her crying and in hysterics left me drenched. It was the evil inside me. It wanted to see her fall. I was going to be the one to do it.

Getting ready for the day was less mechanical than normal. I had a pep in my step and it was due to the fact that my plan was coming together nicely. Last night I might have let him see some of me but it was to get him to trust me. Or so I kept telling myself.

Today was going to be a difficult day. I was going to go and try to make things right with Jean. I know he isn't going to be nice to me, but I hate the way things ended between us. He was the only thing I allowed myself to have in this life. The only friend I had. He couldn't stay mad at me for being real with him. I told him shit was going to go south if he kept letting himself feel things for me.

We will see how it goes.

Monroe

I pulled the door open to Jean's place and walked into a half-empty restaurant. They opened at noon, and it was only nine. It had been a couple days. I hoped he wasn't mad anymore and had time to clear his mind. Everyone seemed to be on their toes this morning, as if they were tiptoeing on eggshells. These men and women were loyal to Jean, but you could tell he was in one of his moods. He must still be pissed at me.

"Monroe, I don't think it's a good time to come by", the waiter from last night told me as I stood in the entrance.

"Nevertheless, I will be seeing him before I leave. Please inform him that I will be in his office." At the other end of the dining room, I heard a bowl crash into the wall followed by some obscene words. He was just going to have to get over his little tantrum.

I waited in his office as I told them I would. It didn't seem like he was in any rush to come and see me. I was fine with it, and I would wait until he was ready to walk in here. As soon as the door opened, I could feel his wrath.

"Monroe," he said as he took his seat. He wouldn't even make eye contact with me.

"Are you going to pout the entire time? Or are we going to be the adults that we are?" he stared down at the floor for a moment then hammered his hands down on the desk.

219

"You embarrassed me in front of everyone in the company and you just want me to forgive you and act like nothing happened?" Was it wrong that this was exactly what I was hoping for?

"Why are you really mad, Jean? It isn't just the fact that I embarrassed you. There is more to it than that."

"Isn't that enough? Isn't the fact that you left with another man, enough? Or the fact that everyone was looking at me with fucking pity in their eyes? Like I was a lovesick puppy! How am I to forgive you for stomping on my heart?" He was breathing heavily with so much hate in his eyes. I might have been wrong to think he would be kind to me and forgive what I had no control over.

"I was wrong to come here." I grabbed my bag and made my way to the door. He was there before I turned the knob.

"Just tell me one thing," he fumed.

"What?" He wasn't a small man and him standing over me with anger running through him had me a bit shaken.

"Do you have feelings for him?"

"Him?" I was confused at first.

"Don't play coy, Monroe. The jackass you danced with last night." I thought about what he was asking me. I thought about everything that happened last night and I was kidding myself if I said no. There was something there, whether I was willing to admit it or not. My need for revenge was stronger though.

"If I told you there wasn't, I would be lying to you and myself. The fact still doesn't change that I don't get involved like that. I am a woman and I have needs just like a man, and just like you. I am sure you took your anger out on one of the women who was throwing herself at you last night. Just because I slept with him means nothing. It was a stress reliever." I sighed and sat back down. There was no use standing there. He wasn't going to let me leave until he was done saying what he needed to say.

His office was cold. Filled with steel furnishings and glass. There was no color in here, making me wonder if there was more to Jean then what he was letting me know. This room was cold and void of any personality.

222

There were no pictures on his desk and everything was neat and in its place.

"You couldn't find relief in me?" Of course I couldn't. Jean made me as wet as a desert.

"You know I think of you like a brother or a best friend." I tiptoed over to him and placed my hand on his cheek. It was something my brother Ira did when I was upset and he tried to calm me down. It helped, though it would never take away the memories or the pain they caused. "The last thing I wanted to happen was for you to get hurt. I love you in my own way, and I am selfish because I don't want to lose you." He gently took my hand in his and turned it to plant a kiss on my palm. He was one of the sweetest men I had ever met. I was a selfish bitch because I was willing to hurt him just to keep him.

"I forgive you. Monroe. Can I try one thing?" he was moving closer to me before I gave him the go-ahead. He was going to kiss me. Not sure what to do, I closed my eyes as his lips gently touched mine. It was nice and soft, but it wasn't a kiss that invoked passion in me. It felt like I was kissing my brother. "How did that feel?" He was looking at me expectantly. Was I supposed to enjoy it? Was he going to get mad at me when I told him, it just wasn't doing it for me.

"I don't feel it. I'm sorry." I released my held in breath. Honesty was the best policy. I didn't want to lead him on and give him false hope. "How did it feel to you?" It was only right that I asked him too.

"I thought it was something I wanted for a long time. I have been dreaming about kissing you for five years already. I built it up in my head so much, it fell short in the end." I couldn't help myself. I laughed. It wasn't what I expected. It was better. He didn't like me anymore. I wasn't the only one who though chemistry was important when it came to loving someone. I was so relieved. It felt like a weight was lifted off my chest.

"You don't know how happy I am to hear you say that," tears threatened my eyes as I looked up at him. I didn't want to lose him as a friend. This was another sign that I was changing. If you would have asked me a month ago if I saw myself needing friends, I would have laughed in your face and told you you were crazy. It seems I have lied to myself and I needed people more than I would admit.

"Jo, why are you fighting? Those girls just wanted to be friends with you." Ira asked me as he cleaned the blood from my split lip. He didn't want the teacher to ask

225

anymore questions. They noticed all the cuts and bruises left from my daddy. Ira had told them it was nothing and I liked to fight the boys in the neighborhood. They believed him, but kept an eye on me anyway.

"They were calling me names Ira! They didn't want to be my friends. They told me they heard stories of me and what I let their daddies do to me." I couldn't help but cry. It wasn't my fault their fathers were all dirt bags who needed their bits cut off. What they were doing to me was wrong and I could feel it.

"It doesn't matter what they call you Jo. They don't matter. They don't know what you're going through. Why should it matter what they are talking about?"

"It does matter Ira. Why are they talking about me when it's their daddies that should be punished? Why are

226

they quick to point at me, when they should be thinking about what these men are doing to a little girl?" I was tired of letting people touch me. I was tired of everyone thinking it was me. I was tired of no one sticking up for me. So, I was going to. I was going to tell my teacher what was happening to me. Daddy told me he was going to kill Ira if I ever told anyone. It was the only reason I kept my mouth shut for so long. I would die if anything happened to Ira.

"It's okay Jo, come here." I flinched from him when he reached for me. I saw the hurt in his eyes as I shrunk into myself. It wasn't that I didn't trust Ira, I just didn't want anyone touching me anymore. The feel of fingers over my skin made me remember all those drunken nights my daddy would have the men over to play.

227

I didn't trust women much. As I recalled, it took me years to get over the feeling of someone touching me. To this day, it gives me anxiety, even when someone bumps into me. I have come so far. I should be proud, but all I can think about is what he did to me, and my mother was no better. I was going to come face to face with her one day, and I would spit in her face.

That day was coming soon. I was going home to see Ira soon.

After the visit with Jean, he invited me to a light lunch. I accepted graciously and went on my way after. I had things to map out. Stage two was getting Vera close. Making her my friend and the way to do that was to get Jean Luke involved. He would be the first person I trusted since Ira, but I just feel safe with him. Tonight, I asked him if he would meet with me over drinks. That there was a business deal he wouldn't want to miss out on. I knew he was close to them because he had something for Vera's mother. The details of what was going on didn't need to be shared with me. That woman was old enough to be his mother. My plan was to embarrass the family and discredit their name. I was going to take everything they worked for just for raising a bitch daughter. It wasn't going to be easy. I was going to have to get close to Mr. Calvin. I was going to have to seduce him, get in his office and find his dirty books.

I was almost positive where I remembered Mrs. Calvin from. About two years ago, the company was under investigation for money laundering. It was a far-fetched notion at the time, I recalled thinking there was just someone out to get the money this woman had worked so hard to get. They just didn't like seeing a woman in a man's position.

Of course, I was wrong and Mr. Calvin just used his wife for publicity. He wanted to make sure no one thought anything different. It was a simple mistake you see, and his not so bright wife was the reason there was money missing. It wasn't true and she wasn't stupid. They devised this plan to make sure the company and the Calvin name went away with no harm. Their ploy almost worked on me. It did until I heard say Mrs. Calvin in an interview. They were asking her questions like 'How could she be that naïve?' and ' How did all that money go unnoticed.' and I thought to myself there is no way in hell someone could misplace all that money. You would have to be a special kind of person to misplace ten million dollars. At the time, it didn't matter to me, because I didn't know these people and given the opportunity to take ten mill, I would have. But now that I know who these people were, I just had to laugh. All I needed was the proof and I was on my way to finding it.

The day went by in a flash. I drafted the plan out to see if there were any holes in my thinking, and of course there was the whole getting caught part. That was the only part I was uncertain about. I was going to play the sex tape to create a distraction. Everyone was going to be scranbling to stop it and find out who did it. I was going to have someone slip in as tech support and search his office. Of course, they aren't going to know where it's coming from.

It's the ultimate hack. All I had to do was get a crew together and with the right kind of money, they wouldn't be able to say no.

I was meeting with this guy at an internet gaming café on the upper East Side. I had an hour before I needed to meet with Jean, this meeting was going to have to be quick. He was already late. From what his ad said, he was a computer programmer. He went to MIT and received his Masters in computer science. This was all gibberish to me, but I knew people and I was relying on instinct to get me through this. Finding a seat was more trying then you would have thought. This place was crawling with geeks who didn't like light. It smelled like an out of date ass. Someone missed the memo on taking showers daily.

At last I did find a seat. "Monroe?" a kid with a funky goatee asked.

"Yes, that's me." Please tell me this wasn't the guy I was meeting with. He barely hit puberty. He was fresh out of diapers. His mother's womb wasn't done healing yet because he just fucking left it. I could do this all day. The shock on my face was apparent. I didn't try to hide it from him.

"Hi, I'm Orlando." Well there is that. What kind of hacking geek was named Orlando.

"This is why there should be fine print on all services offered in papers or online. I apologize for wasting your time, but I don't think this is going to work out." I tried getting up from my seat, but my dress was stuck to something sticky left on the chair.

"Why? Because I'm young?" he didn't look like I offended him. If anything, he looked like he was smug.

233

"I am sure you are fabulous at whatever it is you do, but I need someone who knows what they're doing. This isn't a little kid's game. This is serious." The look of humor on his face was tragic. It made me wonder if he understood me or not.

"Don't judge me because of my age. It would be like me judging you because you are a blonde. I could say I don't trust your dimwitted actions. How do I know this is a sound plan?" He spoke with confidence and the smug look never left his face. At this point, trusting him wasn't going to happen, but working something out business wise, that was something I was willing to talk about.

"Fair enough, though I'm nothing like most blondes," I smiled at him and waved the waitress over. I needed a coffee and a wet-wipe for when I got up.

"I could tell just from looking at you that you were about your business. Someone as beautiful as you must fly under the radar." He was on point with his observation. It was apparent that I didn't fool everyone. Humans see what they are willing to see. If there is something they don't think should happen, to them it didn't. It was a selective process.

"There is a theme with the men in my life lately." I was losing my game if they were able to tell what I was feeling. Getting comfortable with my surroundings, I blamed my environment.

"It seems you have been meeting with awesomely intuitive men." Orlando smiled at me and set money on the table for my coffee.

"Thank you." I offered.

"No problem. My mother taught me to be a gentleman."

His mother deserved an award. The shit society was producing lately was horrifying.

"Shall we talk business?" I placed the coffee on the table and leaned in.

"I thought you would never ask." This was the easy part, getting him in on it. The hard part was coming up with something that wouldn't get us caught. From the looks of Orlando, prison wouldn't be kind to him. Destroying the kid's life wasn't an option. We started talking about what I wanted to accomplish. He was all ears and eager. Taking down a multi-billion dollar, company was on his bucket list. Who would have guessed? This kid was a light. He was determined and driven. It was refreshing to see someone as young as him so goal oriented.

The plan he came up with left wiggle room, and the best part was no one would be the wiser. I thought me going undercover was the only option, but he knocked that off the table. He told me these people would know who I was. By the time I was leaving, we had a plan in place. He told me he was going to get in touch with some college friends that would be willing to help. The kid had a lot up his sleeve. I couldn't wait to see him in action.

I was running late to meet Jean. I called and let him know it would be a couple minutes until I was there.

"Monroe, there is someone here," he whispered into the phone.

"Who?" I asked, confused.

"It's Mrs. Calvin. She is here trying to get me to bed her again, but I told her I was taken. Don't be mad. I told her I was with you, and we worked our shit out." he stammered.

"No, I'm not mad, this is a perfect opportunity." I laughed and waved down a cab. "See you soon, lover." This was going to be the most entertaining thing I get to do in my life.

The cab pulled up to Jean's building and I passed some money to the driver. He ran his fingers over my hand more than was required. His cab smelled as if he hadn't showered in a year, and here he was touching my hand. I bet he hadn't used soap on them either. I was going to have to sanitize myself. First the café, and now this.

Monroe

Walking into the doors, I looked around for Jean. He wasn't the type to leave company unattended. Sure enough, he was sitting at a table with Mrs. Calvin. She was leaning into him whispering something in his ear, her hand placed on his upper thigh and traveling higher.

I did what any other dramatic woman would have done. "I'm here Jean dear! That cab driver was as slow as a snail, but I made it." I smiled at him as I approached. When I made it to him, I kissed him like a desperate woman. I licked his lips, and grinned over at Mrs. Calvin.

She was watching me with hate filled eyes. I extended my hand to her and said, "Nice to see you once again. I hope Jean isn't boring you with his blabber about food and cookware."

"No, we were just talking business, I was hoping to get him to cater Vera's engagement party." Oh Mrs. Calvin was as catty as ever. She wanted to get a rise out of me. Little did she know, all I saw was revenge on the horizon. Plus, I already fucked Roman. Vera could have what was left.

Stop telling yourself lies, Monroe.

I cast my eyes over to Jean Luke to see why he was so still and silent. He was stuck in place with a look of awe plastered on his face.

"Jean dear, you act like I have never kissed you like that before. Don't be rude. We have a guest here."

"That kiss was a bit inappropriate for company, don't you think?" chimed Mrs. Calvin.

"Not at all, it's like I'm here with family and friends," I smiled wickedly. Stupid bitch! What did Jean Luke see in this woman? I could ask the same thing about Roman. He can kept spewing lies, telling me there is nothing going on with them, but he fucked her before. It was evident in the way she was acting. Two things will make a woman want revenge as much as Vera. The love of a man or loyalty and she didn't strike me as the loyal type.

Finally, Jean got the lead out and said something, "I was just telling Patsy I won't be able to cater for her daughter. I have something going on that day. I'm sorry to be terribly rude, Patsy, but me and this beautiful woman have a lunch date." Jean pulled me onto his lap and caressed my bare leg.

"Not a problem, it is a shame that you are taken on that day," The double meaning wasn't lost on me, and I wanted to slap the shit out of her. Roman must be paid handsomely, because there are a lot of bored house wives, Patsy being one of them.

"I am sure there is someone else you know who can cater to your needs." Sarcasm was thick in my words, and I got the response I was looking for when she sneered at me.

"I would say it was a pleasure, but we would both be lying." She conceded

"You think?" I chuckled and leaned into Jean. His heavy frame was comforting to me. It felt good. If I was normal this is where I would be. I would take him up on his offer to love me. I wasn't normal, and if he did love me, if I did accept him all I would do is kill who he was inside. He would end up hating me. I would drain the life out of him until there wasn't anything left to give. I would leave him a dried up husk of the person he once was.

I moved out of Jean's lap and sat in the chair. "Well, that was fun." It was difficult to look him in his eyes. When he kissed me in his office, there was nothing there. The kiss today brought something out of us both. It felt like a flame burst to life. Once Roman walked into my life, my emotions started running wild, exploring feelings in myself I never knew were there.

"What the fuck was that Monroe?" he demanded.

"That was nothing, I got carried away, that's all." My hair was tickling my nose, I swiped in to the side and make eye contact with him. "Did you see her face? It looked like it worked."

"I don't care what worked, that was intense!" He rubbed his face like it was going to take back the last ten minutes.

"You were the one who told her I was your girlfriend. I was just going along with it." The look on his face told me he felt more than just my act.

"What did you want to talk about? Are you going to be leaving soon?" Every time I came into town, I could count on Jean. He knew I was only here for an allotted time.

"I will be in a couple of days. What I need to talk to you about, you might not like." Talking the whole plan out again was draining. Orlando and I had come to the agreement that Jean Luke only needed to know so much.

He was more for information than necessity. I didn't want him to have anything to incriminate himself.

"I need dirt on the Calvin's. I can't tell you what it's for, but I really need you to trust me on this. I have a plan, but the less you know the better. You don't need to get involved in this."

"What kind of dirt?" he asked and placed a plate in front of me that the waiter brought out.

"Anything you can think of. Stuff that is illegal. Do you think you know anything like that?"

"Do you mean did Patsy share anything with me while we were having an affair?" He picked up a strawberry and gestured for me to open my mouth. I took a bite and the sweet juice burst onto my tongue. It was an act lovers shared. Feeding someone else your food was more intimate than lovers sharing a bed.

"Yes, I guess that is what I am talking about." I dipped a strawberry into the crème on the plate.

"If I share these details with you" he waved him hands in a circle. "What will I get out of this?"

"I would hope you would do this just because we are friends, because there isn't anything else I can offer you but my friendship."

"You felt what I felt, right?" Man, I was going to lose my shit. Why couldn't I have normal conversations with men?

"Josephine, where are you, you little slut?" My mother was looking for me. My father was at work and I

was hiding under my bed. My mother blames me. The woman who held my in her belly for nine months hates me.

"Momma what are you doing?" Ira asked as he appeared in the doorway.

"Mind your business boy." Ira walked calmly into the room and sat on the mattress. It sunk in a bit and bumped into my head.

"She is my business momma. If you aren't going to protect her, then I will. You are the one who brought us into this world. We didn't ask for it. Are you so blind that you can't stand up to him? You aren't my mother. My mother was supposed to protect me, and as I see it, Jo is the only family I have." My mother rushed him then. He

247

jumped off the bed and she cornered him. She was going to hit him with the extension cord.

"You little shit-!How dare you talk to me like that!" she shouted into his face, but Ira didn't move. He just looked at her.

"Do what you wanna do momma, but you won't get to hit my sister." he turned his face and stared at the wall as the first blow landed. The cord landed against his face causing it to tear the skin. I watched as she hit him repeatedly. She was only satisfied when he was lying in a bloody heap at her feet.

"Maybe next time you will let me have her!" she spit and began to walk out.

"Never!" Ira let out. He was asking to get it again. I cried into my hand, trying not to make a sound. When she *left, I crawled out and helped my brother up. His face had gashes all over it. I was weak. I had let this happen to him. I wasn't worthy of him or his love.*

"Don't cry Jo," he wiped away my tears. Trying to concentrate on my face, his eye was swelling shut.

"Ira, don't worry about me. You're bleeding."

"I would do it all over again if it meant you would be safe Jo. Sometimes I wish I could leave, just take you and go, but I know he'll find us." tears began to drop from my brothers eyes. He usually kept everything in. He didn't want me to see he was suffering. I cried harder than I had been. The only way anyone was going to believe us is if we both came out, but the fear my father instilled in us was too powerful.

I knew what I had to do. I couldn't let my brother get beat for me anymore.

"Monroe?" Jean waved his hands in front of my face.

"Yes, sorry, I'm just dazed."

"Where do you go when do daze?" he asked and placed his chin in his hand.

"I go somewhere no one should have to." he studied me with fascination. It made me nervous to be under the microscope. "So, are you going to help me?" I asked, changing the subject.

"I will." From there, he went over in detail about everything Patsy had told him. She was tired of taking the fall for her husband. She didn't want to get up there and take the blame for what he had done. She told Jean her husband kept books of everything he did. They were locked in a safe in his office and no one knew where it was because it was located in the floor of the office. There was a switch on a portrait that was behind his desk. It was the man's eye. All you had to do was push it and the safe would raise.

The problem with this was that I needed to get in there before the plan went down to take pictures of the safe. Orlando told me he needed to know that make of the safe and what kind it was. It was easier said than done and with all this going on, I still had to deal with Roman.

I had received an invitation in the mail to Vera's party. I wasn't going to call it an engagement because it was fake. I was going to attend it in a couple days. It was at a building that Calvin hoped to acquire soon. It was a good opportunity to get inside Calvin & Co. to take pictures of the safe. We met with a security guard that worked for them. He wasn't too pleased with the way things were run. Their lack of respect was going to bite them in the ass. He assured me that getting Orlando in there to fix a computer problem wouldn't be hard. There was always someone trying to hack into the grid. That's why they needed security with intelligence. This meant he was Orlando's roommate at MTI.

The plan was coming together beautifully and I would be out of here the night it went down, after I accomplished what I came for. Vera's party is going to be the perfect cover. Everyone they know would be there. The funniest part of it is, it's an engagement party.

Monroe

The day was long and trying. My brain was full of information and I needed to get it out somehow. Writing it all down was the best way I knew, but I couldn't trust anyone. I stripped all my clothes off and sat on my bed thinking. Vera's party was two days away and tomorrow Orlando was going in there as a tech guy, I was glad it wasn't me. They would have picked me out immediately.

For now, I needed to rest my mind. It had been three days since mine and Roman's meeting, and I was getting anxious. Not knowing where he stood or planned to wasn't sitting well. Plus, I missed him. There were only two days left, and I wanted to spend as much time as I could with him before everything crumbled.

A knock sounded on the door and my heart fell. The only person who would come here was him. I strolled over to the door and unlocked in. However, it wasn't him. It was the bellboy and when he looked over my nude body his cheeks flamed. The color was amazing. I loved seeing it on such young, plush cheeks.

"Sorry Ma'am. I have something for you." He handed me a scarlet box with a gold ribbon. A note was stuck on the top. I retrieved money from my wallet, knowing the whole time he was staring at my ass. As I handed him a tip I bit my lip. Poor kid was going to have blue balls for the rest of the week.

The envelope was simple and white with my name elegantly scrawled on the front. I ripped it open and took out the powder blue slip of paper. If I wasn't mistaken, there was a light musky fragrance coming from the note. I inhaled. I was right. It smelled like Roman. Delicious and sweet. I sat on the bed and crossed my legs as I read:

Monroe,

I want to see… Josephine.

I love you,

Roman

I lost all ability to breathe. He knew who I was. It was only a matter of time before he found out. I knew that. I was just hoping it would happen when I was gone. By that time, I wouldn't be traceable. Vera paid me already and I was going to be on an island somewhere, sipping a margarita.

I rushed to my closet and pulled on the first thing I saw. Getting out of this hotel was my number one priority and as I riffled through my clothing a knock came from the door. It was a swift rap in intervals of three, this time I knew who it was.

"I know you're in there, just open up." Roman announced. "I can hear you Monroe." Why was he calling me Monroe when he knew who I was? He was playing a game, but it was a game I didn't know.

I stalked over to the door and swung it open. "What do you want Roman?" In his hands, he held a dozen red roses and a bottle of whiskey.

"All I want to do is talk. Promise." he looked into the room, "Were you planning on leaving, and you weren't even going to tell me anything?" he faked a disappointed look.

"You might as well stop your shit and own up to what you are doing here!" I moved so he had space to come into the room, as he moved past me, I took the whiskey from his hand.

"I could use a drink too," he sighed and sat in the chair. "Is there anything you would like to tell me Josephine? I mean—that is your real name, right?"

"Nope, my name is Monroe. I changed it legally. I don't see why you felt the need to check into me." I said fuck the glass and took a gulp of the whiskey. He was making me nauseous just talking about it.

"I looked into you because there was something about you I couldn't put my finger on. I'm still in the dark with a lot of shit, but it makes more sense now. You being the hurtful bitch that you are, and the need to have everything your way, the control." he smiled as if he just won a prize.

"Good for you! Now I think you should be going." I opened the door for him and waited.

"You aren't going to get away from me that easy. After all, we only have two days left. You shouldn't leave because of me." He placed photos on the table in front of him. "After all, Jean would be disappointed." They were pictures of Jean Luke and me today, when we were having lunch, and right before, when I was in his lap. All this was was jealousy. I could deal with that, all I had to do was get in character and place Josephine on the back burner so to speak.

"That was all show, you couldn't be jealous, could you? All that proves is that I'm an amazing friend." I laced my fingers together and stood there looking into his eyes, and every time I did, it felt like they were stealing my soul.

Two more days. I just had to keep telling myself that.

He got up and stalked toward me. "Jealous of what Jo?" When he said my name, it sent me into a spiral down memory lane. The word alone caused fear to bubble in the depths of my stomach.

"Stop calling me that! It isn't who I am anymore." I took a swig of the liquor. It helped numb the feelings that were locked inside me.

"It was the name you were given at birth. That is who you are!" he took the bottle from my hands and placed it on the table. "Why try so hard to lose who you were?"

"Because she died, and I want it to stay that way. Why can't you just leave me alone?"

"Because I love you, but you make it so hard. I keep telling myself I should just leave you alone like you keep telling me to, but it feels like I'm stuck. I can't leave now even if I wanted to." He rambled frustratingly.

"You don't know what you're talking about, you have no clue what love is." I moved for the bottle, trying to get around him, but he wouldn't let me. I ended up in his arms. I cocked my fist back and punched him in his jaw. It was too much. Him calling me Jo, his touching me. I couldn't bear it and I started hyperventilating.

"You okay?" he asked and released me. I withered to the floor.

"I need air," I gasped and held my throat.

"Breathe, Monroe." He was in a panic not knowing what to do. Black dots clouded my sight, I was on the verge of passing out.

"I'm fine just give me some room." Of course, he didn't listen and he stood over me like a watch dog.

"Ira, don't do this. Ira are you listening to me?" I told Ira everything I was going to tell the teacher. Some of the things he had no idea about, and some he did. He was making his way to the house. He wanted to kill my father for what he did to me. Enough was enough, he said, and if Daddy did kill him, at least he went out like a man.

"Ira, he will kill you. He told me it over and over again. Let's just leave, me and you. Let's get out of here." he stopped and cleared the tears from his face. His eyes never strayed from mine.

"How can I let him live Jo? I told you I was going to protect you, and I failed." he wailed and sunk to his knees. He wrapped his arms around my middle and held on to me. Repeating over and over again how he failed me.

"It isn't your fault, Ira." I said as I comforted him.

"It isn't your fault, Jo" Roman repeated. The eerie echo of my brother's words filtered through my brain. Roman bringing his words to life caused my heart to break open once more.

"What?" I asked confused.

"I said it isn't your fault. Everything that happened to you, isn't your fault. You're going to have to let it go. If you don't, it's going to kill you." I heard everything he was telling me, but it wasn't sticking. Everything was my fault. That day is burned into my memory for all time. Nothing will make it better, or disappear.

"You reading about it on paper tells you nothing about what happened that night. It was my fault and it's mine to bear."

"Is that why you think you can't be loved and that you don't deserve it?" He responded. Pity dawned in his eyes.

"I have no time for this!" I shouted in frustration. He wouldn't know what I was going through. He wasn't there, and he would never get it. There was no point in explaining it to him.

"You have time. You just can't handle what I'm telling you!" He grabbed my face and forced me to look at him in his eyes. "Even if you can't handle me, I am going to tell you, I'm going to tell you how I feel and then I'm going to make love to you, because at the end of the day, no matter how fucked up you or I am, I want to be here. There is no one else I want to be with." He kissed me pushing and prying my mouth open with his tongue. "I am going to love you, even if you don't love me." His kiss softened as he moved me to the bed. He stripped my shirt off and my breasts bounced softly. "I'm going to kiss every inch of your body. I will make you feel loved." His mouth moved over my breast, sucking it in and licking the peak. Everything he was doing was gentle. Every move planned.

"Tell me how to love you?" he asked.

If he had asked me how I would like to be fucked I would have known what to say. But his question left me wondering what the right answer was. "I have no clue. Do what you want with me." It was the same thought I got before my father entered me. I stayed stone faced as he was grunting above me, his sweat dripping onto my face.

"Don't go there anymore. You are here with me. Feel me. Know I'm here and nothing will hurt you." I wanted so badly to believe what he was telling me. More than anything, I wanted him, but I wouldn't let myself be content. I deserved nothing. "If it's control you need, take it."

He brought me back with a simple sentence. Reaching for his belt, I undid it without taking my eyes off him. He was giving me something I required. My mind was fucked up and the only way to express my love was to give into the demons that were there.

Once the belt was removed, I motioned for him to place his hands in front of me. He did as he was told. His smoldering eyes searching my face. I tied his hands together and told him to get on the bed. The last time we were together, he wouldn't shut up. This time he didn't make a sound.

"I am sorry about this Roman" I cried as I tied him to the bed.

"There is nothing to apologize for, love." He brought his locked hands up and placed them around my neck, pulling me down to him. "You will never have to say sorry for what you do to me. Do as you wish, I promise I'll be ok." I nodded my head and moved off him.

Angry tears pooled in my eyes, I was too scared to say anything. If I let the words escape my mouth, everything was going to come out. I secured his hands to the headboard with one of my belts. I watched his hands turn red from the tightness. The joy I was feeling from the color change should have classified me as psychotic.

I was going to show him the only way I knew how to love. All the anger and pain from over the years was built up. Roman was giving me the release my body was calling for. He was willing to lay down his pride to satisfy me. He wanted me to love him, and the only way he knew it was going to happen was this.

"Roman, my intentions aren't to cause you pain, but you consenting to this, you know what this means, right? If you want to back out I won't be mad."

"I'll be fine," he closed his eyes and swallowed. My anger was raw and rage ran through my blood. He knew everything I was running from and he was still willing to stay with me. "I will do anything you want. I wasn't playing with you when I told you I was going to make you feel loved."

"Once I start, I won't be able to stop. I want you just as much as I want revenge on you. You understand?"

"More than you know." He quietly stated.

There was no plan. I had no idea what I was going to do. I knew I craved the pain. Rough sex wasn't enough and if he wanted me to love him, this was the only way I knew how.

I got on top of him and started stroking his manhood. "Tonight, you will only call me Jo. Nothing else." I deserved to be the nameless whore the older men passed around when I was eleven.

I placed my mouth over his cock and sucked hard, running my teeth down it. This caused Roman to flinch and make a strange sound. I popped it out of my mouth and sat on his lap, his dick poking into my stomach. I got another belt from the closet. It was decorative piece. It was meant to cinch the waist. It was made of a heavy metal. I tightened the ends of it around my hand. "You ready?"

"Yes Monroe..." I smacked the belt across his abdomen. It swelled fast, but didn't break the skin. The look of pain on his face thrilled me.

"I told you not to call me that. You wanted to find out who I was. Now you're going to have to deal with what you found out." I hit him once more, but with more force. The air expelled out of his lungs hit my face. This time, blood broke the surface of his skin. I bent over kissing and licking the parts that were crimson.

"I'm sorry. It won't happen again." He sounded as if he was already out of breath. I took the rubber band out of my hair and began wrapping it around his dick.

"Can't have you going limp on me." Hitting him was causing me more pain than it was him. He wasn't looking at me. I kissed his chest and made my way to his mouth. I wanted to taste him. I hungered for his pain. So much that it was driving me crazy. The desire to feel his scream against my mouth was overpowering.

I positioned his shaft at my entrance as I asked, "You still okay?"

"Yes." With that, I sunk myself onto him. I took his nipple into my mouth and bit down on it. He squirmed around uncomfortably

"Do you like this?" It couldn't be that bad, right? It was making me feel sick and powerful at the same time. His pain was turning me on, bringing me to a whole new level of pleasure.

I stopped.

What I was doing terrified me. I wasn't my father, and I didn't hurt the people I loved. Why would I do this to him if I cared about him? This wasn't the way to show someone you loved them. If anything, this was a tactic to scare someone away.

I released his hands. "Why did you stop?" he asked as he rubbed the circulation back into his fingers. I helped and remove the rubber band from him genitals.

"Because I am not my father." We sat there looking at each other. The silence was stressing me out. It had me questioning what he was thinking, or if he was going to leave. This was the real me, and I was screwed up in the head.

"Come here," he moved to me and enveloped me in his strong arms.

"It felt good seeing you in pain. My body loved it. I wanted to feel you scream but my mind is telling me it's wrong." The dam I built broke. Tears streamed down my face. I tried covering it so he wouldn't see what a mess I was.

Monroe

"I know. I know, shhhhh…" He said repeatedly. He didn't leave my side and eventually he pulled me onto his chest as he soothed me to sleep.

I woke in the middle of the night still covering Roman. I hadn't told him, but he was the first man I have slept with overnight. I was always too scared. I had nightmares and it would leave them with unanswered questions.

Roman was snoring lightly. He looked peaceful sleeping. There was no emotion clouding his delicate features. His full lips were plump and calling out to me. I kissed him lightly, my eyes closing at their own will. Funny how when you kiss your eyes close, like a natural response to nearness.

"That was nice, who would have thought you could be gentle?" he caressed my face and laid my head back down on his chest.

"I can be, it just doesn't come naturally to me. With you, I want to be that." I admitted.

"Keep talking sweet to me and we won't leave this bed for days." No matter how good that sounded, I would get out of this bed.

"Let's just make the best of what we have." I threw the covers off me, and forced him onto his back. He helped me lower myself onto his manhood. I gasped when a sensual feeling moved over my body. His willingness to submit to me made me want to beg him for forgiveness. To merge one's soul with another will only lead to damnation. You will strive to complete one another leaving yourself hollowed out. It was best to never love than to hurt for eternity.

I learned the hard way.

It mustn't have resonated with me, it was only going to end in disaster. The look of sheer ecstasy coated his face. I didn't take my eyes off of him as I watched him wither under me. His look was enough to send me over. I was giving him pleasure, and it was turning me on.

"Cum with me" he said, and I released everything, I let it all go, and for the first time in my life, I felt complete. The shock from the joint orgasm left me boneless . I smiled down at him as he pressed further into me. He looked at me confused and wiped at my cheek.

"First I make you laugh and now I make you cry? What am I doing wrong?" he asked.

"You should be asking what you're doing right." I told him, as he licked the tear from his fingertip.

"When you leave, it's going to be difficult. I'm going to miss you." Deep down these were the words I wanted to hear, every fiber in my being told me so. My brain was telling me something different. It said: this is a stupid decision. You know he was out to get you. But maybe that was what attracted me to him in the first place. It was as if we were two pieces of a whole. We fit together like ying and yang.

He was just like me. Damaged.

I might not have dug into his past, but there was something there. In time, I would find out but for now what we had was enough. I was content just lying next to him, having him inside me.

"I'm going to miss you too, but there is no way I can stick around. I have things to do. There is a whole world out there just waiting to be explored." I did love to travel, but doing it alone was getting old. Yes, there were random men and it was fun.

Roman was always going to be my falling star. He was bright and he lit up my dark world for a second in time. But like all shooting stars, it disappeared too quickly. But it still never went away. The memory or the feeling of the time you saw it, no matter how brief it was. After this, I wasn't going to be able to touch him but I would be happy knowing he was out there somewhere, hopefully thinking of me too. It was the only wish I had at the moment.

"I am going to get clean. I have to meet…" he stopped. I didn't need him to finish to know what he was going to say. Today was his engagement party, and he was meeting Vera for some last minute prep.

"All good things must come to an end, but it was fun while it lasted." I kissed him softly and made my way to the bathroom. I had a lot of planning to do too. Today was going to be one for the records, for him and me. I was just going in a different direction then he was.

After we were clean and dressed, I thought it best to check out so I gathered all of my things and placed them by the door.

"This doesn't have to be goodbye." he said.

"There was never a hello. This is just how our hand was dealt." This was harder than I thought it was going to be. Pain seized my heart and I clenched my chest.

"I still would like to see you, maybe call sometime?" I didn't see how that was going to be possible. If the only reason he was here was to work, then why were they throwing a party for them? He didn't have to put on that big of a show just to get even with me, or maybe Vera did. I had no clue. It was final, us sitting here. Our road split off into two separate ones.

"It's better this way, you'll see. Soon you won't even remember my name, let alone me." I pulled him to me and kissed him sweetly. It was my goodbye to the only person I have let see who I truly was. He might not remember me, but I would always know him.

Monroe

I placed my bags in the back of the cab and looked up at the hotel one more time. I was going to miss this city and all of the crazy people in it. This trip had taught me who I am and it brought me to the conclusion that I was okay with being the person I was and the person I had become. Josephine wasn't a bad person. The people who she was given to were the bad people.

The cabbie asked me where I wanted to go and the only place I could think of was Jean's. It wasn't the ideal situation. I didn't want to have any drama before departing but it was the only place I felt safe. It was only until about five today. I had booked my flight to Alabama yesterday. My plan was to edit the tape and get it to Orlando as soon as I could. Jean greeted me by kissing both my cheeks.

"You look beautiful as always," he smirked and rubbed my upper arms.

"Thank you. Is there somewhere I can decompress in private? I have tons of notes to write before everything happens." I pulled my bag in front of me and showed him it as if it explained it all.

"You can use my office. I'm going to be working most of the afternoon prepping. I'll come to check on you in a moment." He left me to find my way to his office. I set my laptop up on the desk and dug in my bag. After editing the tape, I was going to write my notes for my files. I told myself it would be safe because this was the last day, eliminating the chance someone would steal my things.

But the editing was the most important thing. I was meeting with the boy genius in a couple of hours, and it felt like I was running late already. Looking over the video was hard. It showed more emotion in me than I thought was possible. When Roman wasn't looking at me, I would stare at him. When we were sleeping, I would run my fingers along the side of his stomach. There was never a time I wasn't touching him. I thought it was him projecting his love onto me. That wasn't the case. When I wasn't conscious, I would do things that were out of character for me. There was a lot of the same thing for a couple of hours. I worked my way through all the sappy shit, collecting everything that was worth watching.

I deleted everything that showed emotion or love. The only thing I left were the steamy bits. The ones where he was pounding into me. The time where I squirted on his face and he lapped at me until he got it all. This tape was doing something funny to me. I wanted him again.

I stopped when I was satisfied with what I had. I was confident it would get the job done. Now for the hard part. The notes.

Client: Vera Calvin.

I met Vera on the Fourth of June in New York City, New York. The client was involved with someone who worked for her father. She wanted to know if this man (Roman) was in love with her or her money. I was convinced after meeting Vera that her intentions were as she said they were. From what she reported to me, Roman was after her money. Of course, these were all assumptions and I wouldn't have a conclusion until I met with the mark. Vera wanted to marry him and the mark wanted the family company. As time passed, I figured Vera to be a liar. She showed emotions that are characteristic of someone who was bi-polar.

FOOTNOTE: Severe depression noticed. Cannot diagnose clinically.

The day of June seventh, I overheard a conversation in the stairwell between client and mark. What I heard was disturbing. They were conspiring against me, reason unknown at time. I didn't recall ever meeting with these people previously. Confused as to why my client hated me so much, I dug. I concluded that Vera was in love with someone I investigated. He left her and stayed with his wife, causing her extreme need for revenge. I devised a plan accordingly.

SUBJECT: Roman Pierce.

Roman came off as a kind man from our first run-in. After further observation, I concluded that he was in the same line of work I was. Roman was dangerous. His emotions ran rampant and caused problems with my investigation. I did not want to hurt the mark, when usually I could give a fuck.

Writing about him as if he was an object killed me. He was more than that, but remembering he was conspiring against me left me paralyzed. The plan was going to play out, regardless who it hurt. Jo was going to have to sit this one out—for now.

The door to the office opened and Jean walked in. "Are you done?" he asked and sat on the arm of my chair peering over my shoulder at my notes. It was nothing he should see, so I covered them.

"I am, and in time too. I have to get going I have a meeting in twenty minutes." I kissed him on his cheek as I rushed for the door. "I'll see you at five, right?"

"I wouldn't dream of standing you up."

"See you then." When the doors opened, the air felt smug. I waved a cab, but none seemed to notice. I bet if I was in a dress they would all stop, but sadly right now I was in sweats and a fitted tank top.

Of course, Orlando would want to meet me at another dank internet gaming place. He told me they were his people. The people he felt comfortable around. I was paying a pretty penny for his services. You would think he would let me pick the meeting place.

"There you are," he said as I walked into the establishment His reaction changed when he realized I wasn't in the mood. "Someone woke up on the wrong side of the mattress."

"I'm fine. There is too much to do today." I took the CD out of my bag and placed it on the table. "Here is the video. I hope you know what you are doing with it."

"Chill, this isn't my first time at the rodeo. I know what I'm doing." he smiled and fingered the CD.

"What's on there is personal and I would like my face obscured if possible."

"I can do that. What's on it?"

"Nothing you need to worry about."

"Porn huh? You know, this wouldn't be my first time watching it. It would however, be the first time watching a client." He shrugged.

"Keep it in your pants, kid." I joked.

"That isn't possible. Have you looked at yourself lately," he was checking me out over the rim of his glasses. "Really though, I am going to be professional

288

when I watch it. I promise I won't touch myself." This kid was cheeky.

"Whatever. So how is the other half of the plan going?" I was referring to him breaking into Calvin's office.

"My boy is going to be at work in a little over an hour. The Calvin's are going to be busy most of the day running around getting shit ready for the party. The only person we have to worry about is the secretary. Piece of pie." he remarked as he drank from his glass.

"Isn't the saying a piece of cake?"

"Yeah, but I don't like cake. Pie is a better choice." I laughed. This kid thought he was so good he could change a common phrase. "Why don't you talk to me in that sweet, southern accent of yours and I will buy you some?" Of course, he would know about me. It seemed like Jean was the only one left in the dark.

"We aren't all pie loving southerners. I prefer ice cream." I stood and tapped the brim of his hat down over his eyes. It was three hours until the party and I was going to be there in the front row for what was going to happen.

Be still my beating heart. The thought alone had me riveted.

Before the door closed, I heard Orlando say, "This job is going to be the death of me." If he was a couple years older, I wouldn't have thought anything of it, but he's a baby. He deserves a woman who will give him babies so he can pass on his smartness.

Tonight was a new dawn and I wanted to get a dress that showed it.

The dress I chose was in the middle of classy and dangerous. It was a long skirt. It had a train in the back that followed behind me beautifully. The sleeves were long lace that had loops for my fingers. The dress was black and made of leather. I might not have thought through how tiring it would be carrying around the heavy dress, but I was making a statement. My hair sat atop my head in a creative messy bun. To top it all off, my earrings were long, dangly silver skulls. I looked fit for a funeral, not an engagement party but my feelings fit it.

He was really marrying her. The man who declared his love to me last night was marrying a woman who wanted my head on a stake.

It left you wondering how they met in the first place. I thought I was a transaction. I thought he was doing this because he was getting paid, but the more time passed, the more I saw this for what it was.

The valet took my hand and helped me out of my town car. My dress was long. The valet waited for my train to emerge from the car. "You look lovely tonight, ma'am."

"Do I?" I stated and start up the stone steps. I wasn't the only one arriving. There were crowds of people waiting to get in and see. Reporters littered the stairs taking pictures of all the guests, as they should. Some of these women and men were dressed like they were going to the Oscars. It was a sight to see. My eyes glittered with the sequins, fur, and other shiny material.

A man at the door asked me for my invitation. After he determined it was real, he let me in with a, "Welcome ma'am." I nodded my thanks and walked into a long corridor. It wasn't confusing to find where the hall was located. They probably rented the whole building out. There were going to be people sneaking off to the upper floors to fuck against the windows. It was what I would do.

Wicked minds thought alike. I smiled to myself, thinking about all the people who were going to be shagging tonight. Normal people wouldn't think like that, but I prided myself on my outlandish behaviors. The hall opened into a grand ball room, with Seventeenth century architecture. Roman must have been the one to pick the location. I'm sure they had a few choices. It had him written all over it.

There were people on the dance floor already enjoying the fruity drinks glued to their hands.

"I see the invitation made it to you. I wasn't sure where to send it, seeing as you have no address." Patsy said from behind me.

I turned and smiled brightly at her, "I wouldn't have missed this for the world. This is, after all the event of the year, toping all award ceremonies together." I placed my hand over my heart and acted as if I was tickled pink. "You just look divine, Patsy." I let some of my roots show through. Just the politeness.

She looked me over trying to think of something nice to say, but her face showed disgust. "Isn't that an interesting dress. You don't see many like it." It was as close as it got to a complement.

"Yes, I had it made for this occasion, I didn't want to look out of place with a department store dress. After all, look at the attire. It is simply heavenly." She could choke on her name brands. This dress was me. Monroe. There was nothing on this planet like it. This bitch could eat that for dinner.

"Enjoy yourself. Tonight is going to be a joining of family. I am so excited to add Roman into ours."

"I'm sure he's lovely," I smiled and nodded. Thank God that was over. Talking to people like her left people assuming you were in cahoots with them and I would never even sit beside her on a bus.

She slithered off. No doubt to talk someone into eating a poisoned apple. I was laughing slightly to myself at the joke I just told. When my eyes lifted, they made contact with his. One blue, one brown. Both soul stealing. I recovered fast and inclined my head in his direction. He didn't do anything, just looked me over as a couple of men continued to blabber on about what not.

I walked around the room, searching the tables for my name card. When I found it, I chuckled aloud. She placed me at the table with senior citizens. She was a smart girl I had to give it to her. I sat and waited for the brat to make her entrance.

When she finally made her way in, everyone stood to greet her but me. Who the fuck did they think she was? The queen? She wasn't worth the energy it took to stand up. My phone rang and saved me from looking at her any longer.

"Orlando," I greeted.

"I got into the office. I got the books. How is everything on your end, gorgeous?"

"As to be expected." Roman chose that moment to find me.

"Monroe, what are you doing here?" I looked up at him and held my finger out, indicating I needed a moment.

Monroe

"Orlando, I will call you back in a minute." I replied into the end of the phone.

"Monroe, wait. There's something I have to tell you." I heard him say before I hung up.

"I was invited and I thought to myself I do love punishment. Why not sit here and watch the man I care for tell everyone he is marrying someone else? I love a good drama, but don't worry, my lips are sealed." I acted like I locked my lips and thrEw away the key. "You don't want to keep your bride waiting." I looked at him through my lashes.

My hands fidgeted with the tablecloth. I didn't want to look at him. If I did, I would come undone. He didn't say anything further, he just stood there looking down at me until Vera called him over. She looked at who he was talking to and fumed.

"Roman, come and meet my aunt Vera. You know, the one I was named after." She motioned with her thin hand. Vera was the polar opposite of me tonight. She was dressed in all white. To me, it looked like she was over compensating for something. Her dress was puffy with tons of lace marking up the skirt. I hoped someone got drunk and threw up on her. The thought amused me.

"What is a beautiful young lady doing at an old folks table?" an elderly man asked.

"I have no clue. I just ended up where I ended up, I guess." He seemed nice enough.

"Well, either way. At least we will have something nice to look at." He placed his cane on the back of the chair and sat next to me. "I hope you don't mind keeping an old man company."

"Not at all, I would love to," he extended his hand to me and I took it graciously.

"Marvin," he said.

"Monroe," I returned.

"A fitting name, as well." he released my hand and looked over his placement card.

"Flattery will get you nowhere, Marvin." I joked.

"I wouldn't know what to do with you anyway. I'm old, and it looks like you would need a stud who could keep up with you." he laughed and patted me on my shoulder.

"I don't know about stud. At this point I am swearing off all men," I looked over to see what Roman was doing. Vera had her arms linked with him. His eyes focused blankly on the gentleman's face in front of him. Marvin looked in the direction I was trained on.

"If a man doesn't know what he has, then he isn't worth the pot he pisses in. if I was younger, you could bet I would be hounding you." I smiled at him politely. He was trying to make me feel better but all it did was make me think about what I was walking away from.

"One day I will meet someone like you Marvin, and I promise I will only stay if he worships me." If I was going to settle it, would be with someone who treated me like a queen. Nothing less.

Monroe

"Can I have everyone's attention please?" Patsy said into a microphone. "We are here to celebrate adding a member to our family, and what a fine addition he is. When my daughter came to me and told me she was falling for someone in her father's company, I won't lie, I was against it. Everything about it screamed scam. But what are mothers for if not to worry and interrogate future boyfriends? When I met Roman, I knew he would fit right in. He was honest, charismatic, and loyal. I couldn't have picked anyone better to be with my baby, Vera. What I'm up here trying to say is, I love you Roman. You are the son I have always dreamt of." She wiped under her eyes as if she shed a tear. What a crock of shit! That bitch is too evil to cry. If she did cry, venom would leak out of her eye sockets and melt her smug face.

"Bullshit," I said under my breath

"What was that sweetie?" Marvin asked.

"Nothing, just that this was just… great." he laughed at me. Obviously, he knew what I said.

"I agree. My daughter is full of shit and so is that little asshole of a kid she has." I laughed so loud, everyone in the room looked at me. Marvin patted my back. "Just because she's my child doesn't mean I have to like her."

This was turning out to be entertaining. "I wasn't going to say anything, but since you did, I agree." My stomach was hurting from laughing with Marvin. "I think you and I are going to be good friends, Marv."

"I think so too. I wish they had your sense of humor. They are a stick in the mud to be around."

"You would think she'd get your personality." I stated.

"I wish, but she takes after my late wife. They say in relationships, one person is kind and sweet and the other is serious and mean. It's just about evening each other out, complimenting each other."

"Time for tonight's waltz," a man in a top hat said.

"Would you like to dance?" Marvin asked.

"Why not?" I chucked and linked my arm through his. There were only five minutes before Orlando was going to hack into the mainframe, and instead of Roman and Vera's memories playing, it was going to be Roman fucking me doggy style against the door in my hotel room. I smiled to myself. It was going to be historic.

Next time Vera is out for blood, she should be careful about whose blood it is.

The waltz was lost on me. I didn't know where to go. I stepped on Marvin's feet a couple of times. He stopped. "I am the man. I'm the one who leads. Just give me control." If he only knew what he was asking me. I followed his lead and ended up loving the way the dance felt. Marvin was a pro. I could tell he danced with his wife a lot. "My wife was mean, but she did love to dance. When we were on the dancefloor, she would smile and laugh. It made her just as happy as a school girl. Times like those made me fall for her all over again. She was the love of my life. No matter how uptight she was, I will never love anyone like her. Have you ever been in love?"

This question was a plague. "Can't say I have." I looked over Marvin's shoulder and found Roman on the dance floor with Vera in his arms. He was spinning her and she was laughing. She was happy. I stopped dead in my tracks. I let go of Marvin and watched him. He looked at me with saddened eyes and turned away.

"I made this video to share all the love I have for Vera. She's been my best friend since college, and I would be lost without her. This is my gift to you, Vera," she lifted her glass in a toast. "And here is to welcoming Roman to the family!" she drank from her glass

The lights dimmed and the video began playing on a huge white screen. At first, it was pictures of Roman and Vera as kids doing kid things like riding bikes or when they played sports. When the video cut out, I was still standing in the middle of the dance floor with Marvin at my side. When the video cut out and turned to static, everyone looked around as though they didn't know what to do. I laughed and walked back to my table and took my glass in my hands, raising it and downing the contents.

Orlando's voice boomed from the speakers. "This is prepared special for the blushing bride! Hope you all enjoy." The video cut back on but this time it was of me pushed against the door. My face blocked out as I asked so no one would know who it was but those two. The feeling I got in the pit of my stomach was like I was on a roller coaster.

Everyone in the place gasped and rushed around trying to figure out what was going on. They tried turning it off, unplugging it nothing was working. I had to give it to the nerd--he was good. The video was on a loop of three separate occasions of Roman and my meetings. I watched with delight and the people raced around like ants.

I looked over to Vera and her face paled. She looked like she was going to be sick. She started screaming for them to get it off the screen. But Roman? He was just standing there with his arms at his side, fists clenched.

Staring at me.

At that moment, the sound came on, and Roman's voice filled the room. "I am going to have you beg me." he said. "Tell me how you want me to fuck you." The video showed Roman pulling my head back and biting my neck. I might have been the only one in the room turned on from this. Roman still stood unmoving like a stone carving.

"Well isn't this an unexpected surprise?" Marvin piped in.

"Quite," I laughed and watched as Vera started yanking out wires. When that wasn't getting her anywhere, she walked over to Roman and slapped him in the face. He didn't react at all. His eyes were glued to me. "I think I am going to take my leave now. It was a pleasure getting to know you, Marv." He took my hand and kissed my knuckles smoothly.

"I hope no one else gets the pleasure of knowing who is in the video" he said to my shock. "I might be old, but I am not blind, and everything is as fine as I imagined." He winked. What a cheeky old bastard!

"It was my pleasure," I bowed and made my way out the doors, dodging the scrambling crowd trying to save poor Vera any more humiliation. My car was waiting for me at the curb as I descended the stairs.

"This was your great plan? To fucking embarrass me in front of my family and friends?!" Vera shouted from the top of the stairs.

"It was you or me, Vera. I was here to help you and all you wanted was revenge. For what? You have Roman but you're still worried about someone else's husband. If anything, I was doing you a favor Now everyone knows what a heartless bitch you are!" I moved forward never looking back at her.

"This isn't over Monroe!" she shouted into the night. She sounded like she was a villain from a bad movie.

"It was over before you had any idea! Please give your future husband my farewell. It's a shame I won't be able to tell him myself." I grinned. "Ciao, darling!" I waved and got into my car. The driver pulled away and I took one last glance at the building. On the steps, Roman sat, looking at my car leave still stone faced.

Regret moved through me. There was no going back now. Orlando was where I told him to meet me. He was sitting there looking like a lost teenage boy.

"Hey, there you are. I thought I was going to get robbed waiting here!" he got into the car in a hurry.

"I wouldn't have had you meet me here if I thought something would happen to you. Do you have the books?"

"Yes. Do you have the rest of the money?" Smart boy, get the money first then hand over the goods.

I gave him an envelope with cash like he asked for and he handed me a bag with four ledgers in it. "That safe was a bitch to get into. I thought for sure we were going to get caught. It was taking a long time."

"Glad you got out of there on time." I said as I flipped one of the books open. The information went years back. It was enough to send Mr. and Mrs. Calvin to prison for a long time. "You dirty cheaters." I mumbled.

"Right, there was something else I wanted to give you. I was trying to tell you before you hung up" he handed me a package with pictures in it and some letters.

"What is this?"

"Not sure, but it had pictures of Roman and some woman. I thought it would interest you seeing as you two are friendly." He wiggled his eyebrows at me.

"Driver, take our friend here whereever he wants." I looked at Orlando expectantly.

"I have a date at the gaming café," he winked.

"Wonderful." I said and nodded my head at my driver.

"So, where are you going now?" I had no clue, but I knew I was going to live in a bottle of whiskey for a while.

"I have things to do at home, but after that I am going to lie on a beach. Some sand and sun will do me good." I sighed.

"That does sound nice, wish I could go too. But no thanks, the ladies are starting to recognize me. I'd rather stay here to get laid." The café was close so he placed his backpack on one arm and unbuckled his seat belt.

"Just remember, you treat them like queens and no means no. If I hear anything different, I will cut your nuts off!"

He paled. "Good talk. I hope I'll get to see you again but if not, take care Monroe. It was a pleasure doing business with you. By the way, that video," he puckered his lips and made an okay sign. "It was cherry."

"Get out of here, perv! I have places to be."

He laughed and got out. He was an okay kid, and I was going to miss his snarky remarks. Like any other part of my life, this chapter was done and over. Time to start new.

Monroe

‑

Two months later…

Lying on the beach in Fiji, I watched as the local fishermen took their boats out to check the nets they put out this morning. I was thinking about moving here. It was always nice and sunny and I didn't know anyone. After I left New York, I was supposed to go home and deal with stuff there. But when I got on the plane, I was too tired to deal with anything else.

My ticket took me to Alabama, but I got on another flight just as soon as I landed. The beach was more appealing to me, and I needed the time to myself. I had been here for a little over two months. It was time to go home, I needed to see my brother. Roman still crossed my mind all the time. I knew it was going to be hard to forget him. Now that I was here and there was no one with me, or here to bug me, it was time to go home.

"Would you like another drink?" A half-naked man asked.

"No, thank you. I was wondering if you could book a flight for me to Alabama?"

"Yes, I can. I will send confirmation to your room when I'm done." he said and walked away. The thing I liked about this place was that no one felt the need to bug you. I could be alone for days at a time just exploring the island and being with myself.

When I was in New York, I thought Roman was the one causing the flash backs but he wasn't. Even here on the island he haunted me.

"Jo, what are you doing here?" I hadn't seen my brother for months. After I told the teacher what happened to me, they placed me in foster care. I begged them to get Ira out of there too, but they told me they had to wait for a judge to rule on his case. I stayed away as long as I could. I wanted to make sure my brother was okay.

317

"I needed to see you," I reached out my hand to him, but he flinched.

"Go away Jo! There is nothing here for you anymore!" I forgot how much we depended on each other. Now that I wasn't here, Ira had no one.

"I can't Ira. I missed you." I cried to him and tried to reach for him again. He moved further away from me and turned his back to me.

"I don't need you here! Just leave!" he shouted and my mother came out of the house to see what was going on.

"Look who it is! You aren't welcome here anymore, get off my property before I call the cops!" she moved to the steps and looked down on me.

"Momma, I ain't here to cause any problems. I just wanted to see my brother." I raised my hands in surrender.

"You ain't no kin to us! My daughter wouldn't make up lies and tell the whole town trash."

"You know full well that I'm not a liar. You let him do those things to me, Momma! Now you're acting like it was me who started this?" Her anger left me baffled.

"Ira, get your behind in the house!" Ira walked up the stairs and pulled the door open. He gave me one last glance and disappeared.

Time to go home.

***

Monroe

The flight was long, and my body was killing me from sitting in the same position for hours. The best part about being in first class was there wasn't anyone sitting so close. The plan was to arrive at eight in the morning central time, I was going to be jetlagged on arrival.

When my plane touched down, I gathered my things and made my way to customer service. I was going to need a car while in town and a place to stay. I arrived at Birmingham Shutters Worth, Allgood was thirty-two miles away. It would have been a better idea to get a driver, but my mind was still stuck in Fiji. The time alone would be good to process and think about what I was going to do.

Last time I checked, my mother and father were still alive and kicking. I found out later in life why my father never went to jail. He was letting the town sheriff fuck his daughter.

"Is that all for today?" A blonde with a thick accent asked. She was wearing the airport uniform of blue and white with a white bandana tied around her throat. It made me want to choke her.

"Yes, that is all." She must have thought I was exotic with my tan and I didn't talk like I was from the south. I got rid of that a long time ago. "You aren't from around here are you?" Her grin pissed me off and even more when she tried to touch me.

"No, I ain't from here. My country bumpkin ass left a long time ago!" I snatched the key from the counter and went in search of my rental car. It wasn't her fault I was in this mood. It was just the fact that I was in Alabama at all. The air was filling my senses with something and the little girl in me was curling up into a ball. If I wasn't careful, I was going to turn into her.

I had to keep my mind sharp and remember I was here for one thing. It was time I came to peace with what happened. My brother was calling to me. He was in my brain, eating away at it. Passing through the small towns made me sick. The people were all over friendly and wanted to know your life story. They were strolling around the street, saying hi to everyone who passed. I was waved at a couple times and I was tempted to flip them off and smile.

What the fuck were they so happy about anyway? They wanted to help? Too bad! Why didn't I ever get the help I needed? Small towns hold big secrets. No kidding! I was scared to be stoned by all the hateful women in my hometown. I bet most the girls I went to school with were pregnant and married to the person they lost it to. Fucking chumps.

When I finally got into town, the sun was high in the sky and the heat was unbearable. There was no hotel in the area. There was only a small bed and breakfast, run by the family of one of my old classmates. My name was the only thing that changed about me. I looked like I did when I was younger. I was counting on time to wipe their memories. I didn't want anyone to place my face. If my father found out, I don't know what he would do.

I parked my car on the side of the large house and took my bag out of the car. This was going to be fun. The door chimed as I walked into it. I looked at it with contempt.

"Welcome." a bubbly teen answered. She had long light brown hair that was so straight it was limp.

"Hello, I am going to need a room for a week, I might be staying longer. I'm not sure yet." I stated sorely.

"We have rooms available. Is it just you?" I looked around me to see if there was anyone else there.

"It's just me." I said and took my glasses off my face.

"A room for a week in advance is two-fifty, or you can pay by the day. That will be forty-six dollars a day." she smiled and placed a paper in front of me.

"What is this?" I looked over the paper.

"It is a contract agreement stating you are responsible for any damage you may cause." It was different I stayed in hotels all over the world and they just kept your card on file just in case. She saw my confusion and replied, "We don't take credit cards. Only cash."

"Got it." Thank goodness I had cash on hand at all times. You never knew when you would get into a sticky situation. I took two hundred and fifty dollars from my wallet and placed it on the counter. I read over the paper to make sure there wasn't anything in it that didn't seem right. I didn't get people who just signed tings without reading it first.

"Here is your room key, Ms. Wilkes. Hey, there is a Wilkes family from this town. Any relation?" I should have changed my whole fucking name.

"God no!" I said and took my key from the table.

"Do you need help with your bags? My uncle is here" she rushed after me.

"I can manage." I waved her off.

It was worse than I thought. The room was covered in a floral wallpaper that was yellow. From the looks of it, they hadn't changed it since the fifties. I placed my bag on the bed and when it plopped down dust filtered through the air.

What the fuck! They were going to give me new bed sheets. It was completely unacceptable.

"Excuse me!" I said to the man behind the desk. His back was facing me. He was putting paperwork into an old steel filing cabinet. "I need new bed sheets! The room

I was put in has dust all over it." His shoulders shook from what I assumed was him laughing.

"Dust it then! That's the problem with you city folks. You don't know how to do anything for yourselves." He turned and looked at me. The smug smirk that set on his face evaporated when he saw me. "Then again, I guess people from here are entitled as well."

"Nice to see you again, Garth." I stumbled. Someone recognizing me was inevitable.

"I didn't think you would ever show that pretty face of yours in this town again." Garth was the only friend I had here and it was only for a week because Ira told me to never trust anyone in this town.

"Hi Garth." I skipped over to him and waved at him.

Monroe

"Hey Jo, what are you doing right now?" He asked and took his hat from his head. I was convinced that his family was the last decent family in this town.

"Nothing. I was just going to find Ira and go swimming. It is mighty hot out here." The sweat was gathering on my upper lip. I wiped it away.

"If Ira don't mind, I would like to come too. My momma isn't going to be home from my aunts for hours yet." Such a gentleman.

"I don't think he'll care,'" I twisted from side to side.

"Josephine, what the hell are you doing?" My brother's voice boomed across the court.

"Seems like he might care. Seems like he might care a lot." Before I had time to explain that it was just the way Ira was, Garth was gone.

Ira took me by my arm and pulled me into the shade of the nearby building. "Why do I keep having to tell you not to talk to these people? You must like pain."

"Garth isn't like them. He's different!" I crossed my arms across my chest. I was starting to bloom and my chest hurt at times, making it difficult to show my attitude.

"You just want to think he is Jo, but he is just like all the others. They don't give a fuck about us!" Ira was sixteen now and I was just getting into my teens. We had been living in abuse and torture for six years and it was

329

making Ira something he wasn't. I didn't hold it against him. We had both been through too much at our age.

"You and me both." The silence was deafening and the way he was looking at me brought me back to my eleven-year-old self.

" To what do we own the pleasure? You don't want anything to do with us. You lost your accent. I take it you don't want anyone to know who you are." he leaned on the counter penetrating me with his questioning eyes.

"No. Well, this was lovely, but let's act like we don't know each other. I don't want anyone knowing I'm here but I even doubt they'll put two and two together." If he talked, the rumors about me would spread faster than a wild fire.

"Yep. Us country folk don't know no better. We all marry our cousins and get a high education of the fifth grade." He held up three fingers and crossed his eyes. It was funny, but I wouldn't allow myself to enjoy it.

"That may be, but I would still like you to keep this to yourself. I'm only here to see my brother and I am leaving."

"No problemo, city girl." he frowned and started filing papers again.

"I'm not a city girl and you know that full well, Garth." He was trying to get under my skin and I don't know why I let him. I should have just gone upstairs and dusted my own sheets.

"Whatever you say," he chuckled.

331

I kicked the door as I entered my room. Maybe if I acted as if I was from somewhere else, they wouldn't know me. Of course Garth did. I talked to him. He was my first kiss.

It was late. I snuck out my window after Daddy passed out. He would never stay in my room. He would always go sleep on the couch. I told Garth to meet me. He was nervous because he didn't want to get me in trouble. He heard the rumors everyone was talking around town. He wasn't a fool, but he never talked to me about it.

The light from the moon made the creek look magical. I was sitting on a low hanging branch. It stretched out over the water and it was just low enough to dip my toes in. Something moved in the bushes. I looked in that direction and waited for it to show itself. Animals would come here to drink from the creek in the summer. It was the closest watering hole.

Garth popped out of the brush, dusting at his pants. "This place isn't easy to get to. If I'm not careful, my Momma is going to be asking me why my clothes are messed up." He pulled a foxtail off his shoelace and walked to the tree I was sitting on. "Are you going to sit there or come here?"

"Garth, climb to me, its nice up here." He looked at me like I was crazy. "Stop being a stick in the mud, you're already here. Might as well go all the way." I looked at him eagerly.

He began to take his shoes and socks off, placing them on a nearby rock. When he reached for the zipper on his pants, I turned from him to give him some privacy.

The branch swayed under his weight as he moved toward me. He sat right next to me, so close his shoulder rubbed mine.

"It is nice here, I can't believe I've never come here." he nudged me with his arm. Garth was a year older than me and he towered over me. He was going to make a real fine man one day. He was the cutest boy in town and all the girls were gaga over him. He had his pick of who he wanted to spend his time with.

"Plenty of people don't know this is here. You think from the surroundings that there is only brush here and trees. The only reason me and Ira found it was…" I trailed off. The only reason we found it was because we were trying to run away. That night Daddy put it in my behind and made my momma watch. She tried to leave, but he wouldn't let her. He ended up tying her to a chair.

334

"Hey, it's okay. You don't have to tell me. I'm fine with not knowing." he placed his palm against my face and turned my face to look at him. My heart raced in my chest. I wanted to kiss him. At least I thought I did, but it felt wrong. It felt dirty.

I did the first thing that came to mind. I pushed him into the water. He wouldn't get sick. It was warm out and the water was a good temperature.

"What was that for?" he sputtered.

"Why else would I have you meet me here?" I laughed and kicked some water at him.

He swam closer to me with a wicked smile on his face. There wasn't much that people could hide from me. Emotions usually gave them away because they displayed them on their faces. "Jo, I didn't come here to see your secret spot. I came here to spend time with you." His hand came out from the water and he placed it on my knee. "I wanted to get to know you. After all, you are the biggest mystery in this town."

"My life isn't a mystery Don't you hear all the rumors about me?" I pushed his hand off my knee because it was giving me flu like symptoms.

"That isn't who you are Jo. All those people who talk about you don't know who you are. They don't know if those stories are real and it ain't their business." He was the only one who thought like that. It was like the women in town lived to talk and everything that came out of their mouth was shit.

"They make it their business," I spat.

336

"I want you to know it doesn't matter if it happened or not. If you ever feel like you need someone to talk to, I'll be here waiting." He pulled me into the water and as my head went under, I felt for the first time that I wasn't alone. When my head broke the surface, he was there, looking cute with his dimpled cheeks and water droplets all over. Faster than I thought was possible, he kissed me.

"Garth what are you doing?"

"I came here to tell you I want you to be my girl." He kissed me again.

"No!" Ira was right. I shouldn't trust any of them. I liked Garth in another life, then maybe. The shit in my life was enough, worrying about Garth wouldn't be good

for either of us. My daddy didn't care if you were the Major. He would kill you.

"Okay, fine." he backed away from me. "I can protect you."

"Against what? If Ira can't, you can't." The only person who could save me was me.

"You won't even let me try?" He punched the water with his fist.

"No, because I like you, and you shouldn't be involved in this. You will thank me one day, I promise." He didn't like what I was saying. He stormed out of the water. Tugging on his pants, he shoved his wet feet into his shoes.

Monroe

"One day you are going to need someone, and there isn't going to be anyone because you pushed them all away!" It was a demon I was going to have to face when the time came. For now, I was the only one I had the strength to worry about. I let him go and from that day on, he dodged me like I was a bullet.

I didn't blame him.

A thump on the door woke me from my slumber.

"Yes?" I called.

"My uncle told me to bring these to the city girl, and I don't mean any disrespect ma'am, but you are the only one I don't know from around here. The most people we get here are from the south like we is." she passed me the folded sheets.

339

"Tell your uncle he can dust off his eyes next time."
Out of everything I could have said, that it what I chose. I
was losing it.

"I'll tell him, and he also told me to tell you lunch will
be ready in five if you want to eat. He said something
about you needing to eat something. Looks like a twig,
he said." Garth has grown into a douche bag. Great. My
whole childhood dream was shattered.

"I'll be down soon. Thank you." I took out money to
tip her but she was already gone.

This asshole was going to make me change the sheets.
The shower was down the hall. I needed to get the smell
of travel off my skin. I took my time washing. I thought
about Roman running his hands down my body. I found
myself tucking my hand between my legs and massaging

my sweet spot. The whole time, I was fantasizing it was Roman's rough hands skimming all over my body.

The pressure pulled at me, building i up until it brought me crashing down. A quick rhythm sounded on the door. "Other people have to shower, city slicker!" Garth's annoying ass said.

"Leave me alone, Garth. If I didn't know any better, I would say you were trying to get a peek." I tucked the towel around my body and gathered my things. Throwing the door open, causing Garth to jump. "If you wanted to see, all you have to do was ask." I smile devilishly at him and take one end of my towel from its place.

"Stop it Jo, or you're going to get something you didn't ask for." he growled.

"Whatever. Always the knight and never the villain."
I leaned into him and whispered. "I grew to love the
villain." I winked and bit my lip. Of course, I was just
horny and was desperate for human contact but I was
trying to be good. Garth's mouth was slack with
astonishment.

 I closed my door behind me. Lunch should be
interesting.

I descended the stairs dressed for the run I wanted to
get in before the day was over. My iPod was strapped to
my arm. I was ready for anything.

"And you say you ain't from the city," he laughed.
My eyes found him leaning against the counter. I studied
his body as if it was a masterpiece. The years were good
to him and I had been right. He had grown into a great

man. He still looked the same with his black hair and blue eyes, but his face was sharper where there used to be soft curves. The fat from his cheeks was gone and the dimple on his face became deeper. His chin and upper lip were covered in a light stubble. He looked like a cowboy from a romance novel.

I almost broke a rib from laughing so hard.

"What's so funny?" he pushed off the desk.

"You. You talk about me like you aren't a walking cliché." I looked at the ceiling and laughed.

"Are you hungry?" He was quick to change the subject.

"Starving actually, and just because you offer me food doesn't mean you are forgiven for the twig comment." I followed him into the kitchen. The girl is there sitting at the table eating a sandwich.

"Melody, how many times do I have to tell you not to repeat everything I say?" Melody. It was a nice name. It was the name Garth's sister wanted to name her daughter. She didn't tell me that of course but she did take a liking to Ira. Told him she was going to have his child one day and it was going to be a girl named Melody. Ira was handsome, he looked like me but he got my momma's dark hair.

"Your sister's kid?" I sat at the table across from her.

"Yea, she died in child birth. So, now this brat is mine." He smiled at her and ruffled her hair.

"Where is her daddy?" Being nosey wasn't a characteristic I practiced, but Garth is nothing like I

344

would have thought and the fact that he had raised her was amazing.

"Where all daddies go" she replied. I look at Garth confused.

"The Army" he nodded. He was trying to tell me something with his eyes. He wasn't in the Army if she never saw him. Understanding dawned on me. He was telling her this to save her heartbreak. She didn't have her momma and if she knew her father didn't want her, it would be painful. Not all parents were worth hurting over. Take my life as an example. Not everyone is worth loving. She is in better hands with her uncle. At least he would take care of her and love her as she needed.

"Well, your father has one of the most important jobs out there. He fights for our freedom." I gave her an encouraging smile.

"I know, but sometimes I just wish he would come see me." There was nothing I could say to her, so I just listened and agreed.

"Wasn't there a promise of food?" I asked, clearing my throat.

Garth took a plate from the fridge and placed it on the table. "Ham and cheese, enjoy." he said then went back to washing the dishes. "It might not be as fancy as what you're used to."

Monroe

"It's fine, thank you." I swallowed the sandwich without breathing as Garth and Melody looked on.

After I was done, I washed my own dish and started for the door, I started my iPod as I began to stretch. I intended to stop by my parent's house. It was get it over with or I wasn't going to. I would find a way to talk myself out of it.

Running in Alabama was like running on a treadmill in a sauna. I'm sure they didn't even know what that was. People stared at me as they passed, and like I said earlier, they waved and tried to say hi. I ignored them as I tried to think of a scenario where I would come out okay. There wasn't any. My father was still going to be the abusive asshole he was and my mother was going to be his fucking lap dog.

Everything on the street looked the same, except that the houses were in need of a paint job. Their house was at the end of the street and it was blocked off by trees, concealing it from prying eyes. I stopped to catch my breath in the middle of the road as I paced from one side to another. Physically, I was strong. Mentally I was a decrepit old woman who had been abused her whole life. the worst part of that was it wasn't all my father doing the punishment. As a woman, I was my own worst enemy.

The real reason for being here was so I could forgive myself for what happened. The selfish need to see what Roman saw in me was overpowering, and I hoped to be able to love him one day. I was doing this for us. If I didn't bury my past, there could be no future. I walked further in, remembering things on every corner. The feeling of dread took over and clenched at my lungs.

Relax, Monroe.

Mrs. Johnson still sat on her porch in her chair, saying nothing but seeing everything. She looked at me and recognition filled her eyes. She got up from her chair and walked into her house. It was her way of staying out of people's business. My father threatened her time and time again telling her if she didn't mind hers, he would turn her house to ash. When my father said something, he had every intention of following through. I learned the hard way.

If it wasn't for Ira, I wouldn't have come back here at all. I would have stayed in another part of the world. If it wasn't for Roman, I wouldn't be looking for forgiveness.

I would have just accepted my fate and died alone. Being in New York taught me something. If I was ever going to leave my past behind, I was going to have to revisit it.

So far, it sucked.

I dismissed Mrs. Johnson as a chicken shit. I was perfectly able to defend myself now, and I planned to turn that fucking house into dust, with my parents in it. They were going to burn in hell, like I had been for my whole life.

Josephine was going to sit this one out. She was too damaged and a liability. No, they were going to feel the wrath of the woman I had become. This visit was just to let them know I was here. This visit was in hopes of getting to see Ira. Without them, I wouldn't be able to. The house came into view as the trees cleared. I stood in front of it remembering all the suffering it caused. My bile forced its way into my throat and I expelled it into the bushes I used to hide in.

"Jo, you awake?" Ira poked at my face.

"Now I am. What?" I turned away from him.

"We're leaving. Get up. I packed your bag." He tossed my bag to me.

"Where are we going?" I asked and slipped my shoes on. I was in my sleeping clothes, but I didn't care.

"It doesn't matter. Anywhere is better than here." He was right. The attacks on us were getting worse. Daddy was coming home later, drunk as a skunk.

Disgusted, I scrubbed at my mouth.

"What a pretty little thing! Can I help you?" my father's voice filled the air around me. He was standing behind me, not far from what it sounded like. My body became a wall. It didn't move. I didn't blink. I was worried if I did, he would appear in front of me. Be strong Monroe, strong.

"Yes, you can help me. I want to see my brother." I turned to face a white haired man I had no recollection of. My father was an old man now, wrinkled and missing teeth. He was in the clearing off to the side of the house. He must have been working in the garage.

His eyes twinkled as he took me in. "Look at you! What a fine woman you turned into." He took a few steps forward, then thought better of it and stopped.

"No thanks to you." You are stronger than him. You are a different person now. He can't hurt you. You can take him out.

"I think it has everything to do with me" he grinned, his tongue poking out of the areas his teeth were missing.

"It has nothing to do with you!" I pointed at the dirt road. "I am who I am because you are a fucking rapist!" I shouted at the top of my lungs.

"Kitty got balls" his face morphed into the devils and there stood the man who plagued my whole fucking existence. He was the monster hiding under my bed and I realized the mistake I had made. I showed him my weakness. He still saw the little girl I was.

I tried calming myself, "I want to see my brother." I repeated.

"You have no kin here! Get off my land! Unless you want me to remind you of why you left in the first place!" He cackled and reached into the bed of the truck and retrieved his shotgun. "One. Two. Three." he counted.

My mother appeared on the steps of the porch as she had many times before. I blinked, focusing on her.

"Josephine, is that you?" her eyes were covered with glasses. Looks like my father took her eyesight. Is there anything this man wasn't capable of? And the dumb ass was still with him. He was going to kill her eventually.

"I want to see Ira, Momma. Please? I want to see my brother. I will leave and never come back, just let me see him." I begged. I thought I was able to keep Josephine inside but I crumbled when I saw them. It converted me back into her. It stripped everything away and left me vulnerable.

"Get your ass in the house!" he said to her. "I told you, we're not your family. My daughter died when she lied and made up all that stuff about me!" He must have convinced himself so his conscience wouldn't eat him up. He was a fucking monster.

"Momma, don't let him keep me away from Ira. Please momma. You know it wasn't my fault. You saw what he did to me." I would have gotten on my knees if I thought it would help.

"I saw nothing" she said and pointed to her eyes. She took off her glasses, and her eyes were missing from her skull.

"What did he do to you, Momma? You got to leave him. He is going to kill you." I begged.

"Shut your dirty whore mouth, you little bitch! I didn't do that to her, you did." He cocked his gun and aimed it at my head. What was the point of running, he was the best shot in town, drunk or not. He would hit me before I got three steps.

"Daddy, as we speak, the devil is making up your bed in hell. He is going to roast you until you're ash. Then it's going to happen all over again. I will piss on your dead body old man, you hear me?! And Momma, I was kind enough to give you another chance, but now you will rot with him! If I have learned anything from you daddy, it was to keep my word. I promise you, you will die by my hands. After all, I'm a product of you, it's what you always wanted." I vowed there as the shotgun was pointed at me, that there was no forgiveness.

I looked to my mother again, shaking my head. I walked out of their driveway. I didn't care if he shot me. He woke me up then. He made me realize there was no forgiveness for a monster like him. There was only death. He was going to die and I was going to laugh hysterically as his body dropped. If that meant I would be going to hell also, I would take it any day to see this man rot.

My mind was made up.

***

There was no point in hiding my being here. My father knew and he was the only one I was worried about. I needed a drink. The bar in town was a wood building on the outskirts of town. I ran most of the way there, trying to burn off the adrenaline. It was weird seeing all the places I couldn't go into as a child, and all the same people owning them. The inside was the same as the outside. It was covered in wood. Dartboards covered the walls and three pool tables stood in the middle. There were green topped stools lining the bar and a handful of men sitting on them. This is the bar my daddy refused to come to because he didn't get along with the owner. He would drive to the next town over to get drunk.

"Well I'll be! If it isn't little Josephine Wilkes. Not so little anymore, I see. Looking all pretty and well." Sam the owner called out to me as I walked in.

"If I didn't know any better Sam, I would say you were hitting on me," I placed my hand over my heart and took a seat at the bar.

"If that is what you got from that, then it must be true. What can I get you, doll?"

"Just a beer, anything will do." I sighed and took my hair out of my ponytail. I was getting a headache from thinking.

"Coming right up." Less than a minute later, a beer was placed in front of me. I got my money out to pay, but he waved it away.

"Your money's no good here. Think of it as your welcome home." He began wiping the bar down as he spoke.

"Welcome? This town doesn't know that word," I chuckled.

"What happened to the way you talk? I remember you having the cutest southern twang." If he only knew how much I paid to get rid of it.

"I buried it like I buried this town. Can I have a shot too," I chugged half of my beer. He placed a shot of Jameson whiskey in front of me and took my mug to refill it. "Thanks."

"It couldn't have been that bad here." Could it be that Sam didn't hear all the rumors and stories about me?

"Sam, you have become my new best friend." He was handsome for an older man. His hair was graying at the temples with a black streak down the middle. When he smiled, all his teeth were in their places and they were white and straight. His skin was dark from working on the ranch when he wasn't behind this counter. I studied him as he served another man. He was fluid in his movements, I was amazed because he was bulky with broad shoulders. He was made of the best dreams for a small town girl.

"What are you looking at?" Garth said close to my ear.

"Don't you have a business to run? What are you doing here?" God, what was with this town? Everyone seemed like they were following you because there were a limited amount of places to go.

"I suppose it's the same thing you are here for." He signaled Sam without words and a beer was placed in front of him. "I got her next three rounds too."

"Garth, don't act like you're doing me favors. I don't need you pity." The alcohol was getting to me making me catty, and releasing my southern twang.

"You need something. How was it?" he asked knowingly.

"How was what?" Has it got around town already? It just happed an hour ago.

"Don't play stupid, Jo. Half the town knows about it." He answered my unspoken question.

"It went well. So well in fact, that my father pulled out his shotgun and pointed it at my head." I mimicked a gun from my hand at aimed it to my head showing him what I meant.

He flinched, not saying anything. He just nodded. He motioned for Sam again and more whiskey appeared. "If it means anything, I'm sorry. No one should have to have shitty parents like them."

"Agreed!" I downed the shot. "I can't wait to see this town in my rear view mirror." I took another shot.

"You might want to slow down! If you don't, I'm going to have to carry you home and I don't promise to keep my hands to myself." The joke he made was disturbing. I made a disgusted face.

"That wasn't funny! If anything, that is borderline sexual harassment!" Looking him in the eyes, I drained my shot. "You wanna know where I was and what I was doing for years now? I was living in every part of the world. I went to school and got my Masters in Social

Science and Human Behavior. I left this fucking town and made something for myself. I used to ask myself why no one in this shitty town would help me but I couldn't find the answers. It only fueled my hate more." I slurred.

"Helped you with what honey?" Sam came back to where we were waiting for me to answer. I looked at Garth, pleading with him to help me out.

"I ain't covering shit up anymore, Josephine! I won't tell him anything that isn't the truth." A load of good he was.

I exhaled, pivoting my body to face Sam. I cheesed at him and responded. "No one helped me in this fucking town when my father was raping me. No one helped me when he was passing me around to his friends. No one lent a hand when the women of this town were calling me names and throwing stones at me. But the worst part of it…" I was crying now, the tears flowing freely. "The worst fucking part is no one helped me save my brother. Where was this town at then? Everyone wants to know where I went? But no one asked what was happening while I was here!" There it was. It wasn't like it was a big secret. People whispered about it all the time. They just didn't ask my side. They didn't want to know the truth about what was going on in their little town.

Sam looked like he was going to be sick. You could see the thoughts running through his head and as he thought he placed faces. My fathers 'friends' were some influential men in this town. The sickness turned to anger, the anger to rage.

"Now Sam, whatever you are thinking isn't a good idea right now," Garth piped in.

"Hush boy! I didn't ask for your opinion." he pulled a bottle of tequila out and took a gulp from the bottle. "I needed that. Now get the hell out of my way or I am going to shoot you. I don't want to. The bullet is meant for her papa." No, I was supposed to kill him. Not Sam.

"Please let me handle this. I have plans." My head was swirling and my stomach was in knots. Garth was right. I was drunk. A giggling fit took over my body, as the men looked at me funny.

"This isn't funny Jo. I am so sorry. If I would have known…"

"But you didn't, and there is no fixing it now. I, on the other hand, will make him pay. It isn't your place Sam. I can handle this myself. I have been training and waiting patiently to return." It felt as if I were moving.

"Looks like I'm carrying her home." I forgot he was here, his voice kept echoing in my head.

"Don't you touch her boy, or I will shoot your dick off" Sam said gruffly.

"No need to threaten Sam. I loved this girl for most my life. I wouldn't hurt her." The last thought I could recall before I passed out was why was it so easy for men to say those words when it was difficult for me to even think them.

***

Thump. Thump.

Someone was hitting me on the head. My head was going to cave in.

Thump. Thump.

Stop it. Please leave me alone. I can't take it. My head was going to explode.

I opened my eyes, looking around forgetting where I was. The panic swelled in my stomach. I tossed the blankets off the bed, throwing my legs to the floor. My body weighted a ton it felt like I was carrying a cinder block around. I remembered where I was. I groaned. Why did I come back? Now there were men who wanted to kill my father, when I wanted to do it. I was losing grip on my life. It all started in this stupid town. Why would I think I could handle this? Years of abuse weren't healthy, but putting yourself back into it now that was a special kind of person.

I threw myself back onto the pillow and rolled over. I hit something solid with my arm.

No. I didn't. Did I?

Garth mumbled something unintelligent, snoring softly into the pillow. I looked down at myself, checking if my clothes were still on. They were. The same ones I jogged in last night.

"Thank you Lord!" I sent my silent prayer to the heavens. There was nothing wrong with Garth, but this was complicated and complicated was overrated. I had no place for it in my life.

He moved again, this time rolling onto my side of the bed. I tightened my face as if it would help me disappear. His big meaty hand slapped onto my thigh. Panic surged through my veins with a hint of want.

No stupid, you don't want him. Don't fuck your life up again.

A soft laugh was muffled by a pillow. "Why do you look like that?" Garth asked with his face still turned into the pillow.

"Because I don't know why you're in my bed."

"You don't remember?" he became serious.

"No, I don't." I pushed.

"I made love to you all night." Again, I do not make love, but Garth wouldn't know that. We didn't do anything last night. This asshole was making it all up. "You begged me not to stop." He groaned as he stretched. It was another of my will never happen rules.

"Did I? I don't know why I can't remember. I mean if I begged, it must have been great right?"

"It was amazing." This guy had nerve.

I came face to face with him, sitting on his lap. The fact that his morning wood was poking into my ass didn't perturb me. "Stop lying," I said close to his lips. I leapt from the bed and grabbed my toiletry bag and headed out the door. "When I get back, I want you out of my bed."

I wasn't the girl Garth fell for. Even if being here made it seem like that. All I kept thinking of was my blue and brown- eyed angel. I missed him. My shower was quick. It helped me sober up some. Breakfast and a pain reliever were next. I placed the bag on my dresser and looked at my bed again. He was still there, lounging around. On my clean fucking sheets.

"Are you deaf? Get the fuck out!" I tossed my brush and it sailed across the room, hitting the wall and dropping to the ground.

"Is that how you city folk say thank you?" He asked.

"No! We buy you something and never talk to you again. There is too much on my mind right now. I have no time for this." He sat up and the covers fell from his body. What was there would make a saint sin. Lord help me out, please.

Closing my eyes I said, "You have to go. Isn't there a little girl out there in need of breakfast, a father, or something?"

"Melody is at school. The only reason I'm even in your bed is because you can't shoot whiskey." He said seriously.

"Yesterday was shitty! I will not apologize to you for it!" My nostrils flared.

"Okay. I get it. I'm going. We got another city kid last night. So there will be company at breakfast." He left and took his perfectly sculpted body with him. Seems like I kept digging myself into a hole.

Today was the same as yesterday. I was going to see my brother.

Ira was growing into a handsome devil. The girls were throwing themselves at him. He was going to make one lucky girl happy one day. He would be the best husband and father ever.

"Why you over here with that goofy look on your face?" he ruffled my hair as he sat.

"I was just looking at you. One day you are going to break those girl's hearts." I joked.

"No, I am going to do right by my woman. I will treat her like my queen, giving her all the babies she wants."
His smile was dazzling. Every word that crossed his lips I believed.

"I'd be happy with some nieces and nephews running around. A sister would be nice too. Someone to talk with about boys." I teased.

"The hell you will! I will kill every boy who comes near you." he smashed his fist into his hand.

"You are not fair, Ira James Wilkes. How come you get a girl and I gotta be an old spinster my whole life?"

"Why does everything have to be about your whole life? You are so dramatic, Josephine Sue Wilkes." He thought he was funny calling me by that ugly name. When I grow up and get real boobs, I am going to change my

name to Monroe. After Marilyn Monroe. I wanted to look like her. All the boys seemed to like her, but I wouldn't tell Ira that. The only difference would be I'm still alive.

Breakfast better be greasy, or my stomach was going to give in. I regretted nothing but I should have listened to Garth when he told me I was going to be carried out. I bounced down the stairs full of life, today was a new day. Tomorrow would be the same. I was going to plot out my plan tonight, get all my ducks in a row. I rounded the corner into the kitchen to see Garth standing at the stove cooking eggs, bacon and grits. It was just what I needed and it smelled amazing.

"You ready to eat, you lush?" he poked fun.

"I am starving. I think they make the drinks out here with more liquor." I stuck my tongue out.

"That happens when you drink whiskey like a fish drinks water," he chuckled.

"You must think I'm a child. Stop laughing at me." I went to the icebox to look for something to drink. Orange juice sounded too good to be true and lucky me, they had some.

"Jo, here is our guest. What was your name again?" I was still pushing things out of the way to get to the juice.

"Roman." he said.

I slowly looked over the door of the fridge to take a peek at him. There stood the only person I had missed for months. With his soul-stealing eyes glued to me.

"Roman, this is Jo, the town lush." Garth thought he was being witty. He was oblivious to what was passing between Roman and me.

"Charmed." Roman said. I lost my breath. He was just as stunning.

My eyes peeked at Garth and mouthed 'Charmed' copying Roman's words.

I snapped my attention back to Roman, who was still staring at me with his penetrating gaze. Finally, Garth picked up on the tension in the room. "You two know each other?"

"Something like that. You and I know a different Josephine altogether" Roman answered.

"Jo?" Garth asked. He stopped flipping the food and looked between us.

"It's fine Garth." I dismissed.

"Oh, it's anything but, you see. You woke up in her bed this morning, correct?" Roman took a seat and crossed his leg elegantly waiting for a response.

"I don't see how that it's any of your business," Garth said and moved to stand in front of Roman. Men fighting for territory. My life was dramatic.

"It is my business. Care to share Monroe?" Roman quipped.

Stuck and unable to respond, my head pivoted on my neck trying to gauge the situation. I was Monroe after all, so here went nothing. "I was clear when I left New York how I felt. Or did you miss the note. It was on an eighty foot screen."

"All that was, was funny!" he exclaimed.

"You didn't look like it was funny at the time. I thought you were going to lose it." I picked at my nail.

"I wasn't going to marry her, Monroe. It was all a job, just like you. You were there for the same thing I was. How can you be mad at me?" It was different. I was there because Vera hired me. He was there because he was fucking her.

"Did you sleep with her? Did you pin her against the fucking wall like you pinned me. Did you tell her you loved her too?"

"It's was different…"

379

"The only fucking difference is that you are a lying asshole in one of these cases!" I forgot Garth was still in here with us.

"Let me get this straight," he said. "You two were what? In a relationship, or was it just bumping uglies."

"Who is this clown, and why was he in your bed?" Roman fumed.

"Clown…" Garth said, and I stopped him from moving forward.

"I don't have to explain shit to you Roman! You tried to play me, and with everything in my life already being shit, I don't need you!" I pointed and him. "Garth is a friend. If you must know, he was taking care of me because I had a bad day."

"I am going to say this one fucking time, so listen close…he doesn't matter to me." Roman pointed at Garth. "He shouldn't have been in your bed. He shouldn't have even been near what is mine." I should have been put off by his dominance and controlling words, but nothing in life was sexier. Well, maybe him fucking me and saying it.

A devious grin stretched my lips. He was so hot.

"This is my house! You can take your domestic spat somewhere else." Garth tossed the towel on the sink, stalking his way over to Roman. They were chest to chest. "You might think she is yours, but when she is under my roof I will protect her. You should have taken the hint and stayed away. I will tear you apart city boy!" Garth left his warning floating in the air. It sunk in. They were both pissing on my leg.

"I might be from the city, but I am not scared of him. If he wants to throw down, I will smash him!" Roman was lean with nice muscles, Garth was a country boy with a country boy body. All the hard work and long hours on the farm had grown Garth into a mammoth.

Why me, and why when I have a hangover? Roman being here didn't change the fact that I was hungry and Garth was going to join us. My life wasn't spiraling anymore. My life was done, over, finished. The only thing I picked up from love was that it made people do crazy shit, like follow me to my hometown. That's some stalker shit.

"Why does he keep calling you Monroe?" Garth wondered.

"Because it's my name." I said around my grits.

"Jo, I've known you my whole life. I know what your name is." Garth said.

"She changed it, Gigantor—to get away from this town." I had to give it to them they were both being nice, other than their smart ass remarks to one another.

"I changed it before college." I repeated Roman's words.

"But, why? That was your God given name. Why'd you do that?" Garth said and scratched his head.

"God also gave me my parents, so I asked him to take one for the team on this one since I had to deal with them for so long." he just nodded and accepted my words.

"Does he know?" Garth asked about Roman.

"Not everything, and nothing I haven't told him. He's just a nosey bastard." This was the weirdest conversation in my life. Going to town seemed better than sitting here measuring their dicks.

"I'm out. Let me know when you two make up." Ice cream sounded good. This time I was going to pick everything I had ever wanted.

He was still there, Mr. Molt, and when I saw his thick rosy cheeks, I cried. All of my good memories as a child were made here, in front of his store. I stood in line like everyone else waiting for my turn. He was the kindest man in this town, always helping others and expecting nothing in return. There were times I sent him money. He never knew I did, but just knowing I helped him in some way, made me happy.

"I would like a chocolate cone with sprinkles." I said when it was my turn.

"Will that be all for you Ma'am?" He looked up and saw me for the first time.

"Yes that will be all." I smiled through my tears.

"Josephine!" he gasped. Like everyone else in this town, Mr. Molt knew what happened. It made me mad at first, knowing he wouldn't help me. As time passed, I realized it was because my father had a lot of people in his pocket. The sheriff was one of my many nightly visitors. "Wait there. I want to hug you," he said excitedly and came out from behind the counters. The years were good to him. His hair wasn't graying, but his belly was just as round as I remembered.

"It's nice to see you too, Molt."

"Look at you Josephine Wilkes! You grew into a lovely lady, but if course we all knew that." he beamed.

"I keep hearing that, thank you."

I talked to him for a half hour as he served the rest of the customers, eating my ice cream, not caring if the townspeople were looking at me and whispering. Over time, I learned it wasn't my business what others thought of me, it was their problem and I was happier not knowing or caring. I smiled at them as they dragged their kids away from me saying, "They'll let anyone in here." Women would clutch their purses as if I was going to steal it and run off. Too bad, I had more money than all of them put together.

"Don't pay attention to them," Molt said.

"I'm not. This town has stayed the same for twenty years." I tossed the rest of my ice cream into the trash. "I have to go Mr. Molt, there are things to prepare for."

"Come see me before you leave town." The saddened look on his face hurt me. There weren't but a few people who could get to me like him.

I had to go back and deal with the fact that Roman was here and now that I knew what Garth felt for me, it was best to find housing somewhere else. It was in the best interest of both men. Garth was a good man. I needed to let him down easily. Tell him I thought I was in love with Roman. I stayed outside for a while watching the sun move across the sky.

"Are you ever coming in?" I cracked my eyes open and squinted up at Roman. He was dressed in camouflage cargo shorts and a black tank top. His hair was a perfect mess, black and sleek in the afternoon heat.

"Yes, but my mind demanded some space. It's difficult coming from a place where no one talked to you and bugged you to this. My mind was content there. Why would I come back here?" I sighed and kicked the dirt under my feet.

"I checked all the incoming flight rosters to see when you came back. The boy Orlando, you were working with, he told me he didn't know where you were going, only that it had a beach. I couldn't actually find the place you went because it took a week to find that little shit." I laughed at him because it sounded like Orlando. Always one-step ahead of everyone else. If Roman found him, he wanted to be found. I was going to have a talk with that boy genius when I went back to town.

"Stalking is illegal in all states if I recall. You could have just left me alone. We were at your engagement party. Vera was a killer candidate. Daddy's money was calling to you." A bird flew past and I watch as it floated in the air. He was able to go anywhere he wanted to. I was envious.

"I had to. You left me no choice." He declared.

"Roman, the video of us fucking on a screen for all to see were our parting words." I offered.

"Stop it Monroe! Stop acting like you don't care, and that we didn't have anything. I said I loved you. You being you, a chicken shit, ran from me. I told you Vera was all an act. All you had to do was hold it together for one more day." If someone was watching our conversation from a distance, they would think Roman was a mad man, waving his hands about pulling at his hair.

"And let Vera ruin my life, because she's a whore? Right! That's a great plan. No thank you, sir. Taking Vera down was great! it excited me more than you could." I lied. This asshole was going to get taken down a peg or two.

"You're lying." He was stationed in front of me before I could blink. "I do more than excite you." He pressed his nose into my hair and breathed in. "I can smell your desire on your skin."

"And I can smell the desperation on you," I whispered into his chest and bit lightly. Bringing my knee up, I connected with his manhood, not hard enough to damage, but with force to make him back away.

"Why'd you do that?" he doubled over in pain.

"Because you excite me and my desire." I snort.

"I get that you are trying to protect yourself, but if I didn't love you I wouldn't be here. What do I look like coming to God-knows-where-Alabama?" His face gave a sour look as he gained his composure.

"This town is where I come from. These streets are the streets I fought on, but you don't like it here. You say you love me. You should love where I'm from too." I defended the town I hated. Why? No clue, but I felt like this town was me, and it still had my brother and I loved him more than anything else.

"You are from here, but it isn't who you are anymore. And what are you and Garth?" he said his name with contempt. "He looks at you like he loves you."

"He does," I simply said. I hopped onto the hood of the car and laid back. The sun was warming my skin, but the breeze was cool and light.

"Are you sleeping with him? It's the last time I'll ask you," he came to the car and hopped up.

"No, I told you. He was taking care of me because I was drunk." I told him.

He was satisfied with my answer. He didn't say anything. We laid on the car watching the clouds move in the sky. Being comfortable with Roman was wrong. I felt like I should be more scared of what he was doing to me. I should be terrified that he was here, in my town, after stalking me. Him being here only aroused me.

"What's the plan for today?" he turned to me.

"No, idea. I'm just playing things by ear." He took my hand in his, lacing our fingers together and bringing them to his mouth. He kissed each of my knuckles softly.

Someone started clapping. I looked in the direction of the noise. There he was with his gun slung over his back. I yanked my hand from Roman, stumbling from the car trying to gain my footing. My father, Colt spit brown fluid onto the grass, his eyes locked with mine.

Monroe

"Aren't you going to introduce me to your friend?" he said motioning to Roman. Roman was getting off the car with his hand extended, ready to shake my daddy's hand. I pushed his arm down, stopping him in his tracks. He looked at me funny, wondering why I was acting as I was. Confusion was replaced with understanding. Understanding replaced with rage. I shook my head at him.

"Nope, ain't none of your business." my southern twang was more prominent.

"There's my hillbilly princess," He clapped his hands in joy.

"I thought you told me I was no kin of yours. You told my momma not to talk to me, and you are refusing to let me see my brother." Roman must not have known I had a brother. He turned sharply in my direction.

"She is a fire cracker and a locked chest all in one. Didn't tell you things did she?" My father was acting as if he was watching a soap opera. "Jo, this man has nothing to do with our family matters. You might want to tell him to get out of my town before I kill him." My daddy said.

Roman cackled at the threat, placing his hand over his heart and saying, "Bless your heart." In the worst accent I ever heard. He was going for a southern accent but ended up with a cross between Australian and English.

"Something funny to you boy?" The gun was now aimed at Roman's chest.

"You sick fuck! The only thing funny is you thinking I'm scared of you." The look of Roman's face was venomous. Another gun cocked behind me.

"Colt," Garth nodded. "You're not the only one with a gun and by the looks of it, mine is bigger." Garth pointed the riffle to my father's head.

"Now Garth, why would you go and get yourself involved in this? I thought you was smarter than that, boy." The gun in my father's hand never wavered as he spoke to Garth.

"You come onto my land, pointing guns at my guests. In the south, that is just bad manners. You know that. I can't let you kill this man. I haven't had a go at him for stealing your daughter from me." Garth said.

396

"She's a whore! You can do better." My dad switched the gun between the three of our heads. I haven't seen him shoot a gun since I was a kid, but his finger on the trigger was steady and his eyes were sharp.

"That's not how we talk to visiting company and your own blood at that." Garth took the stairs two at a time and positioned himself in front of my father's gun. "Are you going to shoot me Colt? Go ahead. This time there isn't going to be a cover up. Sheriff died years ago. No one here to have your back. There are three of us. Can't leave any witnesses." Garth placed his gun against the car. He raised his hands in surrender. I watched the whole time, worried if I said anything I would bring that attention back to us. My daddy wouldn't think twice about killing me and Roman. I placed my finger against my lips and looked at Roman silently. He was smart, he knew when he was out numbered, or out gunned.

"This isn't over Jo." He looked at me and the devil that he was surfaced. The gleam in his eye was wicked. My father had no soul.

"Counting on it, Pop," I winked at him and blew him a kiss. He responded by flipping me off. When he was gone, my chest stopped cramping. The rush of adrenaline made my body weak.

"Do you want him to shoot you?" Garth asked with an incredulous look.

I shrugged and sat with my back to the tire. "If he was going to kill me, he would have. No, he doesn't want me dead, yet." I gulped in air trying to calm my heart.

"You are the same hard-headed asshole you were back then, Jo. You come here to stir the fucking pot, but instead you tip the whole thing over." Garth rubbed his face and stalked into the house mumbling things under his breath.

"Long history?" Roman asked.

"Too long to explain." I was tired. Right now, all I wanted to do was get naked which gave me a brilliant idea. "You busy?" I asked Roman, standing up and dusting off my ass.

"Does it look like I'm busy?" he answered.

"I could use your help. There is this… thing, in my room it needs some attention." I said seductively. I started walking to the house and he followed. I took the stairs two at a time, getting up them as fast as I could.

The thought of his hands on my body thrilled me, but what made me weak was the idea of him thrusting inside me, Calling me my given name. We were in the room in no time, stripping off our clothes and devouring each other's skin.

"Baby, I have missed you," Roman said between kisses. He grabbed my thighs and picked me up. I wrapped my legs around his lean body, enjoying him completely. We fit together perfectly. My body on his was a form of art.

For the first time in months, I let the truth out, "I've missed you too." He took my head in between his hands and studied my face. When he would say something sweet in the past, I would always have a smart remark ready. Too tired to think of something, I just wanted to feel.

Thinking was overrated.

He walked us over to the bed and placed me on top of the covers. His soul shattering gaze never left me. All he had in his sight was me. As he dropped his pants, his glorious cock sprung to life, making my sex ache.

"You are beautiful," I said, amazed at myself for being honest. He took my face in his hands once more and tilted my face up to him. Kissing my repeatedly, claiming my mouth with his tongue.

"Not as beautiful as you." he said and moved down my body. "You asked me why I couldn't take the hint before? It's because my heart wouldn't let me forget you. Every time I would go somewhere, there was always something that made me think of you. Even Vera and her bitching caused me to smile thinking you were the one who did that to her. You are everything I want in a woman. Everything my heart needs. Plus you are brilliant, and the body doesn't hurt." His words hurt me. They stabbed at my heart, smacked into my skull, and fell to the floor. But more importantly, they chipped away at the ice that covered me.

He took my foot into his hands and kissed the pad of each toe. If I thought feet were disgusting before, he changed my mind. He bit the side of my foot, licking it when he was done. Roman ran his nose down the inside of my leg, sucking the sensitive areas, leaving his mark in each spot he loved. Telling me he would do this every day if I let him. When he met with the crease of my sex, he kissed it like everything else on my body, trailing his thick lips over each spot. Goosebumps broke out over my body as the convulsions started. He wasn't finished with his worship, licking every fold I had, stopping only to place a wet kiss on my thigh.

I was hyper- aware of every movement he made, treading my hands into his hair making him stay in a curtain spot longer. "You want me yet?" he said in a whisper against my clit. He blew on it then took it into his mouth, moaning around it. His torture was relentless.

"Yes!" I get out.

"Beg me. Tell me what you want. Tell me what I make you feel." He slipped a finger into me and began massaging my g-spot. He was putting just enough pressure to cause me pleasure, but not enough to cause me release. His demands were clear as he continued finger fucking me, stopping when he felt my walls grip his finger, the early signs I was close.

"I am not begging!" I forced from my dry throat.

"If you don't, I won't let you cum." The pace in his fingers began to quicken. "You are so wet." he moved his finger replacing it with his tongue. He tasted me and moaned. I could cum just from that sound. He lifted his head and looked at me, his different colored eyes mesmerizing, calling to me. He trailed my juices down my ass, making me buck up. "Stay still." he demanded.

"You are killing me!" I shouted at him.

"Tell me and I will stop," he placed a knee between my legs spreading them apart. "Your pussy is better than ice cream." he said and licked my wetness from his fingers. He sucked them making sure he got every drop off.

"Roman, please." I say annoyed.

"Close, but not there yet." he dipped the tip of his finger back into me, tasting it like cake batter. Not satisfied with his little taste, he dipped his face back down, swiping over my sweet spot slowly. I pull his hair and bring him so close to me that his nose is embedded in my folds.

"I want you to fuck me, please!" I said exhausted.

The tempo in his fingers picks up. "Tell me how." He lowered his head again and sucked my pussy.

"I want you to fuck me so hard I forget… Please I need it. I want you inside me so bad, I can't think of anything else. It helps me forgot how shitty my life is." I explain and wiggle because the desire is so strong I can't contain it anymore.

"Good girl. Tell me how I make you feel?"

405

"You drive me crazy with all your taking when you should be balls deep in me!" I growl.

"Isn't going to make me stop, or get in you faster. The only way to do that is if you tell me what you feel for me. I'm not the only one in this." he smirked and tongued my ass hole.

"You make me feel… like … I'm crazy. Like I can't be with anyone else because you ruined me. You will always be the only man who can please me. The only one who sees me." When the words left my mouth, I felt like crying. Roman stopped and crawled over my body until he was face to face with me. He kissed me on my lips, and I tasted myself.

"Look me in my eyes when I tell you this Josephine." He didn't use my name, only when he wanted to make a point. I took a minute and close my eyes. I focused on his heavy breathing. It calmed me, just because I knew it was him. I pried open my eyes and focused on him. "I love you." Shit.

My eyes shut again. I squeezed hard. "Don't Roman, I can't."

"Stop pushing me, Jo. I love you and just because you don't want to hear it, or the fact that you run from it isn't going to change it. With or without you, I will love you. The months you were gone drove me crazy. I wanted to see you so badly. I traveled to any place I thought you might be in hopes of running into you. When you left, I didn't know what I could do to help you or what to say to make it better. Now I'm positive I can, because I love you. I can't let you torment yourself making yourself think you aren't worth loving. If there is anyone in this world worthy of love, it's you. You should have gotten it when you were a child. You deserved so much more then what you got. Don't let these bad people keep you from me, include me in your life. Let me try and help. Even if I can't help, let me hold your hand as you figure it out yourself."

I felt something wet slide down my face. He was the first person to tell me this. Even Ira never told me, though I knew he did.

"This isn't your fault Jo," Ira would tell me every night after my dad left my room.

"You keep telling me that, but in the end, I'm still the only thing in common in all the situations."

"Stop thinking like that! You have to keep thinking about when we get out of here. You have to stay positive, for me and you." he played with my hair, my head in his lap. It was the closest thing I had to comfort. Tonight, my back was hurting from what the sheriff did to me. He had anger problems and he would hit me with his baton in my back, leaving bruises for weeks. He rode me hard, his fat belly hitting my ass as he tried to keep his small dick inside. I lost the feeling of pain long ago. Him hitting me was just my normal Friday.

"Ira, when are we going to leave? My body is dying," *he lifted my nightshirt a little to look at the damage.*

"Let me get something to put on that." He would make me a lavender, mint and sage oil to soothe my pains.

"No. I just want to feel it." I said. It was a reminder of my failures.

"Love, I think that's what I feel for you. But I don't know because it's my first time, feeling… anything." I replied. "I want to be with you. When I'm not, I think of you all the time. I imagine you inside me when I'm in meetings or out hiking. Your eyes haunt me, and I feel like my soul is with you. You took it in New York and I never got it back. But the worst of it all is that I want you to feel my pain, I want you to live it with me. To help me fight my demons." I wiped at the tears angrily.

My body was a fucking sellout.

"Baby, you'll never be alone again." He laid a kiss on each of my eyelids. As he promised, he kissed every inch of my body. When he was done, he continued to touch and rub all over me, and as the tears dried he inched his way into me, keeping a slow rhythmic pace. He was making love to me. When I tried to thrust up and meet his agonizingly slow movements, he would hold me down.

Eventually I stopped fighting and let the pressure take over, consuming me from the inside. I rolled him over and climbed onto him keeping the same speed as before, it claimed my body as its own. "Tell me you're mine." Roman muttered. His strides became relentless as he came close to the edge.

"No, I'm not. I will not, ever, be yours." I gasped out, unable to hold in my climax. "But I do love you." I got out before I folded onto his chest.

Monroe

In an instant, I was sleeping tangled in Roman. Dreaming of a life I thought I would never have. A life I would have let myself have if it weren't for him. The white picket fence became clearer, as the laughter of children over took my mind. Little did I know, the nightmare was the reality I would be facing soon.

Monroe

My head was pressed against something solid. My face was smashed against a warm body and my lips were wet. I erected my body, blowing tangles of hair away from my face. There was a pool of drool on Roman's stomach. I was mortified. Wiping at it, I tried not to wake him up, praying I got it all off before he woke.

"You drool a lot," he said with his eyes still closed.
Shit!

"Shut up! I can't believe you let me do that!" I
smacked him across his belly.

"I couldn't wake you up. You looked peaceful. I
watched you sleep for a while, moving your hair out of
your face." He got up from the bed and I noticed
something white dried to his thigh.

"Is that what I think it is?" I asked.

"You didn't give me much of a choice. You fell
asleep right when you landed on my chest." he walked to
the bathroom and the sink came to life.

"You could have pushed me off to clean up." I said
disgustedly. If he slept with cum on his thighs, it meant I

had it all over me too. I checked between my legs and sure enough, there were matching spots. "Did you unload a cannon? That's a lot of nut."

"If I recall, it wasn't all me." he appeared from the bathroom, raising his eyebrows at me. His body was nude in all its glory. I rubbed my thighs together trying to calm the fire that was building. "I was going to get in the shower if you want to join me." he reached out for my hand.

If we got into the shower together, I would be there the whole day. I needed to get my ass in gear. There were a shit load of things to do today. "Not a good idea."

We slid down the stairs together. The smell of breakfast was in the air. My stomach rumbled. My mind was spinning, thinking of a way to get away from Roman without him thinking anything of it. I was coming up dry. He would want to come with me, afraid to leave me because of yesterday.

"Morning, lovebirds, I see you guys made up." Garth greeted us and looked at our intertwined hands.

"Garth…" I began but he put his hand up and stopped me.

"You don't have to explain anything to me. After all, I haven't seen you for years." He placed eggs on the table and called for Melody to come and eat.

When she skipped into the kitchen, she waved at me and took her place next to the window. "You still here?" she asked me. "I thought for sure my uncle would have run you off." she giggled and shoved a piece of toast into her mouth.

"Time changes people. Me and your uncle are on two different paths. He couldn't derail me if he tried." I offered but she didn't look like she understood. No one even acknowledged Roman. They knew he wasn't from here and because of that he was irrelevant.

"Garth, can I talk to you a minute?" I asked. "In private?" Roman looked at me with knowing eyes.

"Sure. Melody, mind the grits for me." He passed her the whisk and walked into the hall. "What do you need, Monroe?" he said sarcastically.

"Stop it," I whispered. "Can you keep Roman busy for me for a couple of hours? I have to see Ira and he isn't going to leave my side. No one can be there with me. I have to do this alone." If anyone understood what I was talking about, it was Garth. Making peace with my brother was my burden to bear. Roman was in deep enough that my father would shoot him if he stepped foot onto his land.

"What the hell do you suggest I do? The dude doesn't like me. You think he'll just follow me if I ask him to? I know, we can go hunting. It is duck season. I have a new call I wanted to try out." He was dead serious. The wheels in his head were rotating.

I hit him in the back of his head, "You think taking him hunting is smart? With guns?" I stared at him incredulously.

"It could be a peace offering, after all I hope to be the best man at the wedding." He smirked, leaving me in the hall alone. I heard Roman asking him what we talked about. Whatever Garth said was lost on me as Melody started singing a country song. I gathered my thoughts and went back inside the kitchen.

"Garth asked me to go hunting with him. You wouldn't have anything to do with that would you?" Roman asked, knitting his eyebrows together.

"I did. I thought it would be good for you to make a friend here. You don't understand how close this town is. There are only 665 people in this town, give or take a dozen. You can bet everyone has heard of the city folk walking around here like they own the place. Getting out of the house will be best." I placed my hand on the back of his chair and looked at him adoringly.

"What will you be doing when I'm hunting?" Roman got up from his chair, going to the sink to wash his dish.

"Maybe I'll take Melody to the library. I made a friend there once." I was lying. There was no friend there. The bitch who worked there was the wife of one of my father's poker playing friends. He was my Monday night. After he lost everything to my father, I was a peace offering. He let him have his way with me.

The shouting came from the dining room where my father and his four friends were playing poker. It was a Monday and it was Jace's day. He was going to choke me and spit in my mouth. They all did things to me that their wives wouldn't let them do to them. When the night wound down, my bedroom door creaked open and cast the shadow of a bald man upon my wall. He stood in the

420

doorway letting the light shine on me. He couldn't see my face. It was directed at the wall.

"Wake up Jo" he called to me, entering my room. He closed the door, making sure it made no sound. He crept over to my bed, his weight dipping the bed lower. "Pretty girl," he cooed. The names and the caresses were their way of accepting what they were doing to me because if they didn't do it and they just beat me, they would associate themselves with the monsters they were.

Jace removed the covers from my body, pulling them completely off the bed. He wasn't as fat as the Sheriff but he was tall and needed all the room he could get. The blanket took up too much room, he would say. The light from the moon reflected off his bald head. His eyes were black pits hollowed out where his eyes were supposed to be. He skimmed his fingers over the skin of my leg,

moaning when his fingers made contact with my ass.
"Soft." he kept repeating as he yanked my panties off my
legs. I stayed the same way, not making a sound. Hoping
he would leave me alone, but then again they never did.

"Come back baby!" A voice pulled at me. Blinking
rapidly, Roman's face came into focus. His blue and
brown eyes looked worried. His hands gripped my face,
holding it in place. Behind him Melody and Garth looked
on in horror. "There you are." Roman said in relief.

"Where did I go?" I questioned.

"Where ever it is, I don't ever want to know. Does
that happen often?" Garth looked on in fear.

Roman rolled his eyes still concentrating on me. If I
didn't want anyone to know, he wouldn't say anything.
We spoke without words, our eyes communicating with

one another. We came to an agreement. Garth was on a need to know basis. He needed to know what we wanted to share. Right now, I wasn't willing to share anything. The pity in everyone's eyes enraged me. If they found out I was fucked in the head too, it would only get worse. Roman was the only one who knew. He was the only one who understood.

"Garth. Hunting?" Roman got to his feet like nothing happened. I was grateful for the subject change.

"Have you even shot a firearm before?" Garth asked in doubt.

"Don't be daft! They have shooting ranges in cities." Roman said. He handed me a glass of water and told me to drink.

"Daft? You city dwellers like making up words."
Garth chuckled. "Let's get out of here so you can show
me just how good of a shot you are."

"Better than you, I bet." Roman challenged.

Garth just looked at him like he lost him mind. No
more words were exchanged as both men went to get
dressed to hunt. Roman probably didn't have the right
attire for duck hunting. He was going to be extremely
uncomfortable. Something told me Garth was aware of
this and he wasn't going to say anything.

Roman was in the room looking through his bags,
"What do you wear to hunt ducks?" he said. I laughed
and told him he would have to wear clothes he wouldn't
mind trashing.

"Trash? I didn't bring anything I can trash." he complained.

"You are going to be crawling around in the mud. Wearing something expensive would be stupid. I suggest you go to the general market in town and buy something." I told him.

"Hunting is big in this town isn't it?" He went with black pants and a white t-shirt.

"They like guns and they like shooting things. Make sure you keep your head down." I kissed him on his neck causing a tremor to run through his body.

"Look Monroe, when I'm not here, don't go running looking for trouble. Stay here." he demanded.

Who the fuck did I look like listening to him? He knew it wasn't going to keep me here. I was out the door once I lost sight of Garth's truck. My Nikes carrying me into my memories and my hell. The people of this town understood that it was me now. No one waved to me, and as I passed. They all averted their eyes. I was a plague and no one wanted me. It delighted me to see their discomfort. I waved to them shouting my greetings as they cast their eyes to the ground.

Music streamed into my ears from my ear buds. My playlist choice was war music. It was what I listened to when I was going to a meeting or doing something I needed motivation for. The street was in the distance and my legs hit the pavement harder, getting me to where I wanted to be. This morning when I took a shower, I came up with a plan. It wasn't my best idea but it would work for now.

Waiting in my bushes until he left was my plan. When he was gone, I would go to the house and try talk to my momma. No, I hadn't forgiven her but I wasn't getting into the house without her. I also wanted to know why she was blind. When I was in front of Mrs. Johnson's house, I stopped. As I caught my breath, my heart was threatening to pound out of my chest.

Mrs. Johnson was sitting on her porch looking at me. I waved at her, but she acted as if she couldn't see me.

"Child, do you want to die?" I was shocked she even spoke to me. Even when I was younger, she never talked to me. She just watched.

"If that's what it takes to see my brother." I replied, moving further onto the street.

"He ain't going nowhere. You might as well wait till they're dead." she shouted after me.

"I plan to help them along with that." I jogged the rest of the way to the bush. I ducked into it and stilled myself. I placed my iPod into my pocket. Now all I had to do was wait. It didn't take long for him to come out the door. He was wiping his greasy hands on his already dirty shirt.

"You better not let anyone in this house, you hear me?" My daddy shouted into the house. There was no reply. He shut the door with force, causing the hinges to rattle. His belly poked out further than the rest of his body as he skipped down the stairs. His feet hit the mud with a soft oomph. He jumped into his truck and reversed out the driveway. The truck screeched as it hobbled down the road. Once I couldn't hear the truck anymore I raced to the door, pulling it open.

I stopped dead in my tracks as the familiar scent assaulted my nose.

I told Ira to leave it alone. I told him not to go home. The front door screeched as he pulled it open, red dust flying off the creases. Ira was sixteen now and he took his share of beatings protecting me, but him hearing me talking to the teacher today caused him panic. He told me he was a failure. If he couldn't keep my safe then him getting beat was for nothing. He was going to end my daddy. He was going to make him pay for touching his own daughter and for being a sick fuck. I couldn't stop him and a part of my hoped he was successful because it was the only way to get out of this. The first time I tried

429

to tell someone, they just placed me in foster care, Ira got beat every day I was gone. Daddy told him if I didn't come home, Ira was dead anyway. I came home.

This time, I told the teacher who just moved here, hoping she was different. She wasn't from this town. She might have been different. She wasn't. After I told her, I found out she was the niece of the Sheriff and she was just as nasty. She called my house. Momma answered and told us to get our behinds home. I told Ira I was going to do it alone. I didn't want him to know all the details. I didn't want him to think he was a failure but he stood at the door of the classroom listening to me talk. When I came out from the room, he was there, looking at me like I betrayed him, which brings us to now.

He was walking home to kill my father. Which I knew wasn't going to happen. We were going to get the shit beat out of us for talking to the teacher. Daddy said what happened in this house was family business and if you weren't family, you didn't know our business. My momma was sitting in a chair in the living room, waiting with a switch in her hand. The switch (or branch) had little sharp metal pieces stuck into it. It was momma's design. She made it when daddy started going into my room at night.

"You opened your lying mouth, telling your teachers stories again." she directed her attention to me, but Ira moved in front of me blocking her view.

"You don't get to talk to her anymore! You lost your fucking right!" he shouted at her. She was up so fast, grabbing Ira by his hair and tossing him into the wall.

"Are you a tough guy now? You think you scare me?" she asked, spitting her words out at him. "I asked you a question, boy!" she kicked him in his face. Blood began to drip from his nose.

"Jo, get your ass over here! I am going to teach you a lesson. Running your mouth to people about telling them your dirty little lies, you whore!" Momma growled at me. The strap was raised and it made contact with my arm. It would have been my face if I hadn't blocked it.

Ira stood and moved in front of the strap, taking it in his hand. Blood dripped from his clenched fist. "I won't let you hurt her anymore! And if anyone is a lying whore, it's you Momma! You are just as worthless as daddy! You let him do this to us! You let him fuck your daughter! He does it because you can't please him! Do you like hearing that?" Ira was yelling so loud, his voice was *bouncing off the walls. "You are a fucking disgrace!" He pulled the branch from her and began hitting her with it. She backed herself into a corner, covering her face from Ira's lashes.*

The door behind me opened, and a hand locked into my hair. It pulled me off my feet. I was dangling in the air. My father was behind me with a gun to my back. "I leave for an hour and you guys start attacking your mother!?" he cackled. "Get up!" he shouted at my momma. She jumped to her feet, looking at an invisible spot on the ground. Daddy walked up to her and slapped her across her face. Hard. Her skin welted right away.

Snapping out of it, I quietly made my way around the house. No one was here, or so it seemed. A hand touched my shoulder and I jumped back.

"What are you doing here Josephine? If he comes back and sees you here, he'll kill you." My mother said. Her glasses sat on her nose as they had before.

"I need to see my brother. You going to tell me no, Momma? After all you put me through?" I swallowed my tears. I would not show emotion. They didn't deserve my tears.

"He'll kill me if I let you." she stated. It was a fact. There was nothing she could do or say to stop that man.

"It'd be better than living like this. When I left,, you were dead to me already." My words were angry.

"Then why come back? You should have let us die here!" she cried.

"I didn't come back for you! I came to see my brother. You are nothing to me Momma, nothing, you fucking hear me?" her hand slapped me across my face.

I laughed darkly, a copper taste filling my mouth. "You can't hurt me anymore, you worthless fucking bitch!"

"Get out of my house! Leave, or I'll call Colt." she ran her hands along the wall looking for the phone. I had the advantage because I could see where it was. I pulled the phone out of the wall and threw it into the sink.

"Call him on what? Are you that brainwashed? Do you depend on him for everything? Does he make every decision for you?" I circled her, studying her.

"Why are you blind, Momma? When I left, you were fine. What happened over the years?" I implored.

She remained silent, not even looking for me. Her cane tapped the floor a couple of times. It pissed me off. I reached for her glasses, taking them off her face. Where her eyes used to be, there was nothing. It was scarred craters. Something gauged out her eyes. There was nothing there but scar tissue.

"Momma, what happened to your eyes? Did he do this to you?" I demanded. She was trying to cover her face to hide the mutilation.

"No one did this to me! I did it to myself!" she screamed, shaking me off of her.

"What do you mean you did this to yourself? Momma it isn't your fault for what he does to you. I promise." I grabbed her arms and pulled her to me. I thought maybe she was like me. Maybe she thought she had to do these things, that there was no other way.

"Stupid girl, he didn't do this to me, I did! The night he forced me to watch the things he did to you. I couldn't stop seeing it. One night I was drunk. I took a spoon and scooped them out." she chuckled. She tapped her cane on the floor and moved it about, mapping out her route.

"You took your own eyes? Why the hell would you do that?" If I thought I was confused before, my mind lost all understanding. Both of them, they were made for each other. Something dawned on me then. I was given the worst parents in the world. Nothing was wrong with me, they kept telling me there was, but in all honesty I just got the shit end of the stick.

"I told you not to let anyone in the house." My father appeared in the hallway. My mother curled into herself, leaving me to fend for myself.

"She came in on her own, I didn't hear her till it was too late," she explained. It didn't make any difference to him. He hit her in the head with the end of his shotgun. It knocked her out.

"Josephine, you are a glutton for pain! Here I thought I made sure you wouldn't come around. But here you are." he said, spreading his arms wide. "And in good time too. I was getting bored. I could use a little entertainment." he laughed.

"No way you're touching me!" I shuttered as a fresh wave of fear ran through me.

"You act all hard, like you aren't scared of me anymore, I can smell it on you," he stuck his tongue out and licked the air. "I can taste it, better yet, I can still taste that sweet ass on my mustache." he smacked his lips and stalked toward me.

"You can try!" I challenged and waved him on. Immediately, I took a defensive stance. "Fight me one on one daddy, no guns, no weapons. If I win, I get to walk out of here." I wanted to haggle for Ira, but getting out of here alive was the most important thing right now. "And if you win, I won't fight you. You can have me." He liked the sound of it because a light flashed in his eyes.

"How do I know you're telling the truth?" he asked and scratched his chin.

There was no way I was losing. He didn't know I practiced twice a week every week of the year when I left. "I swear on Ira, I will keep my word." It hurt and I felt like I sold my brother out, but right now my life depended on it. "Just promise me you won't shoot me. No weapons."

He thought it over, rubbing at his week old stubble. "Deal, but you run, I'll kill you." he put his gun down. I took the time to look at my mother, still crumbled in the corner unconscious.

My father started circling me. It was am intimidation tactic. I stood in the middle of the room, counting, estimating, contemplating. What I learned was more than self-defense. It was controlling your mind in a stressful situation, one where you might not think straight. Everything I was taking in, everything I was plotting were simple ways to kill him or disable him with the area and things I was given.

My father was a predator and most predators attack when you least expect them to. Having the upper hand was important in this case, you not only had to know what you were going to do, you had to calculate what he was going to do. My father was like a bomb. There was a timer on it. You could expect he was going to explode but there were things that played into it. Environment, pressure, and most critically, the simple triggers. One false move and you're dead. I trained with my father in mind Years of getting beaten helped me prepare myself.

He stopped, titled his head and rushed me like a linebacker. Tackling me to the ground caused me to hit my head on the edge of the stairs. Black dots flashed in my sight. I recovered quickly, jabbing my out stretched hand into his sternum, leaving him breathless. I used the table as leverage to flip him off of me. I gained my footing, kicking him in his face as hard as my leg would let me. The blood spurted from his mouth in slow motion. It excited me.

He spit the blood out as he attempted to stand, "That the best you can do, bitch?"

"I'm just getting started, Daddy." I tossed back. He adjusted himself until he was able to stand up straight. I wanted to look in his eyes as I took his ass out. He moved for me again. This time, I sidestepped, making him fall into the china cabinet. His head hit the glass, shattering it. I gave him more time than he deserved. Before he got right, I kicked him in his ass, ramming his head into the shards of glass.

"Want to keep going old man? You should have just let me see my brother!" I hollered at him.

"You will never see him as long as I'm alive!" he said, spitting blood onto the carpet.

"I'm willing to help you with that!" He swept my feet out from under me. I landed flat on my back, giving him the advantage. He climbed onto me, backhanding me. I saw stars. A sharp white light blinded me.

"Stupid whore! You think you can fight me and win? You have lost your fucking mind!" His fist impacted my nose. The pain was excruciating. I heard the bridge of my nose snap. He broke my nose. The blood was dripping into the back of my throat, gagging me as it sputtered out my mouth.

Monroe

My heart was hammering into my ribs. I needed to calm down if I was going to get out of this. I closed my mind off to everything around me and found my trainer's voice in my mind.

"You know how to get out of this, Monroe! Thin!. What do you do when you are down, bleeding and unable to overpower your attacker?" My teacher instructed. For this practice, he had me laying on my back as he hovered above me. It was a position I was uncomfortable in, but he told me it could save my life one day. "If he is on top of you, beating you, what are you going to do?"

I thrust my hips up and my father flew over my head, landing on his face. Adrenaline pumped through me, making me stronger than I was. "Get the fuck up!" I screamed. I was losing my voice from all the yelling I was doing. This time, I didn't wait for him to get up. I

444

round house kicked him in the face, his teeth flew onto my mother's face. "Do you still want to fight, or can I leave? Because it sure looks like I won."

"The battle not the war! You can leave but I will be seeing you again, my sweet Jo." he said from the floor. I walked over to him and stared down at him. He made eye contact with me and I spit on him.

When I got out, I threw up. Everything in my stomach mixed with the dirt and leaves in the yard. The pain from my nose was creating a huge migraine and I probably had a concussion. Jogging home wasn't an option. I took my phone out of my pocket and dialed Garth's number. He told me he would be there in three minutes. It usually took eight, which meant he was at home and not hunting anymore. I wonder how their hunting trip went.

Getting off the street was a priority. If my father drove by and saw me walking or jogging, he would run me over. He wasn't going to take getting his ass beat lying down. The next time I saw him, he was going to try putting a bullet between my eyes. I hobbled over to Mrs. Johnson's house and she was there like always.

"Can I sit here for a moment?" I asked. She took in my look, and the blood on my clothes.

"I don't think that's a good idea. If ya daddy finds you here, if he thinks I'm helping you, he is going to burn down my house." she shook in fear.

"If you don't fucking help me, I am going to burn your house down with you tied down inside! You think he's bad you have no damn idea what he created." I snarled at her. She snapped her mouth shut, waving me over to the porch that was blocked off by a divider. I ducked down, holding my arm close. It started hurting when I ran from the house. It might be broken.

Not even a minute after I hid on the porch, I heard my daddy's truck approach slowly. It stopped in front of the house. "You see where that whore daughter of mine went?" he asked Mrs. Johnson.

"She ran off down the street." she said. I watched and her face morphed into one of pure terror. She was deathly afraid of my father.

"If I find out you're lying, I'm coming back for you, you hear me, Mick?" He didn't get out of the car and Mrs. Johnson nodded her head vigorously.

"I got it. She was on the phone when she went by, if that helps." she stood up, looking at my hiding spot briefly. It was enough to give my hiding spot away. I took her ankle in my hand, squeezing it tight. If she threw me under the bus, I would end her.

"She called those stupid fucks that are in love with her." I heard something slamming against the steering wheel and then he revved the engine, taking off.

"You were the one who told him I was at the fucking house! You're his snitch! What have I ever done to you? All my life, I have been getting beaten and abused by him and you never once lifted a hand to help me. Now, you're telling him shit that can get me killed. You know that, right? You know he will kill me the next time I see him? And once he figures out you helped me, he will kill you too!" I was convinced this town was hell on Earth. All these people were blinded by fear and no one was willing to take a stand and do what's right. Getting out of here was the smartest thing I have ever done in my life.

I moved from her porch without even looking at her. She was going to burn with this whole town and I was going to be the one holding the match. I stuck to the bushes. I had to keep moving. Staying in one place would give my father time to find me. Garth should be getting close if not right on top of me. When I spotted his truck, I moved half my body out of the bushes, but behind him was my daddy. Garth put his truck in park. He found me with his eyes and shook his head just enough for me to know what he was talking about.

I slipped back into the trees as my father slipped out the cab of the truck. "Where is that tramp? She called you to come get her?" My daddy accused, looking all over Garth's truck. He held his hunting rifle. It was the one he won from Jace in a poker game.

"Don't know what you're talking about. I came down here to get some black berries. Me and Melody were going to have them with ice cream after dinner." I had forgotten there was a fruit stand at the end of the road. Garth was slick in his comeback.

"I know she called you," Daddy said calmly.

"Colt, if there isn't anything else you wanna talk about, I got to get going. Thanks to you, my only two guest were scared away. I don't know where your daughter is. Should we be calling her your daughter? After all, a father doesn't abuse and fuck his daughter like she's a common whore off the street." Garth spit out in repulsion.

450

"You mad boy? You weren't man enough to take it," my father laughed and placed his hand on Garth's door. "You mad because I tasted that sweet pussy?"

Garth pressed his fingers into the side of his temples trying hard not to say anything else to my father. "Are we done now?" he ground out through his teeth.

All my father did was slap his hood and moved away from Garth's truck to let him drive. It seemed like I was going to be in these bushes until it was safe for him to come back. The world became wobbly and my head swam. Hitting my head on the staircase must have given me a concussion. I got on all fours and placed my head in my hands. I was breathing in slowly, trying to get my vision to stop moving. How long I was there was a mystery to me but when I opened my eyes again, the sun was setting in the sky. The area I was in became dark.

Headlights from passing cars aggravated my head, I felt like I was going to pass out.

"Jo!" Garth's voice rose from the darkness.

"Over here," I called out. Leaves crunched under his feet as he made his way to me. I felt him as he stood over me looking down at the damage.

"Oh Jo, I told you not to go! You never listen." he clicked his tongue. He bent down and picked me up. I locked my hands around his neck so I wouldn't fall.

"I can walk, put me down." I said, tapping on his chest. I was tempted to feel him up. His chest was nice and strong under my fingers.

"Are you harassing me, Jo? You have a boyfriend, remember?" I did remember, but right now Garth was my

452

savior. Roman would have come, but he couldn't go toe to toe with Colt. He would have been killed. I liked him too much for that.

"Yes, I do recall. Where is he right now?" I asked and placed my cheek on his chest.

"I told Mel to keep him busy while I got the berries. They have no idea what is going on but once they see you, I ain't going to be able to lie." Garth said.

"I just want to sleep," I yawned.

"No you don't! You have to see a doctor. There's a nasty looking bump on your head." he put me into the passenger side of the truck and made sure all of my limbs were in the cab first.

"He is looking for me. I can't go to the hospital." My voice was cracking and I felt like I was going to vomit again.

"If we go back to my house, you can't sleep. That means I am going to bug the shit out of you until I feel you're okay." Garth said as he put the truck into drive.

"I got him good, Garth, he looked worse than me right?" I asked hopefully, because by the time it was done I was dizzy. Focusing became a chore, so I couldn't see the damage I had caused.

"Yep. You got him good. His eye was swollen and his lip was busted."

"Garth, he was missing teeth too. I knocked his teeth out," I mused. The feeling I got when I saw his teeth fly, or when he tried to take me down but missed due to my bad assery.

"Well, he didn't have much to begin with. Let's hope he can't chew his food." He made me feel like I was doing something right. The way he joked with me put me at ease. Today was a big step for me. I accomplished something. I had shown my daddy I wasn't going to lay down and take it anymore.

I knew when we got to the house because the engine turned off. Garth didn't say anything as he got out and helped me into the house. There wasn't much to say after a day like this. He understood what it meant, and he was willing to wait for me to talk about it, Roman on the other hand, wasn't going to be so understanding. Technically, I didn't lie to him, I just bent the truth. Which could or could not be amusing depending on the way you looked at it. The look on his face told me he wasn't amused.

"Before you start anything, she isn't well, and it's best to let her rest." Garth told Roman as soon as we walked in. "If she wants to tell you what happened then let her tell you, don't try to force it out."

Roman leered at us, switching between Garth and I. "You bring my girlfriend home bloody and ill and you want me to just what? Let her vent to me when she is able? If you know anything of the person I know, you would know she isn't going to tell me shit, and if I want to know what it was, I'm going to have to pry it out of her." Roman was mad, but I could tell he was worried more than anything. Today could have been rough on him, and I wouldn't have known it. Putting someone's feelings before mine will never happen. I was used to it being me for so long. It was going to be a learning process, one I was willing to take on, because when I looked at him, I wanted to make sure he was alright. His feelings mattered to me and at the end of the day, he was my happiness.

"I'm sorry you were worried." I told him as I hobbled into his arms. When he wrapped his arms around me, his body relaxed.

"It's okay. Right, now all I want you to do is rest." he helped me up the stairs, but before I disappeared down the hall I turned back. "Thank you for everything, Garth. You're one of the few people I trust. Well, maybe not trust—just yet, but I want to. That has to count for something."

His understanding eyes spoke to me in volumes. Today everyone learned something. Whether it was about them, or something they could do, it was something and it made you feel alive. If you didn't pick up on the life lesson, who was to blame?

"Are you going to tell me what happened?" Roman said, closing the door behind us.

"Not right now. Can you help me out of these clothes?" I lifted my arms above my head and waited.

He slid my shirt over my head, tossing it to the floor. Next, he helped me take off my pants. Unable to help much, I kicked them off my feet. I sat on the bed like I was asked. Roman slipped into the bathroom. "Come here, Monroe. I am going to bathe you."

"You don't need to. I can do it." I stepped past him, making my way inside. Garth and Melody stayed downstairs to give us privacy.

"You can, but I have to watch you anyway. Just let me clean you." he said sitting on the toilet and skimming his fingers in the water, testing the temperature. "It's good. You can get in now."

I stripped out of my underwear and bra and lowered myself into the hot water. "This feels nice." I closed my eyes and sank further into the tub.

His gentle hands moved over my body, cleaning and caressing. It felt like he was dragging thousands of tiny feathers along my skin. My head rolled to the side. I was losing consciousness. And fast. I got little glimpses of things: Roman pulling me out of the water, Garth rushing into the room. Both of them wrapping me in a blanket, the hood of the car as lights flashed over it, and then a bright light.

After I saw the light, there was nothing. I must have died, but there was nothing significant. No pain, No angel there to hold my hand and lead me up a golden staircase. Giving into the pressure in my head, I faded into the darkness.

"She doesn't need to wake up to us fighting. Shhhh…" I was not sure who was talking, but it sounded like they were talking over a bullhorn. It was bouncing around in my head. I rubbed the spot the pain was originating from. There was a lump there big enough to have its own zip code.

"I told you! See?" they exclaimed.

"You both didn't graduate from the ninja school." I groaned. Cracking my eyes open, I tried to see who was making that horrible noise. Sitting in the chairs by the window, were Roman and Garth. "Nice of you guys to interrupt me from my impending doom. I thought I was dead. "I told you guys, no hospital."

"It was either the hospital or you dying. What would you have liked us to do?" Roman asked. He pulled his chair to the side of my bed, grabbing my hand in his. I pulled away, not liking the way it made me feel. I wasn't on my death bed. I also was not a child.

"You are an idiot! It doesn't matter now. He knows I'm here. He has people all over the place. Why do you think I left here when I was twelve?" I followed the tube sticking out of my arm. I needed to get out of here.

"Who are you talking about?" Roman asked dramatically. "The whole time we have been here, you've been acting weird, and that's saying something because you are naturally so." Garth kept quiet, listening

462

to the exchange. I looked to him for help and all I was met with were troubled eyes.

"I am going to give you guys some time, hopefully you hash this out." Garth said walking out of the room. Dickhead.

He was leaving because he thought Roman had a right to know but in the end it was my choice to tell or not. "Help me get out of this?" I motioned to the wires and plugs I was connected to.

"No, not until I get some answers." he refused, sitting back in his chair.

"Fine, I'll leave by myself." I yanked the IV from my arm, pulling everything else with it. My father wasn't going to get me because I was stuck in a bed. The only way I was going to lose was fighting, if I died that way, I would die happy.

If my brother fought, I was going to fight. I wouldn't let him go through it all alone. He was being picked on by the older boys in school because of the way he dressed. They didn't care what our lives were like, they just wanted to make things more difficult for us. I tried getting Ira to stop, telling him he didn't need to fight. They best way to get to people was acting like you didn't care. It pissed them off. They felt like they were entitled to your rage, that if you didn't get mad it made them obsolete, and it did. If you gave them your power, it left you with nothing.

"Ira, you wanna go swimming?" I asked hoping it would take his mind off what was really going on. Ira was becoming a man so letting someone pick on him that wasn't my father, wasn't going to pan out. He took too much in life and he would fight to stay alive. What people didn't realize was that if a person was a survivor, all they understood was the fight to stay above water.

"Get home Jo. I'll be there soon." he said and moved past me.

"If you fight, Ira James I will be there too. I will fight with you. So if you think I'm going home, you thought wrong." I kept pace with him as he stormed down the street. He even tried to run away from me, like I didn't know his tricks.

"You can't come, Josephine. It would give them more to talk about. The only guy there who brought his little sister. The teasing will never end." he sighed and stopped once he figured I wasn't leaving.

"Do I look like I care? How come you can protect me, but when I try it's shameful?"

"Because I'm a man, I don't need my little sister's protection." he hollered into my face. His words cut me. He was insinuating that me being a girl was a weakness. I stopped following him, and he came home that night bruised and bloody. His injuries didn't stop my daddy from beating him some more. The fact that Ira came home covered in blood told daddy he was ready to start fighting back, and daddy didn't take kindly to threats. I knew it was going to come down to who was the leader of the pack. Ira was going to eventually grow bigger then

daddy, stronger. My father was going to take him out
before it got that far.

"Roman, I need no one!" I shrugged into my clothes.
If the flash back taught me anything, it was you had to do
things on your own. Being alone didn't make you a bad
person, it made you stronger. I could do this alone. I
would show them all.

"Monroe, the whole point is that you don't have to.
Everyone needs someone, you can't hold it all alone," he
pointed out angrily.

Josephine was gone. She wasn't going to make an
appearance again. Me and my daddy had a date and I was
going to keep it. If there was any future for Roman and
me, making things right was the only option.

Monroe

"My whole life, I have been kicked down, beat, and left alone. If you think that's bad, when I got older my father started coming into my room at night to touch me. At first that was all it was, him touching me, running his fingers up my leg. It was as if he knew it was wrong and he had to work up the nerve to keep going. I was eight, and from all I went through with him I was too scared to defend myself. When I would try, he would tell me he was going to kill my brother, who was the only one I had. My mother was no better. She blamed me for what my father did. She would hit me in my face and tell me I was the devil because I was so pretty, that I tempted these men into my room.

"Anyway, when he finally became confident enough, he started playing with my pussy. Fingering me, and licking me. Doing that didn't last as long as the touching.

He must have wanted to graduate from foreplay. He wanted to fuck me. The night of January 8, 1995 he came to me and pulled down my princess panties. I remember those underwear better then I remember my social security number. My brother stole them for me. The feeling I got when he tossed them to the floor was something no little girl should feel. I lost more than my virginity that day, he took my soul too." I stopped and gauged his reaction. His face was a blank slate. I took it as a sign to continue.

"He would rape me almost every night, unless he was too drunk to get up. This happened for two, almost three years. When I started maturing, or as he called it becoming a woman, he started trading me to his friends when he lost in poker. He priced me high, and told them they could do anything they wanted to me and I wouldn't fight it. I wasn't stupid. If I did try something, he would beat me until I couldn't walk." I choked on my words. They tasted like vomit. "And they did what they wanted. Some liked to choke me, others would beat me till I bled. I have scars on my back from where the sheriff would hit me with his baton. He broke my skin on more than one occasion.

"But I think the worst part was having the town talk about me, and everyone thinking it was my fault. Instead of helping me, the threw stones at me. Every woman in this town hated me, including my mother. It continued until I was fourteen, until…"

"You don't have to, just stop." he said with conviction.

"You think I'm sick now, right? I shouldn't be alive, I should die?" I was crying so hard my tears were mixing with my snot. My face felt like it was puffy with redness. I couldn't stand looking at him. He was looking at me with distaste. As if I were trash left on the street.

"Look at me," he commanded. "I would never think of you like that. You are worth more than all of them put together." He took my face in his shaking hands, making me look in his eyes. Fire consumed them. "I will kill them. All of them."

No longer able to move, I dropped to the floor, sliding along the bed. I was weakened by the energy it took to relive it all. All the pain, all the loneliness, it would all be worth it when I piss on my father's lifeless body.

For the next three days, Roman and I went over all the details about the town. It was from years of collecting, and following the people in it. We devised a plan that would leave nothing standing in the end. I told him I would be happy to kill my family. All the others will receive judgment in time. Roman thought it best to end it all. To new beginnings, he said. I found out that he was a hired hitman at one point in his life. He had been keeping some secrets of his own.

No wonder he didn't flinch when my father threatened him. We talked about everything. He told me it was better for there to be no secrets. He told me why he was with Vera. She found out about what he did, and hired him to kill me. He told her he didn't do things like that but he could help her get information on me. When he met me and figured out she hired me too, he tried backing out, but she held his past over his head. Shit hit the fan when Vera realized Roman had a thing for me. She told him she would tell me everything if he didn't act like he was in love with her, fake party and all.

In the end, I ruined the party and played the movie even though I was in it too, he knew I was the woman for him. He said when he looked over at me and saw the joyful expression I was giving her, he was lost. Guess I was more powerful than I looked. At first, I was nervous knowing he could kill me with one move, but who was I to judge him? He never once made me feel like I wasn't safe.

I trusted him.

When we were done, this town would be leveled. Fucking Bonnie and Clyde had nothing on us.

Garth was in the kitchen like a good housewife making breakfast for us on our last night here. He had nothing to do with this and we agreed he would sit this out. He didn't know that yet. We just told him we were going to leave. There were too many memories.

He hugged me tight at the door. "Take care of yourself." he lightly nicked my jaw with his knuckles. It reminded me of the night on the pond. Sitting in the tree with him, the young man that turned out just how I hoped he would.

"I'll try." I pushed up and kissed him on the mouth. It wasn't sexual and it wasn't a come on. It was what it was, a goodbye.

Roman was already behind the wheel of the car with the windows rolled down. "Garth, I would say it was a pleasure, but I'd be lying." he joked.

"You are finally right about something." he smirked.

I started this life with one person I could trust. Thinking there wasn't anyone out there worth anything, I was taught love was for the wealthy. Love didn't live in the slums. There was a song I heard once that said love was for the poor. Obviously she didn't know what poor was. I was lucky I found Roman. There was a lot we still had to talk about, but for now, it was enough.

We made our way out of town, and I stared in the rearview watching my past disappear. It wasn't the first time but I hoped it was going to be the last.

"Where you going, little one?" The driver of the big rig asked. He told me his name was Ron.

"Anywhere you can take me." I said and blew hot air onto the window.

"You got family I can call?" his words snapped me out of my fog.

"I have no family. They're all dead." I spoke softly, looking at him through my stringy hair.

"Sorry to hear that." It was the last time we talked. I looked out at the mirror, watching as Allgood shrunk into nothing. Little did I know, it was going to be the last time I saw it for years.

"You okay? You went somewhere again." Roman made me wonder what I looked like when I zoned out.

"No place special." I stretched.

***

When he told me we would be camping, he wasn't lying. This place didn't have restrooms. We were meeting one of his contacts here in a day. The only directions he gave the man were coordinates. Roman was professional in everything he did, making sure there weren't any foot prints to follow. He left his rental four miles in the opposite direction. It was us and the woods.

Judging by what we carried on our hike, we would be living off the land. I knew plants we could eat, and hunting wasn't something new to me, I just hadn't done it in a while.

"You sure this is how to go about it?" I asked him, placing my bag on a rock.

"I've done this before, don't worry. My friend is going to bring everything we need." Roman muttered over his shoulder. He busied himself clearing the area, counting steps, testing the strength of branches. He mapped out an escape route just in case we were compromised. His words not mine. All this work and the sun was fading fast. I started gathering food we could eat berries, sweet grass, things like that. He put the tent up and built a fire. He pulled out army rations and passed me one. "You need to sacrifice for the greater good. It won't be long before we are sitting on a beach somewhere." he kissed the tip of my nose.

"I can deal. I've lived with Colt. There were times we went to bed with nothing in our stomachs. More often than not, actually." I didn't tell him this to get pity or have him feeling sorry for me. It was a statement of facts.

There wasn't anything I could do and Roman refused to let me help any further. He was used to being alone. It didn't hurt me. I was tired. I couldn't wait for him to get everything in order so I could sleep. He shuffled around doing things that only made sense to him, periodically talking to himself under his breath. By the time he was done, the sun was sinking behind the horizon, leaving us with only the light from the fire to see. If I thought his eyes were magnificent in the daylight, at night with the orange glow of the flames, the were transcending. If I doubted my feelings for this man before, I was completely enamored with him now.

"What are you looking at?" he observed.

"You," I said moving to where he was. I sat in his lap, facing him. I was studying his incredible features. I didn't have any impure thoughts when I started, but the more I touched, the harder he became. His hands slipped into the back of my shirt as he drew circles on my skin. "Has anyone ever told you that your eyes penetrate the soul? Or that your mouth alone can make a thousand virgins weep in pleasure?"

"Never." he admitted.

"Such a shame, I guess it makes sense for me to be the first one." I grinned, moving off him. Before I got my second leg off, he grabbed my calf.

"Where are you going?" he asked knowingly.

"Just to sleep. I'm tired." I faked a yawn.

"Let me help you with that."

I felt him between my thighs as I rode his face like a bike. The possibilities were endless. My sluggish body became alert with his tempting words. He took the initiative, taking me by my neck and kissing me with a fierce passion that made my toes curl. The tent seemed like the plain choice in places to bone. Not to him. He kicked my bag off the rock I placed it on when we arrived.

He tugged my clothes off and told me to sit. "Open your legs more." he huffed. I opened my legs as much as comfort allowed. "Damn, that's nice!" he cantored to me. He devoured every inch of my sex, licking his lips as he dropped between them. His tongue flicked over my tender nub, shocking me into bucking. His soft moaning and slurping made me weak, and I could feel the need

481

overtaking me. Not only was Roman the best sex I ever had, he is the best head I've gotten. He made his tongue move and disappear like a magician.

"I'm going to cum!" a throaty moan escaped.

"Do it. Cum for me baby," he countered, his delicious words forming over my clit. The power flowing through me exploded, knocking him down as I kicked back.

The rock pocking into my ass made the pleasure more concentrated. Roman said something to me, but my mind was still overtaken with euphoria.

"Get up. I am going to fuck you on the tree." He forced.

Getting up was a task I needed Roman for. He lifted me into his arms, placing my legs around his midsection.

My bare back scraped on the bark of the trunk. The sharp bite of the bark sent waves of pleasure about my body. Sleep was forgotten as Roman's thick cock entered me. We both groaned together as we moved in harmony. Together as one, fighting for our own selfish needs but wanting the other's pleasure just as much.

"You're mine. Your pussy is mine." he grunted out. "I fucking love you, Josephine!" he called into the night air, as we collapsed against the tree. He called me by my name. He hadn't done that before.

"Josephine?" I test.

"Yes. Josephine. I love you" he kissed my head. "I love Monroe, the woman you have become and I love the girl you once were. Both strong in every way. Both hold my heart." he kissed my lips. He helped me into the tent, leaving our clothes scattered around the campsite. We fit ourselves into one sleeping bag. It was hard but we managed.

Sleep was quick and restful.

I woke when I heard someone kicking a tin outside our tent. Roman covered my mouth, telling me to stay quiet. He took his gun out from under his sleeping bag, getting out of the sleeping bag as soundlessly as it would allow. He motioned for me to cover my head and stay still. He unzipped the mouth of the tent just enough to see out. When he put his gun down, I assumed it wasn't anything dangerous.

"What the fuck are you doing here?" he stormed out naked. Whoever was out there was going to get an eyefull.

"What do you know? I was going to get Melody some new shoes and I saw a very expensive car sitting on the side of the road four miles up. And you can imagine my shock when I realized it was your car. You told me you were getting out of town. It's not nice to lie, Roman," Garth clicked his tongue. "Jo, you in there? How you doing? No, don't come out. If Roman's appearance is anything like yours, and I'm sure it is because of the clothes scattered out here." I heard something scuff against the ground. "Out here, be a lady."

"Fuck off, Garth!" I shouted out of the tent.

"Garth, we didn't tell you for a reason. This has nothing to do with you." Roman said in frustration. "I know you have a thing for her, but she made it clear."

"Roman, stay on task. That has nothing to do with right now." I reprimanded.

"What she sees in you, I will never know, but you are right, she made her choice. I'm partly to blame. I should have tried harder when we were younger. She pushed me away and I didn't even try. For that Jo, I'm sorry."

"No need Garth. But it still doesn't change my mind about you being in this. You have a little girl to protect, to make sure no one does this to her. Allgood is still covered in creeps." I mused over covering my nipples or not, it wasn't like he could see but being exposed with two men out there brought something ugly out of me.

My daddy came into my room and told me Jace was coming in with another man, and they were both going to have me at the same time. If I fought, I'd regret it.

At ten past eleven, my door opened and two men entered my room. One I knew and was familiar with. The other was not from around here. "Hey Jo." Jace greeted. Every time he came in here, I wouldn't talk to him. I lay in my bed, unmoving. "This is Grant, I met him online. He was excited to meet you. Don't be rude." He slipped his hand under my blankets and into my panties. "Grant, come here" Jace called him over to the bed and he slipped his wet fingers into Grants mouth. His fingers were covered in my juices and the sick fucks were licking his fingers as if it were candy.

"Sweet," Grant smacked his mouth loudly. "You sure we won't get in trouble?" he asked. His questioning it meant he knew it was wrong.

"No, Jo ain't gonna tell a soul, right Jo?" Jace asked me. I shook my head as he pulled the covers away from me. Jace took Grant's manhood in his hands and stroked it through the pants. "Jo, get over here. Get on your knees." This was sick. I didn't want to do this.

"No!" I took off for the door. My hand made contact with the knob, but I was yanked back by my hair.

"Colt, she is trying to run!" Jace called to my daddy. The door opened and my father's silhouette filled the room.

"Jo, if you don't stop your shit!" he backed handed me but I didn't fall because Jace was still attached to my head.

"I don't think I can do this!" Grant said nervously.

"No, don't go. Stay. She is going to be a good girl." Jace promised him but I wouldn't. I'd rather get my ass kicked then let them both have me.

I was wrong. My father was relentless in his punishment. I should have shut up and taken it. That week, I was left without the use of my legs. They thought I broke my back. My father told them I fell down the stairs, slipping on a skate.

My clothes were flung into the tent. Roman peeked in to look at me. His shirt was barely covering his manhood.

"Get dressed. Garth refuses to leave and he can't be here when… my friend gets here."

"Garth, let's take a walk. Get you back to your truck." I said hopping around the tent on one foot, trying to pull my pants over my hips.

"I'm not going anywhere" he said stubbornly, turning his head toward me as I walked out of the tent, my shirt hanging halfway on me. "Get dressed properly before you greet people." his eyes told me he liked what he saw.

"Shut up, you prude. We have to go now." I grabbed his arm and turned him in the direction of the woods.

"Why?" he responded.

"Because there is a man on the way here. He will kill you if he sees you." I pushed at his back until he began to move.

"Friend of yours?" Garth directed his question at Roman. Roman just shrugged the insult off. "What are you doing Jo? Revenge isn't going to make you feel better and Roman must have lost his mind helping you."

"Garth, this is why you were left out the loop. You always want to run head first into something without thinking it through." I said and pushed him harder. He must have heard something when we were forty feet into the woods. He covered my body with his and dropped to a crouching position, his big beefy hand covering my mouth. Someone was walking close to us. Whoever it was, was heading in the direction of the camp. It could be a bad thing or a good thing.

"We have to help Roman," Garth whispered in my ear. I shook my head dramatically. He looked at me like I had lost my mind. I signaled for him to uncover my mouth so I could talk.

"That might be his…'friend'. It's best to leave him to it." I wiped the sweat from my mouth. There was no point in moving. They would hear if we continued through the brush. Staying here was the only option we had. The space was so small I was almost in Garth's lap. I told myself I should have been uncomfortable being so close, but I didn't. Garth had an appeal to him. I wanted to trace every muscle on his body. Yes, I know I shouldn't think like that if I tell someone I love them, but love was new to me. My response to Garth had me wondering if love was limited to one person, or could you love more than one person? Garth was a good guy and I know we had some moments in the past. Could he have been my first love? Back then, when Ira would tell me to stay away from him, Garth didn't care if Ira beat him up. I'm the one who messed it up when I pushed him away.

"What are you thinking about?" Garth asked. His chest was raising and falling rapidly, as if he just got done running a 5k marathon. He must have noticed my thoughts. My mind was always in the gutter one way or another. I bit my lip thinking of what I could have done with a body like his. Garth had sandy brown hair. His jawline looked like an artist craved it out of stone. It was strong and dependable. His eyes were black and could penetrate the skin.

"Nothing, just how ugly you are!" Laughing I bumped in to him.

"No you weren't," he moved closer to me.

"Garth, no!" I pushed him back. "I was thinking about you, not being ugly, but what a fine man you turned out to be. Probably the best man in that town, it still doesn't change the fact that I'm with Roman."

"If you didn't push me away all those years ago. If you didn't have the parents you did. I can't help thinking I am the one you're supposed to be with." he confessed. I thought of that from time to time. If I was normal and I met Garth, I would have fallen in love with him and had a ranch where I could watch him tending horses in the hot sun, and I would bring him cool iced tea or lemonade.

"That happened in another life." I admitted, placing my hand on his cheek. No matter how I looked at Garth, if I let him in as I let in Roman, he would have run. He would have left me and all my fucked-up-ness and if he told me he wouldn't, he'd be a liar, because I would leave me and all my head cases. I figured out I had more than one when I was nine. My brother would tell me if I just closed my eyes and told the voices to leave, they would. They never did. I just became good at hiding them from others.

Josephine. Josephine. The little drama queen.

"Stop talking!" The voices made their way into my dreams, turning them to nightmares. They called me names. Invisible hands pulled and tore my skin. Teeth ripped chunks of skin out. I screamed for them to stop, but all they did was laugh. Unseen hands would slip into my underwear and fondle me. I tried to move them but there was nothing there.

495

Monroe

Don't pretend you don't like it, Josephine.

The voices slithered around my skin, coating it in evil. When I would get up in the morning, I would scrub my body until it turned red. I rubbed so hard, blisters would appear.

"I think he left." Garth said. He was in a crouch looking over the bush. He didn't know when I left, when I would slip into the past. I knew then Garth was just a good friend, and no matter how much I liked his body, he wasn't the one for me. Roman noticed everything about me. It might have been because of what he did work wise. Roman just got me.

I rushed out of the bushes through the tree line at the campsite. I looked around frantically for Roman. "Roman!" I called looking in the tent. He wasn't there.

"Over here, I had to piss." he came out of the woods buckling his belt. Without pause, I ran into his arms.

"Jo, it was only ten minutes. You miss me already?" He asked and kissed the top of my head. I did miss him, and I knew he could handle himself. My previous thoughts caused this burst of affection.

Without answering him, I asked. "What happened, where's the stuff?" I looked around him because there was nothing here.

"Don't worry he left it in a car, down the way. It was too much to carry with him." he pulled me back to him. "I like when you get all lovey." he smirked and kissed my lips. Not a soft and sweet kiss I was prepared for, but a heated all thought consuming type of kiss.

Garth cleared his throat. "Better time to do that, like later."

"No better time than the present, cowboy. You never know what could happen." Roman said against my lips.

"Stop it." I said and moved from him, but I didn't let go of his hand.

"How do you expect me to stop when you do this to me?" he grabbed himself pressing his hard-on into my stomach. Good thing Garth couldn't see or hear him from this distance.

"I expect you to act like a gentleman," I chastised.

"You and I both know I'm not a gentleman," he made a kissy face at me.

"It's your best quality." I told him. I started gathering all my things, putting them into the backpack.

"You wound me, love." Roman said in pain, going on to act as if he had a sword sticking out of him chest.

"I get it," Garth said out of the blue. To be honest, I forgot he was here.

"Get what?" I look at him funny.

"Why you like him. He makes you smile. You forget about things when you are with him." he observed.

"Like, dude, she loves me." Roman added with a huge smile on his face.

"Whatever it is, I get it." Garth motioned to us.

Talking stopped as we made our way to the car. Roman's friend had left everything, I didn't blame him. It was quite a hike. Mosquitoes buzzed past my ears I smacked the air in hopes of shooing them away. I should have packed bug spray but I wasn't thinking. I left everything in Roman's car. He told me to pack light. For it being hot, the ground was muddy. My feet sank in every few feet. Roman was in front of me, Garth was behind me and when my foot would slip Garth was there to pick me out of it. I was in all senses a strong woman. I could hold my own in a fight. I knew how to take care of myself but hiking this stretch of land was going to be the death of me.

When we finally got to the car, my legs were covered in mud. The men didn't seem to have this problem. They told me it was because their boots helped them stay above the mud. I was going to have to get me some when everything was over. Being prepared for every situation is what made me unique. The car was a lemon. Its back window was smashed out and all four doors were different colors. I had no clue how they managed that. I stood back. My OCD was going crazy with the door colors. I was thinking of ways I could avoid touching them, or ways I could fix it. Of course there was no way, it was my brain's way of trying to work it out.

"Here's the plan: we need to drive this car to mine. Garth is here to make friendly with any police who stop us, since he involved himself. There are enough weapons here to imprison all of us for a long time. The goal is to not get caught." Roman briefed us.

"Couldn't be that hard, it's only three miles from here to the car. If we take this way, we can get there without being seen. No one really knows it's even a road, except the locals. We could be worse off if Colt is out and about today. He doesn't drink in town. " Garth told us about the hidden road, the one my father takes.

"Doesn't matter. If we do see him, it just makes my life easier. I won't have to search for him to kill him." Roman retorted.

"What is it you actually do Roman?" Garth questioned. "At first I thought, maybe you were in banking. You know, the money type. I was trying to figure out what it was Jo saw in you. After all, you are one ugly son of a bitch. You didn't come across as a man that could lift a bale of hay or ride a horse. To me, those are the best qualities in a man."

"Best things in this damn town, but in the big world out there education is the best strength. To answer your question, no I was not in banking. That's too boring, I need something a little wilder." Roman joked, as he rotated his hips.

"Were you a stripper? I can't think of another job that does that," Garth joked making fun of Roman.

"Nope, still cold. But I think you could do it," Roman called to Garth.

"Boys stop. We have something we should be doing, not telling jokes." Getting whatever was in this car to a safe location was the goal now. Killing my father was in sight, and I was going to reach it by nights end.

Roman told me to get in the back and duck down. He handed me a blanket to cover myself . Garth told Roman he would drive, just because if a cop did pull us over it would be easier to get out of trouble. Roman made a comment about Garth being the town sweetheart, making Garth elbow him in the gut. It was as if they were bickering brothers. I couldn't stop it if I wanted to.

I hid myself under the blanket that smelled of oil and gasoline, squeezing myself between the back seat and front seats. I held my breath, too nervous we would be pulled over, but mostly because the smell. "Are we there yet?" I asked the men.

"Shhh... In another five minutes. The road Garth chose was bumpy with lots of twists and turns. The car must have hit a huge pothole. My head bounced and smashed into the seat.

"I can see the car. Who is that?" Garth commented.

"Jo, stay down." Roman demanded. The way he was talking, there was no way I was going to get up. This car wouldn't be hiding anything if they chose to look through it. If it was someone other than the police, they weren't going to get close. Roman and Garth would stop them

"Hello officer, what can I do you for today?" Garth asked. I exhaled loudly. I hoped that Garth would be able to get us out of this.

"Garth." he paused, no doubt to tip his hat to Garth. "I got a call from Colt telling me there was an abandoned car out here. I called it in and they said it was a rental from the next town over."

"Yes, officer. It's mine," Roman added.

"Why would you leave it here?" Officer whatever his name said.

"I ran out of gas. I called Garth to come and pick me up and here we are." Roman's voice was steady. His acting abilities were phenomenal. If it was me he was talking to, I would have believed every word he was telling me, and not just because I liked him. From my professional standpoint, he would have convinced me. It made me wonder if he lied about other things. If he could get away with this lie when we were clearly in a stressful situation, he could get out of anything.

"Colt was blabbering about a man stealing his daughter in a foreign car, but if you know this gentleman, Garth I'll believe you over him any day. That man is nuttier than a squirrel." The officer gave a hoot. "I didn't know he had any kids. From my understanding, they couldn't conceive. Probably why he's such a cranky thing. It ain't right when a man can't father a child."

506

Colt didn't deserve any damn kids. The ones he had are forever fucked in the head.

"If you guys got this handled, I'll just be on my way" he offered. His footsteps stopped in the distance and I heard a car door slam. The car engine revved and he was gone. Both Garth and Roman let out the air from their lungs.

"Let's get this show on the road. The sooner you guys finish what you're here to do, the sooner my life can go back to the way it was" Garth admitted as he got out of the car. I popped my head up, looking around us.

"Jo, get in the car, no one will see you in there." Roman called over his shoulder as he removed bag after bag from the trunk of the beat up sedan. The windows in the rental were tinted. He was right. No one would see me even if they stared hard. I got into the back seat as fast as I could, looking at Garth as I did. He was studying Roman, watching everything he did. Garth might be a country boy and he might have a thick twang but he was very observant and intelligent. He noticed things almost as well I did.

Once everything was in the right car, Garth asked Roman what he was going to do with this car. Roman told him to leave it, that it was like a shopping bag, just there to hide the purchases. Of course, Garth being Garth, he refused. He told Roman he could use it for parts.

"Take it if you want. We gotta go." Roman told him and got behind the wheel.

"Where are you guys going?" Garth asked.

Monroe

"This is the end of the road for us Garth. If things go south, you don't want to be involved in it. I can only get me and Monroe out of it. I can't take you and the kid with us. That life wasn't meant for you guys." Roman called out the window of the car.

"Stop calling her that!" Garth shouted at the car as we took off. To him, I was always going to be Josephine and becoming her again, well it didn't seem that bad.

"Ready?" Roman asked as he took my hand and kissed my palm.

Monroe

The street my father lived on had a lot of abandoned houses. Either from natural disasters or just foreclosure. We chose one at a distance. Roman told me it would be better if we needed to leave in a hurry. The thing about this town was there was no ramp to get on the interstate. We would have to drive through other towns to get out of here.

I remember when I was younger, the old lady that lived here made pies. You could smell them at my house. I was going to ask her for one one day, but Ira asked me if I remembered the story of Hansel and Gretel. If I wanted to live, leave the old lady's pie alone.

"She doesn't seem like she eats kids." I told him. I stuck my tongue out at him.

Monroe

"Does Momma look like she beats her kids? She goes to church every Sunday. She has bible study with these bitches in town. Don't let the appearance of someone fool you." Ira smacked me in the head.

You would think we got hit enough, but we would hit each other in the head every time we thought the other made a bad decision.

"It's just pie." I said, earning myself a dirty look.

"It's just an oven of fire. You want to die? Or worse? In some places they cut hands off thieves." He grabbed my hand and moved me away from the window.

"Hey babe, where'd you go?" Roman waved his hands in front of me. "How many fingers am I holding up?" he asked.

I only heard the first part. "Babe? Are we an old married couple now? That word is only used when you don't fuck each other anymore." It made me nauseous. When I got older, I wanted to have just as freaky of a sex life. I was going to be sixty with my tits locked in bondage.

"It is not! If that's true then why do all the young kids call each other Bae?" I couldn't gauge if his question was real or sarcastic.

"Because they are dumb and they think by shortening something, it makes a new word" I made a disgruntled nose. "Have you seen what they wear? They call it theirs, when all it is styles taken from other generations."

"I didn't ask for a history lesson, Josephine." he scolded playfully.

Whenever he called me by my name, it caused butterflies to flutter around in my stomach. "What are we going to do now?" I asked him. There was still five hours left of day light. We weren't going in until three in the morning. It was time enough for Colt to think he was safe in his bed, lying next to his brainwashed wife.

"Now we're going to go over details. You are going to tell me what type of furniture there is. Usually I go to a place and scope it out, learn routines and all. You know what I'm talking about. That day at the coffee shop, you were sitting there waiting for me. You knew I was going to be there because you did your homework. It was a way to gauge the situation and me. If I gave you a bad feeling, you wouldn't have taken the job. Same thing with my line of work. I have to make sure things will go my way. But in this case, I am going to be relying on you. You are

513

the one who knows this house." he was right, detail was everything.

"Alright where do we start?" I inquired.

The rest of the night was filled with maps and furniture placement. The only thing I wasn't sure of was the upstairs. The only thing I had to go on were memories. When I was there, the only thing I saw was the living room and glimpses of the kitchen. It looked the same, but I couldn't be sure. It meant we were going in there blind. I told him about my old hiding spots, place I would avoid stepping because they made too much noise. I relived my childhood each night in this house. It couldn't be too much different than I remembered. My father was a lazy asshole who liked things the way they were.

When the clock read two thirty, Roman told me to get my things together. We were going in light. If we needed to come back and get something, he would be the one to. I slung my bag over my shoulder.

"Are you okay?" Roman worried. He helped me strap on my gun under my black cotton jacket. Everything I wore was dark. It would be impossible to spot me when I put on my mask.

"Yes, I'm good." I stammered.

"You sure you want to do this?" he inquired.

"I've wanted this my whole life! Of course I'm ready." he looked at me like I was making a mistake but he wasn't the one who had endured all the things that I had. He never asked me after I told him. He never said,

"Hey, don't you have a brother?" Ira was the one thing that was off limits.

"Alright, you remember everything I said? There is no room for error. We go in, do what we need to and get out."

"I remember, Roman," I huffed and moved out the back door. The street was eerie. There was no sound at all. Not even the crickets chirped. The town turned into a ghost. Something that was once vibrant with life no longer breathed. A lone light from Mrs. Johnson's house lit the way. I stopped and looked into a crack in her curtain. There she was at the table, alone. A puzzle was scattered about the table, half complete.

"Let's go." Roman whispered to me. I remember nights on this street and hustling. People littered the sidewalks as kids played in the street. Running around tagging each other. Ira and I never played with them. I just liked watching. It was the life I was meant to have.

We stealthily moved into the brushes, picking and choosing where we would step. The leaves hadn't fallen yet. It was only the middle of the summer. My mind was scattered, my thoughts would linger on unimportant things. Roman got on his knees to boost me over the fence leading to the backyard. Once over, I looked up to the starry sky. it was amazing. I stopped dead in my tracks. There he was. My brother. I forgot everything else around me as I walked over to his grave. Tears poured from my eyes as I sank to my knees in front of him.

"It's been a long time Ira. I have missed you, brother." I said around my sobs. Roman gave me space, staying back in the shadows. "My brother, that night I will never forget."

"Boy thinks he has balls!" My father hooted and hollered to no one in particular.

"He didn't mean it, Daddy just let him go!" I cried as my father held Ira up by his neck. His eyes started rolling back in his head as he lost consciousness. I was hitting my father in the chest, begging him to let my brother go. I would say anything to get him to stop. This was all my fault. If I hadn't told Ira the truth, he wouldn't have tried to stab my father.

"Protecting your slut of a sister! I told you I was going to kill you one day. Today is that day you little shit! Then I'm gonna fuck your sister until she bleeds." my father said devilishly.

It was no secret that my mother favored Ira. I would catch her babying him when she thought no one was watching or sneaking him some food. It was her way of showing love. It did not give him a repreive from the beating. If Ira defended me, it would boil her blood. She loved him . She hated me, but Ira cared for me like I was his own.

My mother came into the room and saw my father holding Ira's lifeless body against the wall. "Colt, let him go." She said weakly. She knew if she defied him, he would kill her too.

"Stupid bitch! Stay out of this!" he told her and lifted Ira higher. His face was turning powder blue from the lack of oxygen. My father was happy when he felt Ira wasn't going to get up. He moved toward me. "Get over here, whore! You'll pay for hitting me! You couldn't save

*him if you wanted to. He got what was coming to him!"
he grabbed me by my throat and forced my body against
his.*

*"Daddy, please let me check him! Let me call the
ambulance. I'll do anything you want me to! I won't
fight." I said desperately. I would do anything to save my
brother's life.*

*"It's too late for him. He's dead. You'll do whatever I
say anyway. In this room. While your dead brother is
watching!" My father was Satan. He was evil and there
was no saving him. You could actually feel the waves of
evil coming from his body.*

*My mom ran to Ira's body, smacking him in the face
trying to get him to breathe. I watched and wondered
what I did wrong for her to never love me, I wasn't a bad*

kid. I didn't do anything to hurt her. Her tears leaked on to my brother's face and rage consumed me.

"Get the fuck away from him! You have no right to touch him! You never were a mother to us! Your tears are worthless, just like you!" I shouted to her. Her head swiveled in my direction. She gave me a sad look and stood.

"Colt, let her go! You took one of my children already! One is enough." My mother never stood up to my father. Fear ruled her life. A hearty laugh bubbled through my father. It was the most frightening sound I have ever heard. He pushed me to the ground and kicked me in my stomach. Bile splashed onto the floor as the impact of the kick emptied my stomach. My father dragged my mother from where she knelt in front of my brother to the kitchen chair in the corner of the room. He

told her to get in the chair and he tied her to it with duct tape. This would be the second time she allowed him to tie her to a chair. I couldn't feel sorry for her, I wouldn't. She deserved everything she was getting. After all, she was the one who chose to stay with him.

"You want to go against me? I will make you regret your decision." My father shoved something into my mother's mouth. He taped her eyelids open so she would have to witness whatever he was going to do. After he was done with her, he propped my brother's lifeless head up, peeling his eyes open. His dead eyes looked at me, straight into my soul.

"Your dear brother is going to watch as I take everything from you. Make him proud Jo! This is what he gave his life for, to protect you!" My dad smiled wickedly and took off his pants. My mother was crying silently *from her chair. "I am going to fuck your daughter! You will watch everything. I will fuck her like you wish I'd fuck you."*

There was no fight left in me. My brother was dead. It was my fault. My father wouldn't have killed him if it wasn't for me. He continued to say it as he screwed me. He kept his word and made me bleed from where he entered me and from his blade.

I dusted off Ira's headstone. "Brother, forgive me." I choked out.

"I told you he would never forgive you, stupid bitch." My back stiffened at my father's words. " I knew you couldn't stay away. I saw that fancy car on the outside of town and I knew it was you. I've been waiting for you to come, Jo. We didn't finish what you started." I turned slowly to face him. I wiped the tears from my cheeks, standing tall as I addressed him.

" I told you I was going to see my brother whether you liked it or not, you sick bastard!" I retorted as I shifted my weight to the balls of my feet. If he came at me, I would be ready.

"And I told you I would kill you! I said I'll watch as your life leaves your body." he stalked me as he spoke.

"Ain't going to happen Colt! The fuck I look like? The scared little girl is gone, and you aren't anything to me. If you recall, you told me I wasn't any kin of yours. I called you daddy, even when you hurt me. I grew up believing pain was love. That the only way you could love someone is by hurting them. You told me I killed my brother, but I didn't. I couldn't have stopped your psychotic ass if I wanted to! I have dreamt about killing you for fourteen years now. I trained myself, patiently waiting for today." I cackled.

"You don't have the balls to kill me child. You aren't a murderer, but I am," he lunged for me. I was swift in moving out of his way. He rammed his head into my brother's headstone. I took it as a sign. Ira was here to help me out.

"You're getting old Colt! You can do better than that," I mocked. "Get up and fight, old man!"

He stayed down, covering his now bloody face. I grabbed him by his neck and helped him up. He spit blood into my face and smiled a toothless grin. "Gonna take more than that to take me down, Princess!" He encased my neck with his hands and squeezed. I looked to the spot where Roman used to be. Panic took hold of me when I saw he wasn't there any longer. Monroe, the strong woman I was, became the whimpering child in seconds. It left my brain blank. I did not know how to get out of his grip. I had been left alone like I had been for most of my life. Did I expect anything else? Even from the man who claimed to love me?

Ebony swirls danced in my vision. I caught movement from behind my father, Roman approached soundlessly, stalking forward. His hand came up and sunk a needle into my father's neck. Colt let go of me, placing a hand over the spot the needle entered. The sedative took ten seconds to kick in. My father dropped like a fly at my feet.

"Let me look at you." Roman searched me. He touched me all over, lifting my hair, studying my face.

He didn't know at that moment I was at war with myself. I felt abandoned by him just seconds ago, but my mind was telling me he didn't leave, that he was there with me. He wasn't going to leave me.

"I'm fine. I just need to catch my breath." I gulped down air like it was my first time breathing. Roman left me alone. He took Colt and lifted him onto his shoulders.

"I'm going to start preparing. Take your time. He won't wake for a couple of hours." He gave me one more glance before he moved into the house. My mother usually heard everything, I worried about when she would show her face but with my father incapacitated, my mother would be a piece of cake.

Forgetting the real reason I came, I took a knee in front of my brother's grave. "I will avenge you, Ira. He will pay for what he took from us." I swiped the snot from my nose. "So much has happened. I don't know where to begin. I went to college and I graduated. I made a name for myself." I stopped. "I'm here because I met someone. He's great. His name is Roman. I think I might be in love with him. I know I vowed to never love anyone. I promised you because I felt like it was my fault. I want to know that you are okay with me being happy. Please tell me you want me to be happy?" I sobbed into my hands, muffling the words I kept repeating. "I miss you so much! Please forgive me for not stopping him. I tried. I would have given my life for yours. Everything you did for me and I couldn't stop him from hurting you. I was so scared." The sobs wracked through my body. I collapsed on t top of my brother's grave, looking up at the night sky. One thing I did miss about Alabama was the vivid night sky. "Give me a sign,

Ira. Something to let me know you're fine, wherever you are." I prayed to the sky. A star shot across the heavens, followed by three more. I smiled around the tears. Every time I asked my brother for something, he would give it to me and say, 'What are big brothers for?' ruffling the top of my head playfully.

Now I had to forgive myself.

"Josephine, everything is set up," Roman's voice echoed in the dark.

"I'll be back, Ira. To say goodbye." I leaned into his headstone and kissed it. After all the time I was away, it took me just seeing him to burst my heart open all over again. I could feel him watching over me, telling me to be strong. Now it was time to end the life of the prick who took him from me.

I met up with Roman at the back door. He was covered in a plastic smock. Booties covered his shoes and rubber gloves were stuck to his hands. He held the door open for me, but he stopped me when I got into the hallway. "Jo, your mom didn't make it. She's in the corner in the living room. Her body has been there a while from the looks of it. She's bloating. Wear your mask. In this heat, the smell is toxic."

I was not sure how to feel. She didn't love me and she treated me like I was a parasite. "Saves us the trouble then. Let's get on with it." Roman tied my father to a chair in the living room, the same way he had done to my mother years before. He was still knocked out. Blood poured onto his greasy shirt and my mother's head laid at his feet.

Showtime.

Monroe

I dressed in the plastics Roman handed me, tucking my hair under a shower cap. Roman told me we couldn't leave any evidence. He broke a tiny capsule in his hand and held it up to Colt's nose. Colt shook his head and came to, confusion painted on his face.

"Hey Colt," Roman said gently. "You're going to behave while Monroe talks to you." Roman moved to my side, waiting for me to take the lead.

"You and I both know this was a long time coming. You just didn't think I was strong enough to get here." His face became red as he struggled to get free. "Isn't going to do any good Colt. You're staying right there. Poor Momma didn't have a choice either, did she?" I pointed to my mother's rotting body. "Leaving your wife to decompose. You couldn't even bury her. After all she dealt with." I punched him square in the nose. Reflexes and all, it felt extraordinary.

Giving him a chance to talk wasn't for his benefit because I was beyond words. I did it because I wanted him to piss me off. My father's mouth wouldn't stay closed. He was going to talk himself into his death. I removed the gag.

"You stupid cunt! I'm going to skin you when I get out of this." he threatened.

"Now now, Father. I could have sworn you loved tying people up. I wanted to bestow you the same kindness you gave me. It's only right. This seems fitting. You, me and this knife." I exposed the knife my father once used to cut me open. In fact, he had used that knife the last night I saw him. "Memories!" I cooed, sliding the knife over his exposed throat. Roman did such an amazing job securing him. He couldn't even move his head.

"Jo, you think this is going to scare me? That if you intimidate me with everlasting life in hell, I'm just going to beg you for forgiveness? Once you let me out, I will kill you!" He said menacingly.

"Wouldn't that be lovely?" I probed. "You won't be walking out of here Colt. Get used to the idea of hell, because you will be there shortly." I placed the knife on the table. I picked up all the different instruments Roman laid out for me.

It looked like Colt was finally getting it. He never thought I would come back for him. He was convinced I was so terrified I would just forget. He was partly right, if you had asked me five years ago, I would have told you to fuck off.

"Monroe, time is ticking," Roman called to me.

"Monroe?" My father questioned in disgust. "Why would he call you that? And who is he?"

"Well, Colt, this isn't the way I intended to meet Monroe's parents, but none the less here I am. I am Roman. Roman Pierce and I'm in love with your daughter." Roman said politely. He stuck his hand out mockingly. "Guess you're a little tied up at the moment." He was my hero.

"You're just a murderer! I can smell my kind miles away. Is he the one who talked you into this, Jo? You ain't that person. You wouldn't hurt me, I'm your father.

534

I gave you life." he pleaded. His life was already mine. I had no mercy for him.

"Funny, the person who gave me life is sitting at your feet, dead. By your hands Colt, and I didn't even like her that much. Seeing her down there is harder than I thought it would be. But when I think of you in her place, I don't have any fucking emotion!" I picked the knife up and licked it. The cold steel pressing against my tongue felt good. I purred, closing my eyes. When I looked back at him, Colt was vibrating with desire.

"You learned that from me," he said darkly.

"Yes, all my fucking anger problems, the inability to feel emotions. I got it all from you! Be proud daddy, your little girl is screwed up, just the way you wanted me!" I chuckled, tossing my head back. I ran my hands over my body, stopping when my breasts filled my hands. "Too bad the only thing I'm thinking about is making love to him." I pointed the knife to Roman. "Because he's making all my dreams come true. I'd be lying if I told you this wasn't turning me on. I'm consumed in lust."

"Monroe." Roman warned.

"Okay. See daddy? He keeps me in line. He doesn't have high expectations, because he knows what makes me tick. Matter of fact, he knew before I even told him. I hid everything from everyone. I vowed I would never love anyone because you took Ira from me. You murdered him in front of me and made me watch his cold dead eyes as you fucking raped me over and over again!" I screamed into his face. Some of my saliva splashed out and landed on his cheek.

"You deserved more! I should have killed you instead of your brother! At least he would have helped out around here." Colt replied.

"You are a demented bastard! You should have been locked away, but she," I kicked my mother in her back. "Let you do what you wanted!" Without thinking it through, I took his knife and slit his throat. I watched as the blood pooled onto his potbelly, collecting right above it. The sight of him gurgling and struggling to get air made me feel childlike. I imagined my younger self, standing over his draining body and I giggled, delighted. It might have made me just as troubled as him. You could even say I had lost my mind. At that time, yes I had. The bloodlust was so strong. I wanted to rub his blood into my naked skin and dance with his decapitated body under the moonlight.

I did none of it. Instead, I rushed into Roman's arms and cried as he cradled me like an infant. I lost track of time. When the sun made its way onto the horizon Roman studied me. "We have to get the bodies out of here. Both of them." he pointed to my mother and father.

"I don't want them next to my brother!" I cried.

"Of course not. I was thinking an unmarked grave somewhere in the woods. You stay here and cleanup. I'll move them." He kissed me sweetly. "This doesn't make you a horrible person, you know that right?"

I was a terrible person who just killed her father. His actions didn't justify mine, but I couldn't stop thinking I had helped the world in some way. My father was a sick man. Nothing a doctor could prescribe was going to help him. Killing him was the only way to insure he wouldn't hurt anyone else. The look on his face when I licked the knife was enough to tell me he would do it again. He was just waiting for someone to leave their kid alone in a park, or walking home from school. A predator never stopped hunting.

"I'll work on being okay." I promised and kissed him back. He left me without another word. Time ticked by as I gathered all the knives and tape and stashed them in the bag. The blood from my mother's body stained the hardwood floor, there was no removing it.

A car door slammed outside and Roman came in with a black plastic bag. He started getting the bodies ready for transport, tucking them in, making sure the blood didn't spill out. Watching him work was exciting. You might think dating someone who was hired to kill people was not a turn on. It wasn't the strangest thing I've seen.

I handed him the bag full of torture devices so he could get rid of them . Roman was everything I needed in a man. He was caring, he was willing to let me express myself and he could protect me.

"Keep staring at me like that and I will end up screwing you in your old room." He warned. It would be the first good thing to happen in this house, but I couldn't. Too many bad things happened here. I couldn't associate Roman with it. He was my light at the end of a dark tunnel and I could see it approaching.

"Later. On the plane." I smiled and smacked him on the ass.

Monroe

A Year Later

I sat at the bar waiting for Roman to meet me. It had been four months since I saw him. We were dating now and I couldn't be happier. He had taken a job for a former employer for the last couple of months and I was so excited to see him. I couldn't stop moving. I tapped my foot on the barstool and waited impatiently. The airport bar was slightly crowded. It was the five o'clock rush.

Last minute planes and layovers. I did what I did best. I watched people.

San Francisco was bustling with different kinds of people. Tall, short, fat, skinny, and all colors in between. Joy filled me when a little girl gave her father a kiss on his cheek, handing him a picture she drew. It made me envious in ways that I shouldn't have been to see the love they shared. It was beautiful. I wiped a tear from my face. I wondered if I would have nieces or nephews right now. I always said my brother would have made a great husband and father. He would protect them. No one would be able to hurt them

The city of Allgood had an investigation into my parents' disappearance. They didn't find anything. Roman and I also decided to leave the house standing for Garth and Melody. They told me it looked like they just up and left. Roman made sure to move my father's truck, driving it to an unknown spot where it sat rotting, just like my father. When he was out doing that, I took the liberty of packing their things and putting them in Roman's trunk. I brought them to California with me. I threw them in the Pacific Ocean. I found stuff of Ira's that I kept. A book he would read over and over. It was the only one he had. A shirt of his, it still smelled like him, like sun and dirt. Warm and kind just like him.

Hands covered my eyes. "Guess who?" A warm voice tickled my neck. Last year, this would have sent me into a panic. Today, right now, I knew whose hands were covering my face. I didn't worry about the boogieman anymore.

"If you don't stop playing and kiss me," I told Roman. He let go of my face and kissed me chastely.

"That's all I get after months of celibacy?" I teased.

"You will get more when we get out of here." he said excitedly. He took me by my hand and began sprinting through the airport. Everyone turned and looked at the spectacle we were making. He made me feel loved and desired, as if I was the only one he saw, as if I was the only one in the world. I was giddy with glee as my feet raced to keep up with his long strides.

We only made it to the car before all of our clothes had been stripped off and I was straddling him in the passenger seat. The windows in this car weren't tinted. People passing by looked in, but averted their eyes once they realized what was going on. No sex for months had left me sensitive. Once he filled me, I came.

"Missed me that much huh?" he mused, pumping into me.

"You. Have. No. Idea!" I said breathlessly as exhaustion took hold of my body.

I licked his neck, sucking it into my mouth. His exquisite movements brought me back to the edge. I placed my hand on the roof on the car and I rode out my orgasm, calling out Roman's name. It stuck in my throat, taking the air with it. "Breathe baby." Roman told me. I wasn't sure that I wanted to breathe. If I had to choose between air and having him balls deep in me, I'd choose him every time. His pace quickened as he drew nearer to explosion.

"Fuck, that's mine!" he moaned and thrust into me one last time, his seed spreading in me. He brushed the hair from my face, looking me over. "Did I hurt you?" he probed.

"No, Roman. I'm pregnant, not sick." I said sarcastically. Being pregnant wasn't in our plans, but here we were. When I found out, I was going to get an abortion. I felt I wasn't ready for this. Roman didn't need to know, I told myself. But I remembered what we promised. To tell the truth no matter what it was.

"Roman we need to talk." He was just getting out the shower. A towel was hanging off his midsection. He swiveled his hips and winked at me.

"Jo, you don't have to ask when you want me. I understand you have needs like a man and I will happily give it to you." he boasted.

546

"No, you idiot! I have to talk to you about a serious matter." I scolded.

His face fell as he tried figuring out what it was I needed to talk to him about. "Jo, I know this isn't how you thought it was going to be . Relationships are difficult for anyone. I'm not saying you aren't normal, but you should give it more time." he babbled. He thought I was going to leave him, that this wasn't what I wanted.

I snickered, "You think I'm going to leave you? Why would you think that?" I patted the bed next to me.

Once he was sitting, I began to talk. "When I left Alabama, the first thing I did was go to a free clinic. All those years of abuse left me wondering if I was ever going to be able to conceive. Not that I wanted a child.

547

But I thought I might as well know. The doctor told me my cervix took an extreme amount of abuse. Her words not mine. It was the last time my father shoved a blade inside me. She asked me if I had been raped. I told her it was foreplay and I liked it. The last thing I needed was for her to investigate me. I was only fourteen, with nowhere to go. She would have sent me back to them. I couldn't hide it from her. She told me she dealt with girls who had gone through this, and she could help me. I wanted to take her up on her offer so badly, but I kept lying. She let me go, but not after telling me I probably wasn't going to be able to have kids."

"Okay, it's fine if we don't have kids. With what you and I do, it wouldn't be the best idea anyway." he admitted shaking his head at me.

"You told me to be honest with you, whatever it is." I sighed.

"Yes, anything." he nodded again.

"That doctor was a cunt. She lied. I'm pregnant." I blurted out. I repeated it when he didn't say anything. "I have a baby in here." I patted my flat stomach. He was thinking all the same things I thought about, I could tell. "I was going to get an abortion but I thought you might want to know."

"Yep." he said in shock. "A baby! A baby! What are we going to do with one of those?" He freaked.

"I told you I was going to go to the clinic and…" he cut me off.

"No, we need to think this over a bit more.. Killing it wouldn't be right. My mother always told me kids were a blessing, but they came to you when your life was all over the place." his face still looked uncertain.

"Keep it?" That option never crossed my mind. Why would it? I was crazy. I couldn't raise a kid. It would be just as messed up as me. The kid wouldn't have any hopes at surviving.

"Don't over think it. You'd be a great mother, you have me." he kissed my head and smiled.

"Are you telling me you want to have a baby?" We hadn't talked about this yet. It scared the shit out of me.

"Yes. I would be a great father, and I love you. People do this all the time. They don't question if they can handle it, because they all know they can't. No one is ready for parenthood, I assure you." Roman patted me on the back as if I were a toddler.

"It doesn't assure a damn thing." I sighed.

"I know you're not handicapped Jo, but I worry about my little bean in there." He placed soft kisses on my tummy.

"Bean? Pot roast? Is there a food name you won't use to describe our child?" I demand. Getting my clothes on was a challenge, the car was limited in space. My stomach wasn't big enough to cause problems yet. I was only four months along. The night I told Roman I was pregnant, he left to Seattle on business. We didn't talk about what he did. I really didn't want to know. He came home and it was all about us. My work was over. I was going to miss the money but I wanted to stay home with our child. Roman was going to look for a regular job once we had enough money in the bank. I was planning to find a job in counseling. My experiences could help others. The death of my father, the way he died, was eating at me. I would have nightmares about him. He would skin me alive, telling me he would be waiting for me in hell.

Hell was where I was going. Raising my son in a healthy environment was my only goal. He would never know the pain I went through. All he would see is mommy and daddy and if anyone hurt him like I was hurt, my father's death would look like a fucking picnic.

Roman and I pulled into the parking garage of our apartment. It was raining lighting and I was tired. I wanted nothing more than to crawl into bed with him and rest. And maybe eat something.

"Home sweet home!" Roman called from the top of the stairs. "I'm going to get in the shower. I'll be out soon."

From the door to the couch, I left a trail of clothes as I stripped them off. Being pregnant made me feel like my blood was boiling. I turned on the TV and the news blared to life.

"The bodies of an elderly couple were found on a construction site in Allgood, Alabama. Authorities say the bodies remain unidentified and are waiting for DNA results. We will keep you updated as the story progresses."

Fuck!

"Jo, if you ever kill someone, don't bury the body. Put it in the ocean or a swamp, that way a wild animal will

eat at it. No body, no problem." Ira said between licks of his ice cream.

"Why are we talking about this? I'm eating."

"Because there might be a time when I'm not around to protect you. You have to be prepared." he smoothed back his black hair.

"I ain't a killer, Ira James! And I don't like talking about this nonsense. You won't kill anyone either, you hear me?" I demand.

"There will come a day, Jo. Just be prepared" He told me seriously.

"Roman!" I hollered up the steps.

I heard the water turn off. A couple of seconds later, Roman was running out of the bathroom. He caught himself on the bannister before he slipped and fell. "What? Are you okay? Did something happen?"

"They found them!" I cried.

"Get your shit together! We are on the first flight out." He hurried to the bedroom, getting our things ready to leave. After we left Alabama, we got forged papers, new identities. Roman had his but he didn't worry about it. On other cases, he didn't know his mark. He had no connection. This time, with my parents it was personal. We kept a duffle bag of money, papers and contact information. It was time to leave the country.

Within the hour, we were on a plane. Headed to the only place I ever thought about living, Fiji. We sat in first class, biting our nails. This plane ride was going to kill me. My nerves were all over the place.

"We are going to be fine. Stop worrying." Roman comforted me. We were officially outlaws. Why would I bring a child into this? Why would I think this was a good life for him? "Our child will be fine. Our past doesn't determine how we love him. He is going to be raised knowing he is loved. He will be raised knowing he has a family that will do anything for him. We are leaving everything in the past for him."

New home. New life. New family.

It reminded me of the time Ira asked me what I wanted most in the world. Even as a child, I knew what I wanted. Happiness. I wanted a life were I didn't feel pain. A life where the voices in my head didn't take over. I wanted to be like Suzy down the street. Normal. It was simple. I wanted a family, one who loved and cared for me. When I told Ira this, he said. "Jo, you have that. You have me." he pointed to himself.

He didn't know how much those words shaped me as I grew. Even with my brother gone, I felt him. He was with me guiding me whenever I was lost. I got lost a lot, and he helped find my way.

"Jo, if you learn anything from me, let it be the love I have for you. In our lives, we were given darkness and pain but also a small amount of light. God gave me you. I wouldn't trade you for all the good things. You are worth it all, and I would do it all over again, just to keep you. If I'm not there in the future, remember that I love you. God did right by me when he put you in my life. He made sure I wasn't alone anymore." I was little when we had this talk. For some reason, it choose right now to come out.

"I will. Now can we play?" I said to him.

"Sure kid, whatever you want." He smirked and ruffled my hair.

I will always remember the love he showed me. He gave his life to protect me. I will make you proud. Every day, I will strive for it. I rubbed my stomach absently.

"What do you think of the name Ira?" I asked Roman.

"I think it's fitting. It's perfect." Roman placed his hand on my stomach, followed by his head. "Ira, you like that name?" he asked. My stomach fluttered.

"Did you feel that?" I asked. I was only four months along. He couldn't be kicking yet, could he?

"It was light, but yes." Roman beamed. "Ira it is, little baby."

There was a chance for me. I could be happy. Forgetting the past and moving forward was the only option I had. Me, Roman and my son Ira. That was happiness. That was life.

I could feel my brother with me, smiling at me. He was proud of me. He would never be disappointed in what I did. The pain I faced growing up didn't equal all the problems I created. I had to forgive myself and let it go.

"Jo, one day you will be a great woman. One day, people are going to be looking to you for answers and all you have to do is remember my words. Tell them there is always good that comes from bad. In darkness, light will guide your way, all you have to do is ask. Your life is going to be filled with love and light and I can't wait to see it."

559

My brother was my light in this dark world. He got me this far, why not keep pushing on? I looked at Roman, talking to my stomach.

We are the answer. We are the light.